I don't say this lightly: Angharad Walker is the real deal. This is a stunning debut – a blisteringly dramatic and emotional book that has stayed with me from the first moment I read about these children caught somewhere between the real world and . . . another place.

I'm still in two minds about what really happened, but this book is all about exploring the scary parts of life and the blurred lines between truth and lies. In Angharad's words: *I've intentionally invited questions about what's real and true in Dom and Sol's world, because the 'truth' in this story is simply the parts that really matter: friendship, courage, and those intrepid steps towards freedom.*

These are the truths that make *The Ash House* everything a classic children's book should be, and more!

**BARRY CUNNINGHAM**
Publisher
Chicken House

# The Ash House

## ANGHARAD WALKER

**Chicken House**

2 Palmer Street, Frome, Somerset BA11 1DS
www.chickenhousebooks.com

Text © Angharad Walker 2021
Cover and interior illustration © Olia Muza 2021

First published in Great Britain in 2021
Chicken House
2 Palmer Street
Frome, Somerset BA11 1DS
United Kingdom
www.chickenhousebooks.com

Chicken House/Scholastic Ireland, 89E Lagan Road, Dublin Industrial Estate,
Glasnevin, Dublin D11 HP5F, Republic of Ireland

Cover and interior design by Helen Crawford-White
Cover and interior illustration by Olia Muza
Typeset by Dorchester Typesetting Group Ltd
Printed and bound in Great Britain by CPI Group (UK) Ltd, Croydon CR0 4YY

FSC
www.fsc.org
MIX
Paper from
responsible sources
FSC® C020471

1 3 5 7 9 10 8 6 4 2

British Library Cataloguing in Publication data available.

PB ISBN 978-1-912626-97-7
eISBN 978-1-913322-58-8

*To my parents, with endless gratitude.*

## 1: THE NEW BOY

He wanted to change his mind as soon as they turned off the main road.

'Perhaps I should speak to my old doctor,' the boy said to the man driving him. 'Just in case.'

'We're here now.' These were the first words they'd exchanged since they left the hospital at dawn.

'I know, but maybe just to check . . .'

The car slowed to a crawl and the driver turned around to look at him.

'The people at the hospital told me you either try this place or get discharged. Which is it?'

The boy looked at the dripping, bristling trees through the windscreen.

'I'll try it.'

'OK, then.' The car picked up pace again.

They passed a cluster of trees, where he noticed an old

phone box with half its glass panes smashed in, then there were green fields, a stream, and towering horse chestnut trees surrounded by shining conkers. They turned a corner and started down the long, winding driveway. The main road disappeared behind a wall of evergreens.

After a twist in the drive, he saw a dirty gold gate and a boy perched on top of it. The car drew closer and the boy uncrossed his arms and climbed down, bouncing on the balls of his feet and waving. The new boy leant forward in his seat to get a look at him, but the droplets on the windscreen distorted the other boy's face, smudging it in places. The driver got out and went to speak to him.

Alone in the car, the new boy wanted to go back to the hospital.

He wasn't sure that this was the right choice after all. He remembered the stiff fingers prodding his muscles while his foster dad tapped on his phone. More questions. More tests. A night in the hospital, when strange dreams crept out of the shadows and twisted around his sleeping thoughts. A rough shake at first light – a porter ready to usher him out and, of course, the promise the night nurse had made about this place, before driving all day.

The driver came back. He opened the door and stuck

his head inside.

'Time to go, then,' he said. When the boy didn't move, he added more kindly, 'Always funny, isn't it? The first day at a new place. But you've got a new friend right here. He says he's going to show you around.'

The new boy told himself that he didn't care about friends. He clicked the door open, then stepped out into the relentless rain.

The other boy was tall and thin, and his brown hair was wet through. His shirt was soaked and the peaks and grooves of his shoulders, collarbones and ribs showed clearly through the fabric. An old pair of binoculars hung around his neck on a leather strap. His face was pale and perfectly round, like his body had let go of every ounce of fat except on his cheeks.

'Hello. I'm Freedom. I'm going to help you find your way around.'

The ridiculous hippie name was almost enough to make the new boy jump back into the car and tell the driver to take him back after all, no matter what had been promised to him.

'You can call me Dom,' Freedom continued. 'The others do.'

'OK.'

'There's Wisdom, too, but no one calls him Dom.

*I'm* Dom.'

'Right.' This boy seemed as simple as he looked.

The driver clapped his hands together. 'I best be off.'

'OK.'

'OK,' Dom echoed, even though the driver clearly hadn't been speaking to him.

The new boy guessed that Dom was about his own age, and was the daydreamy, dopey sort of boy who lived with a target on his forehead. At his old school, boys like that got beaten up and thrown in the skip down the road on their first day, no questions asked. He'd need to keep his distance, otherwise he might become a target too.

They stood side by side as the man drove away so fast that the car screeched.

When he was out of sight, Dom asked: 'Want to see the house?' He was hopping from foot to foot in excitement.

'Sure.'

The new boy followed Dom through the golden gate. It squealed open in the rain. He felt his resolve wobble again, and he reminded himself why he was there. After all, he told himself, things certainly couldn't get any worse.

## 2: DOM

The new boy and Dom stood side by side and watched the man drive away. The new boy was dressed differently to everybody at the Ash House. Dom's trousers looked like they'd once been a part of a smart suit, but now were stained, shredded at the hem and short enough to reveal his muddy ankles and trainers. The new boy was wearing tracksuit bottoms that didn't have a single rip or stain. For the first time that he could remember, Dom felt self-conscious. He wanted the new boy to like him more than anything.

He pushed his sodden fringe out of his eyes. Clothes could change. He just wished that the sun was shining when the new boy saw the Ash House for the first time: the way the smoke eased off the building and smudged the sun, the way tiny grains of ash mixed with pollen in the summer and were whipped by the wind so that they settled in the children's hair and under their eyes. It wasn't so nice in the rain.

Dom opened the gate and reminded himself that patience is a Niceness.

He led the new boy up the rest of the driveway to the front of the Ash House, stealing glances so that he could see him catch the first glimpse of the soft, opaque walls, the towering chimneys, the glossy windows lined with black powder. He wanted to see his eyes widened and hear him catch his breath. Soon the gate and the drive were out of view and nothing stood between them and the house. They stopped walking.

'Here it is,' said Dom. 'The Ash House.'

He admired the walls seeping into the air. The house's outline blurred and billowed as the wind scuffed it. Its smoke drifted over the glassy, rain-soaked grass, infusing the world with the smell of bonfires. Twin torches were staked into the ground outside the house, burning despite the rain. Dom put his hands on his hips and beamed.

'It's brilliant, isn't it?'

'What's that burning smell?'

'Come and touch it!' Dom cried excitedly.

He dragged him over the grass, ignoring the rain tapping on their shoulders. Dom could smell the walls as they got near: wood, air, coal and something fragrant, all caught together in the moment they're set alight.

'Look.' Dom pressed his hand into the wall. It was warm, and Dom knew it would burn him if he pressed too hard for too long. He whispered the reverent words they used to show their thanks for the ash and the Niceness of their names: 'Freedom is a Niceness.' His pale palm came away with a perfect dusting of grey powder. 'You do it too.'

The new boy held up a finger and stroked the wall gently. It came away smudged with the same grey.

'OK. So it's a dirty house?'

'It's not dirt, it's *ash*. The Headmaster made it.'

'But—'

'What was I thinking!' Dom smacked his forehead. 'We have to give you a name first.' He set off towards the front doors.

'I already have a name,' the new boy called after him.

'What is it?' Dom was turning the iron door knob.

'I . . . I . . .' He pondered the question and hiccupped, as if he was suppressing a gasp. He touched his forehead, leaving a dark smudge above one eye. 'I-I don't know.'

The hall had a high vaulted ceiling and a stone floor. There was a small table with an old telephone, and a stool next to it. By the door was a larger table with a metal bowl and a wood panel engraved with words mounted on the wall. Dom took the new boy towards the bowl first.

The bowl was filled with metal badges, each one the size of a large coin. Dom rummaged through them, picked up one or two, scrutinized them, and put them back, while the new boy watched him with reluctant interest. It was a tricky decision – one the Headmaster had always made.

Finally, he chose one. The badge was perfect – not as shiny as some of the others, but it was weighty and was perfectly smooth. He could run a finger all around it and not feel a single nick or groove. He held it out to the new boy.

'Solitude,' Dom announced.

The new boy looked at it sceptically.

'Is it a coin?'

'It's a badge.' Dom pointed to his own, pinned over his heart. It was bright silver and had an engraving of a bird. 'See? Freedom. You should be Solitude, because you arrived alone and sometimes being alone is a Niceness.'

The new boy looked at his badge. It was dark grey and had a wolf's head engraved on it. Since he clearly didn't know what to do with it, Dom pinned it on to his jumper for him.

'Solitude,' Dom said again, enjoying the sound of his friend's new name.

'So you're all named after . . .?'

'Nicenesses.' Dom tapped the mud off his shoes. 'You'll meet all the others soon. You'll learn them all.' He then led the way across the hall. A window high above them sent down a single beam of blue-grey light.

There were several doors with dusty handles, a grand staircase leading upstairs, and a stone staircase going down to the basement. But Dom ignored these and headed for a door at the far end. Its wood was smooth and shiny from use.

They stepped outside into a concrete courtyard veined with moss. The rain had got worse.

'So, that's the classroom, and over there's the canteen,' Dom said, pointing to the single-storey, barn-like buildings. 'For lessons and mealtimes – I suppose that's obvious . . .' He laughed nervously. The new boy looked unimpressed. 'They don't look like much, but we can all fit inside. We're going this way . . .' He set off across the courtyard, towards an overgrown path that led away from the house. Solitude fiddled with his badge, and then glanced up to see where they were going.

'What's that?'

'Dorms.'

Solitude stopped walking.

Dom turned around. 'It's where we sleep,' he explained. The Headmaster had said that it would take the new boy time to get used to everything.

'It's a greenhouse.'

Dom frowned. He turned back to the dorms, trying to see them through fresh eyes. 'Well, it's not really green.'

'No, I mean, it's a place for plants,' said Solitude. 'You can't sleep in there.'

'We can. Come on, I'll show you.' Dom set off with renewed excitement.

Other than the Ash House, this was his favourite building. It was nearly as tall as the house itself, the glass had a blue-green sheen, like a beetle's back or a black-bird's feather, and its frame was made from ornate wrought iron, turned orange with rust. It had a floor to split it into two storeys: boys upstairs, girls downstairs. The girls walked through the front entrance to get to the shadow-filled maze they slept in. The boys went around the side and up a spindly metal staircase to reach the upper floor.

As they climbed the stairs, Dom told Solitude about a day a few years ago when they'd grabbed old buckets and clothes they couldn't wear any more, tied lengths of rope and bungees around themselves, and walked over the roof and down the sides, cleaning the glass. For the rest of the day the whole building glittered like it was moving under the sun. They'd sat on the lawn and watched it. They were soaked, rubbed raw from the ropes and had green sludge lodged under their fingernails, but it was worth it to watch the clouds drift over the glass. But in a few weeks the ash and rain and sludge had claimed it back.

'That's why we don't clean the outside very often,' he finished.

They reached the top of the stairs. It was still the warmer side of autumn, so they hadn't covered the gaps in the glass panes with blankets and carpet yet.

Dom let Solitude go inside first.

He took a moment to look about his new home.

'I don't understand. It looks like you put this together yourselves.' He turned to Dom. 'Where did you say your Headmaster is?'

'We're not sure.'

'But he's not here?'

'No, he's away.'

'Yes, but . . . Dom, how long has he been away for?'

Dom squinted and thought. 'Three years this winter.'

## 3: SOL

The dorm was a forest. Mosses, vines, algae and leaves covered every surface. They knitted themselves over the glass roof, draped over metal beams, carpeted the floor and twisted into soft cushions on bedframes. A few late-blooming flowers decorated the roof high above their heads. It smelt of the outdoors. The light glowed through the cleaner panes in some places, while dirt and plants cast green shadows in others.

There were two rows of beds with an aisle down the middle. Some beds were rusted metal frames; others were thin mattresses on the floor.

Solitude felt bewildered. He knew that buildings couldn't be made of ash and smoke, and these children couldn't have lived in this greenhouse on their own for years on end. But that's not what Dom was saying.

He had been expecting a healing refuge for children like him. Something between a school and a summer camp. But this wasn't it. The Ash House was like the end of a world that had been left to decay, forgotten by everyone who had ever cared about it.

Dom walked down the aisle, pointing to each bed and saying a name. When he reached the end of the aisle, he said: 'This is where I sleep.' He was pointing to a mattress and a bright yellow blanket on the floor. 'And this one is yours.'

Solitude was relieved to see that he had a proper bed. He didn't like the idea of sleeping on the floor, where bugs and spiders could reach him.

Dom beamed at him. Solitude knew he couldn't let this madness go any further. He needed to find an adult.

'Dom, I want to use the phone.'

Dom frowned at him in confusion. 'The phone?'

'The one in the house.' He had been told everything would be provided – he didn't need a mobile, a towel, books, not even spare clothes. He felt vulnerable, lost in this strange world with nothing of his own to hang on to, not even his name.

'But it's not ringing,' said Dom.

'What? No, not to answer it – to call someone else's phone.'

'That's not how the phone works, Solitude.' Dom spoke to him as if he were a toddler. 'You have to wait for it to ring first.'

'I just need to speak to someone. I think there's been a mistake.'

'But no one has called for you,' Dom said. 'The Headmaster said the Ash House might be confusing for you at first. Can I call you Sol?'

'I need a minute.' Solitude sat down on the edge of the bed and held his head in his hands.

'It's OK, Sol.' Dom patted his arm, apparently thrilled with the new nickname.

They heard the clang of shoes on the metal staircase. Sol listened to the chatter punctuated by laughs and shouts. It was like his old school – the real world – was echoing in his ears in this strange place. But whenever he tried to picture the real world, it was foggy and distant in his mind, like a memory that didn't really belong to him.

'Everybody wants to meet you,' said Dom.

They burst into the dorm, ripping off jumpers, kicking off shoes, shoving and pulling and laughing. They came down the greenhouse towards Sol and Dom. When they saw the new boy, their noise lulled and then bubbled up again even stronger.

Sol guessed there were fifteen new faces. They all wore the same tattered, mismatched, dirty clothes as Dom. Their metal badges bumped against their chests and their sleeves were pushed up over scrawny arms.

A few of them jumped from mattress to mattress down the room, while others shouted at them to stop. Some ran their fingers through trailing vines as they talked. They were happy, unselfconscious. Sol felt himself bristle. He tried to take in each face and decipher the group dynamics.

He was relieved when one boy surged ahead of the pack. He was small and wiry, with floppy dark hair. When he smiled his teeth were straight and white. This had to be their leader, Sol decided. Best to start distancing himself from Dom.

Sol shuffled to the end of the bed and put on his bravest smile. He held out a hand and the floppy-haired boy reached for it, but before he could take it, someone tripped him and he stumbled forward, somersaulted and skidded across the filthy floor, landing crumpled under a tangle of leaves. The other boys laughed.

'Nice try, Wisdom.'

An enormous boy now stood in front of Sol. He was nearly the size of a grown man, with colourless hair that was cut into short, ugly clumps. His mouth was a straight line across his face. But that wasn't what drew the eye. A fascinating scar ran from the parting of his hair, down the side of his face and over his eye socket in a

C-shape. The eye was bright and beady inside the puckered flesh.

The other boys fell silent after the enormous boy had spoken. Sol had been wrong about the other boy. This was their leader.

'H-hi,' Sol said, holding out his hand again.

'I'm Concord,' the boy said. The badge on his chest was gold and showed two hands shaking. Concord made no move to take Sol's hand. 'Who are you?'

'Con, this is Solitude,' Dom interjected. Sol felt a flush of irritation towards him.

Concord looked at Sol's badge and nodded with approval. A few of the boys chuckled. 'Makes sense,' he said.

'I said we should call him Sol,' Dom chirped again. 'I made him touch the ash and then we came straight here.' Sol edged off the bed, putting as much space between him and Dom as possible.

Concord nodded. 'What do you think about the house?' he asked Sol.

'I've . . . never seen anything like it,' he said honestly. The boys all smiled and nodded at each other. 'I was wondering . . . why is it called the Ash House?'

Dom erupted with a childish laugh. The others joined in.

Sol stepped back. The laughing crowd made his neck feel prickly and hot.

'The Headmaster made the house out of ash,' said Concord, the only one who didn't laugh. 'He named it that. Then he gave us our names.'

It felt like they were closing in on him, their smiles and Concord's stare forming a wall that blocked the door. Sol felt the itch in his neck spread towards his back.

'I need to use the phone,' he explained to Concord.

'I already told him—' Dom started to say, but Sol cut him off.

'Yes, you've told me nothing but a load of rubbish since I got here, so why don't you go back to whatever mental place you broke out of?'

As soon as the words were out of Sol's mouth, Dom's round, smiling face dropped. The laughter and smiles from the other boys dried up too. Concord reached out, grabbed the neck of Sol's jumper and dragged him slowly across the floor until Sol had a close-up view of the split skin around Concord's eye.

'You will not speak to Dom like that,' Concord said very quietly. 'That is not a Niceness.'

Others behind him nodded firmly. 'Definitely not a Niceness,' someone echoed.

'Dom has the most Niceness of us all,' Concord continued. 'And he is my best friend.'

Sol thought of Wisdom being thrown across the room just moments earlier. The rules in this place were totally upside down. He wanted to pull away and stop staring at Concord's face, but the boy was bigger and stronger and held him there with unshakeable strength.

'I only meant—' Sol started to explain, but Concord didn't listen.

'Since you clearly have no Niceness, we don't want you here. But we will wait and hear what the Headmaster tells us to do with you.'

Concord pushed Sol so hard he fell backwards on to the bed and smacked his head on the metal frame. He yelled and gripped his head, squeezing it until the pain subsided. When he opened his eyes, the boys had drifted away in groups towards their beds.

Only Dom hung back. He placed a blue blanket on the foot of Sol's bed, before turning away to his own mattress.

After dark, Sol lay under his blanket – which was surprisingly thick and soft – and stared up at the shapes the moon cast on the glass. The fifteen other boys in the room slept, some murmuring, some tossing and turning, some twitching and itching in their sleep, so that the dorm felt like one creature with lots of limbs.

He longed for sleep. He decided that tomorrow he would find a way to contact someone – anyone – and get himself out of this place.

He tried counting himself to sleep.

One ... two ... three ...

He shuffled his shoulder blades deeper into the mattress. When he shut his eyes, the pattern of the leaves above him was replaced by Dom's face, hurt and confused.

*I don't care*, Sol told himself. He'd only met Dom that day. What did it matter if he was Concord's best friend? It wasn't like he'd said anything that bad – at his old school, he'd been teased and bullied far worse.

But every time he rolled over, he thought of Dom placing the blanket on the end of the bed.

'Sol?' Dom's voice wormed its way into his restless thoughts.

'What?' Sol whispered back.

'Why aren't you sleeping?'

'I'm just thinking.'

'Do you need another blanket?'

'No.' After a pause, Sol added, 'Thank you.'

'That's all right.'

Then, after a longer pause, Sol whispered again, 'Dom, I'm sorry about what I said. I don't think you're mental.'

'You do a bit.'

'No, I really don't.'

In the darkness, Sol heard Dom prop himself up on his elbow.

'Sol, honesty is a Niceness.'

'OK, so I think some of the things you say sound a bit mad. But isn't being sorry a "Niceness" too?'

He heard the smile in Dom's voice. 'It is. So is forgiveness.'

'So you're not angry at me?'

'Of course not. You're my friend. You can't stay angry at your friends.'

Dom rolled over. Within minutes he was snoring softly.

Sol lay awake for longer. His mind still whirred, but now with other thoughts. New friends. A place where nobody knew him and he could get better.

A place where the pain couldn't reach him.

He tried counting again. On the mattress next to him, Dom's breath caught in his throat, making a wet clicking noise like a frog.

One . . . two . . . three . . .

The leaves that crawled over the roof of the green-house were bent double by a sharp wind that he could hear but not feel.

One ... two ... three ...

He couldn't remember who had told him that being here would make everything better.

One ... two ...

He had to get better.

One ...

## 4: DOM

The new boy slept longer and deeper than the rest of them. As the first pink and orange light seeped into the dorm, illuminating the leaves so that you could see every vein, Concord came over to Dom's bed. He stared at Sol, who was sleeping on his side with his mouth hanging open.

'It's not right,' Concord whispered to Dom. 'We've never had a new person before.'

'But the Headmaster said . . .'

'I know, I know.' Concord waved away Dom's excuses. They had been best friends for as long as Dom could remember. They often knew what the other was thinking or feeling.

'Con, I think that Sol could really have some brilliant Nicenesses.'

Concord raised the eyebrow above his unscarred eye.

'I do,' Dom insisted. 'He showed me last night. If we

just give him a chance.'

'We need to see what the girls think about it,' said Concord.

Dom nodded. He had woken up in his usual good mood, but he had to admit that if the girls and Concord decided to dislike Sol, the new boy wouldn't enjoy living at the Ash House very much. He picked his binoculars up off his pillow and fiddled with the focusing wheel while he worried.

'I'm on duty this week,' said Concord. 'I've got to go. I'll see you at breakfast.'

He left as the rest of the dorm began to stir.

When Sol finally woke up, Dom pointed him to the showers. The bathroom was at the opposite end of the dorm, behind the thin dividing wall where they hung their coats and stuffed their clothes in cubbyholes. Sol was reluctant to use the rusted taps and stand on the once-white tiles with black grout between them, which no amount of scrubbing could budge, even though the water was hot and gushing.

They were the last ones to trudge downstairs, just in time to see the girls emerge from the ground floor of the dorms. Sol stopped and stared at them, hanging back a half-step behind Dom as if he was suddenly shy. They turned to look at Sol, their expressions guarded. Dom raised his hand and a girl towards the front of the group nodded back.

Dom felt a twinge of disappointment. He used to be just as close to Liberty as he was to any of the boys, even Concord, but since the Headmaster had left, a rift had appeared between the girls and boys. No one talked about it, but Dom sometimes felt he was being left behind on a shore as they drifted away.

It was a morning like any other, only different in every way, because Dom had Sol. Usually he sat with his three best friends: Concord, Merit and Justice. But today he sat tall in the middle of the long table with Sol on his right and fielded questions. Happiness and Temperance served breakfast – hot porridge with a tiny drizzle of honey.

Libby sat opposite Dom and Sol, her curls barely contained by tight braids. She watched Sol closely, while the boys asked Sol question after question. What did he think of the Ash House? Did he like his name? Didn't he love the dorm?

Sol had his mouth full during each question, so he only had to answer with a cautious nod. Then Dom would sweep in to expand on his answer.

'He's here so we can all teach him about Niceness,' Dom explained. 'And he can help us with chores. I think if it goes well, the Headmaster will send more and more new boys.'

'Or girls,' Libby added.

'He has a lot to learn about Niceness.' Concord appeared behind Libby, his bowl balanced in the palm of his hand.

'That's my point,' insisted Dom. 'The Headmaster says—'

'Can I ask something?' Sol spoke up suddenly. The whole table's attention snapped over to him. 'You said the Headmaster has been away for three years. So how do you know what he wants you to do?'

Dom shifted in his seat. None of them liked to talk about the Headmaster being away. Even Concord glanced at his feet. But Dom felt it was his duty to explain.

'He's going to be back very soon. In the meantime—'

'When?'

'When what?'

'When is he going to come back, exactly?'

Dom felt everyone's eyes on him. He took a deep breath. 'Just as soon as he can. Until then he phones every day to check in with the person on duty and let us know any chores he'd like us to do.'

'Who's on duty?'

Dom couldn't help but notice that for someone so reluctant to answer their questions, Sol seemed to have a lot of his own.

'I am, this week,' said Concord. 'We take turns.'

Sol stopped scraping at the last of his porridge. 'So ... there aren't any adults here? No teachers or parents or anyone? Just us?'

'Par-ents,' Libby sounded out the word. Heads tilted to one side.

'You don't have parents?'

'What are parents?' Dom asked.

Sol looked scared, suddenly, which Dom thought was strange. His green eyes were wide and worried, and his voice became high-pitched as he tried to explain: 'Parents – your mums and dads? The people who made you and raise you and look after you!'

'He means the Headmaster,' said Concord, though he sounded confused.

'But where do you think you all came from?' Sol demanded.

'The same place everything comes from,' Libby replied. 'The ash.'

'The ash.' The words were repeated and murmured around the table.

Sol put his spoon down. Dom thought he was starting

to look a little sick.

'So you don't have families?'

'This is our family,' Concord snapped.

'And we have the whole place to ourselves!' Dom felt himself speak a bit too loudly and with a bit too much enthusiasm, but he felt the questions spiralling towards a bad place and wanted to stop it. 'Isn't it wonderful?' He beamed at them all.

'We're totally alone?' Sol asked.

'Solitude is a Niceness, Sol.' Dom laughed with delight at his own brilliant joke until the rest of the table joined in.

Dom explained the daily routine to Sol as they left the canteen and headed into the Ash House itself. Sol paused to look up at the smoking walls. Just then, a bird swooped overhead and whirred towards the classroom.

'Is that a drone?' Sol asked.

'That's a bird.' Dom pressed the cool brass of his binoculars to his eyes and watched it fly over the classroom roof and head out over the grounds. 'It's doing its usual route, making sure we're all heading in for assembly. Nothing to worry about.'

Sol hesitated, looking around for more. Dom steered him inside. They followed the chattering group to the staircase that led down to the assembly room, which Sol kept calling a 'basement'.

'Is he not coming too?' Sol asked, when he noticed Concord sit down on the stool next to the phone.

'He needs to wait for it to ring,' Dom explained. 'Because he's on duty. At the end of the week it changes. It will be me soon, but it might be a while until your first go. Come on.'

They left the natural light behind them. Rows of seats were set out in the assembly room, facing a small stage. Dom made sure Sol sat in the front row, next to him. He felt certain that Sol – the most exciting thing to happen at the Ash House in his entire memory – was here for a reason. Right at that moment, the Headmaster was probably telling Concord what it was, and they would teach him about Niceness together.

Dom was so lost in these thrilling thoughts that he didn't mind waiting for the assembly to begin. In fact, he was one of the last to notice that the wait was unusually long. Too long. Bums shuffled in seats and trainers scuffed the floor. Sol let out an irritated sigh. Dom twisted round and caught Libby's eye. She always knew what to do before the rest of them. But she just gave Dom a confused frown. No one could remember the last time someone spent this long speaking to the Headmaster.

When Concord walked down the stairs, every muscle in his face looked strange. Dom felt like his hands and feet had been dipped into icy water.

'He didn't phone,' Concord croaked to the room.

In the three slow-moving years he had been away, the Headmaster had never failed to phone the Ash House.

## 5: SOL

Concord's words were immediately lost in a clamour of children's voices. They all shouted questions at him and each other. Some of them were out of their seats, hands in the air. Others were holding their hands to their mouths, eyes wide. Dom stood up, then sat back down straight away and tucked one leg beneath him.

Concord held up his hands and the noise eventually lulled.

'I'm sure he'll phone tomorrow and everything will go back to normal. In the meantime, we have chores and lessons and lots to do. I'm sure he'd want us to go on as normal and remember our Niceness.'

This was followed by quieter questions, the biting of nails and the nodding of heads. Everyone reluctantly got ready to leave and Concord climbed down from the stage. The colour was returning to his face, but his head was bowed.

'What was that all about?' Sol asked Dom, who was still sitting with his right leg underneath him and his chin resting on his left knee. He was chewing his thumbnail.

'The Headmaster always phones us. He's never forgotten before.'

'Maybe he's running late.'

'But he always phones straight after breakfast.'

'Perhaps he'll phone at lunchtime.' Sol had no idea why he was saying these things, but they brightened Dom up.

'Do you think so?'

'Sure, why not? He might just be busy or have lost reception.'

'Lost what?'

'Phone reception. You know – if he's somewhere without any signal, he might not be able to call. Where did you say he is?'

'We don't know. That's the worst part. Anything might have happened to him. What if he has lost these signal things, or if he's in trouble, or – or, or sick?'

Sol hoped more than anything that Dom didn't cry. He just didn't think he could handle it. He was relieved when Libby came over, fiddling nervously with the end of her braid, and squeezed Dom's shoulder.

'It will be OK,' she said.

'Thanks, Lib,' he replied.

'Of course it will.' Concord barrelled over. He was flanked by Dom's other friends, Justice and Merit. Justice was a nervous, restless boy who had that sort of skin that was so pale it looked translucent in some lights, while Merit was darker than Sol, with brown eyes, long, curved eyelashes and a calming voice.

'The house will protect us,' Merit assured them.

Concord looked pointedly at Sol. 'If we remember our Niceness.'

Sol felt his dislike for Dom's so-called best friend reach boiling point. Just because he hadn't started on the right foot didn't mean Concord had to single him out every chance he got.

'It's just a house,' Sol said. 'A house can't do anything. We're alone.'

'We're not alone,' Dom insisted. 'The Headmaster phones us. *Every* day. He looks after us and makes sure we're OK, and will be back very, very, very soon.'

'I don't see what he can do over the phone,' said Sol. 'And three years is hardly soon.'

Dom opened and closed his mouth several times. But the others didn't mind wading into the conversation on his behalf.

'You don't know anything about it,' Libby said. Sol

thought she'd been aloof at breakfast, but now she seemed to openly dislike him.

'No one asked you,' added Merit.

'You've only just got here, you have no way of understanding—' Justice was nearly shouting, but Concord held up a hand and cut him off.

'That's a good point. You *have* only just got here.'

Sol glanced nervously at each of them. Dom was staring at his feet.

'What do you mean?'

Concord glared at him. The colourless fuzz of his hair blended in with the wall behind him. 'You turn up out of nowhere and now we don't hear from the Headmaster. Anyone else see the connection?'

Sol felt a puddle of silence forming around where he and Dom sat.

'The outside is not a Niceness,' Concord went on, 'but you've come here with it all over you, carrying who-knows-what on your shoes or clothes or skin.'

'Carrying what? Diseases, you mean?' said Sol. 'I'm not carrying germs. If anyone were, it would be you lot. Do you even get doctors or dentists in here?'

Justice sucked his breath in loudly. Libby swore. Concord took a step towards Sol.

Dom stood up so quickly that his chair clattered.

'We'll be late for lessons.'

'But he said—'

'Con, leave it. We should go.' Dom looked down at Sol, looking annoyed at him for the first time.

Sol didn't see what was so outrageous about what he'd said, but he seemed to have overstepped some line.

Concord made a sort of growling noise under his breath and walked away, taking most of the group with him.

'Don't make jokes like that again,' Dom warned.

'OK,' said Sol.

Dom tilted his head to one side as if he was about to say something else. Then he shrugged.

'We really do have to go,' he said. 'Just forget about it. Like you said, the Headmaster will call very soon. Everything will go back to normal.'

'Yeah.' Sol followed Dom up the narrow staircase. 'Whatever that means here.'

The Ash House didn't seem to need any adults. The children moved like clockwork. There were no bells, no shouting, no bossy person shepherding them from one place to another. They stuck to a careful routine which they judged by a sundial near the front of the house, which Sol couldn't read, but they hardly needed that either. The days at the Ash House were so familiar to them, every movement was a habit. When it was time for a meal, they ate. When it was time for chores, they worked. And when it was time for lessons, they piled out of the main building and went into the run-down barn opposite the canteen.

Sol followed Dom. He noticed that every time he was outside, he stopped and squinted at the sky, looking for the drones. Sometimes he used his binoculars, sometimes he simply shielded his eyes with his hands.

They went into a building that looked like it had been put up years ago in a hurry. It was made of corrugated iron and had a metal and Perspex roof, which made a din when it rained. Inside was one large classroom with rows of old-fashioned wooden desks.

Sol's desk was at the back, with no one to his left or right, only Dom's bony back in front him. He began to relax for the first time since arriving at the Ash House. He knew classrooms and how they worked. He scanned the group, making the most of the opportunity to observe everyone together without their eyes on him. If Dom wasn't the school loser, who was? It seemed to be Wisdom, who was given a wide berth by everybody. Dom's group was made up of Concord, Merit, Justice and three girls.

The girls were Liberty, Honesty and Sincerity. Honesty's hair was cut short and she and Sincerity wore trousers and shirts similar to the boys'. When Libby sat down, she turned around to look at something, and Sol thought with surprise that there was a shadow of Dom in her face: the slow smile, the slanted eyes, the round cheeks. But then the light fell across her face differently and he wasn't so sure.

The seven of them were the loudest in the room. Concord sat on his desk and rested his feet on the edge of Dom's chair, chewing the end of a pencil and throwing dark glances at Sol.

Sol was given a few sheets of paper and a pencil. Then Honesty dragged the door shut and a light came out of an overhead projector. An image formed on the wall in front of the desks. A film started to play. Everyone fell silent and sat up straight in their chairs.

It was a lecture series from a long time ago. The film must have been made before any of them were born. The man speaking to them wore a multicoloured tie and ugly brown blazer. Sol stifled a laugh and looked around, but everyone was straight-faced and listening carefully.

It was the strangest lesson Sol had ever sat in. The teacher picked out Truth as the Niceness of the day, and they listened to him for thirty-five minutes while he talked about what it meant, why it was important, and how they should behave so that it was a Niceness they had. After the lesson on Niceness they learnt about chores and running a household, then they learnt about Mercy as another Niceness, then they learnt about leadership principles and how to bring people together to solve a problem.

By this point, Sol was bored stiff. Each lesson was either a long, philosophical lecture, or a how-to guide for the Ash House that he barely followed.

The others all made precise, organized notes. Sometimes the man in the film asked questions and paused to allow discussion. They all politely debated among themselves. By the time lessons ended and the projector showed a blank, yellow square of light, Sol had put his pencil down and was staring at wispy spider webs on the wall.

Dom turned around in his chair and gave Sol his big, stupid smile.

'What did you think?'

'It's not what I'm used to,' he said honestly. 'Do you have any teachers other than ... him?'

'Yes, we have five.'

'Are they all films like the one we just saw?'

'Films?'

'Films.' Sol explained the word by pointing at the wall opposite the projector.

'Oh! Yes.' Dom then repeated the new word happily: 'Films.'

Sol looked at his lacklustre notes. 'What happens now?'

'Chores. Then tomorrow more Niceness, leadership and survival skills.'

'OK,' Sol said. 'Don't you do English or history or something?'

'History of the Ash House?' This idea prompted a smile from Dom so wide that Sol thought it might pop his cheeks.

'Of the world, idiot.'

'Well, la-di-da.' Concord turned around too. He placed a hand on the back of Dom's chair. 'Look who's in training to be Headmaster of the world.'

Justice and Merit, alert to any hint of a fight, turned their attention to Concord and Sol.

'I just meant that "history of the Ash House" isn't exactly a school subject,' said Sol.

'"School,"' Concord repeated with a sneer. 'Now you're just making up words.'

Concord and Dom placed their notes and pencils under the lids of their desks. Sol looked around at the tired furniture, dirty walls and flumes of dust floating in the light of the projector. It was only when he stood up to leave that he noticed the neatly painted writing on the wall behind him.

'What's that?' he asked, even as he worked it out for himself.

'It's us,' said Dom, who was tidying his notes inside his desk. He sounded pleased to change the subject. 'We need to add your name soon.'

Sol saw that Dom was right. It was a list of their names. He spotted Freedom. Concord. Liberty. And also Amity, Reason, Calm, Joy, Patience, Prudence . . . It was the same list as the engraving in the hall of the Ash House. Then Sol noticed something unusual.

'Why is there a gap?' he asked Dom.

Near the beginning one name had been covered with white paint. Sol went closer and made out the name Clemency showing faintly through the paint. Sol struggled to remember even half of their names, but he was sure he hadn't heard anyone say 'Clemency' since he arrived.

'Why is it painted over?' he asked.

Dom appeared by his side, draping the binoculars around his neck. He ran his fingertips over Clemency's name.

'She's not here any more,' was all Dom said in reply.

Sol was aware that the room had gone quiet behind them. He turned around. Everyone left in the classroom was looking at the wall, lost in thought.

Concord put a stop to it. He climbed over his desk and placed a hand on Dom's shoulder.

'Come on. We've got chores to organize.'

Dom nodded and they turned to leave.

'What do you mean, she's not here any more?' Sol asked. 'Was she allowed to leave?'

'She . . . well, once . . .'

Sol noticed that Dom's usually pink cheeks had turned pale.

'Dom, how did she leave?' Sol demanded.

'Leave him alone. Come on, Dom, don't listen to his Nastiness.' Concord took a protective hold of Dom's arm.

'How? How did she get out? Where did she go? Just tell me!'

'Shut up about it,' Concord snapped. 'She didn't *go* anywhere.'

It took a moment for Sol to realize what Concord meant by this.

He needed air. The palms of his hands felt clammy. He tried not to think about what that meant.

'What's wrong, Sol?' Dom asked.

'Um . . .' Light started to fray at the edges. It was a sensation he knew well. A few specks of black flicked across his vision. Flies, Sol told himself. It's just flies or dirt.

Dom was saying something else, but he missed it. Concord stepped closer.

'He asked you a question,' he said.

'Sorry,' said Sol as he edged around his desk. 'I . . . I just . . .' The black was multiplying like bacteria under a microscope.

Concord was blocking his way. Justice stood behind him, his white hair blending into the sunlight in the doorway. Sol wished that the boundaries between different types of matter – brick walls, the wooden doorframe, his own skin – would stop wobbling.

'Do you know what I think?' Concord asked. 'I think you're a test. The Headmaster is testing us. He wants us to see how you have no Niceness. You don't belong on that wall.'

In an awkward jerking motion, Sol tried to grab Concord's shoulder to stop himself falling. He missed. The black dots swelled and consumed Justice's face, Concord's face, the sunlight, the entire world.

The prickling ran up the back of Sol's legs, straight as

a line of ants. Electricity stroked each of his ribs and hopped from vertebra to vertebra until finally, as he braced himself, it gripped each of his shoulder blades and twisted. The pain took the air out of him. His neck seized up. It was something he had felt before, too many times before, but each time he was awed by the all-consuming horror of it.

He felt it in his molars, his eyeballs, his fingernails. His back burnt and burnt and nothing could make it stop. He knew it didn't take long for his body to shut down and save him from the worst of it, but it never seemed to do this quickly enough.

He hoped the floor wasn't filthy. He hoped they didn't laugh at him.

He heard footsteps, voices and chairs scraping. Was he really still in a classroom? It was impossible that the pain that was searing his shoulder blades could happen somewhere so mundane.

He heard Concord say, 'I didn't even touch him!'

Libby's voice was quieter: 'He shouldn't have been talking about her.'

Sol couldn't see anything. He tried to say Dom's name. Then the pain pulled him to a place where no one would reach him. He let it.

## 6: DOM

After Sol collapsed in the classroom, Concord carried him up to the dorm. Libby had stood at the bottom of the staircase and watched them go, two lines creased between her eyebrows. Dom stayed with Sol while the others finished the rest of the lessons. He sat on the edge of the bed, put his elbows on his knees and held his chin in his palms so the weight of his head would stop his hands from shaking. Occasionally he heard a bird hum close to the dorm, then disappear quickly. He hoped it didn't watch too closely.

Sol barely moved. There were moments when he almost woke up, but then he would clench his jaw, groan and drift off again.

When lessons ended, Merit was the first up the stairs and into the dorm. He brushed away the leaves that tried to tangle with his hair.

'Is he up?'

'No,' said Dom.

Merit handed him an apple. Dom took it but was in no mood to eat.

'You don't have to look after him.'

'I do.'

'You know what I mean. The others are coming.'

'Tell them to be quiet when they come up.'

Dom heard Merit call down the stairs to the other boys. The cobwebbed ivy on the glass panes above his head kept his corner of the dorm in shadow. It felt like sitting in a tree. Usually Dom felt safe here, but seeing Sol so ill made it hard to feel safe anywhere.

The boys filed in slowly and quietly, until everybody was gathered around Sol's bed.

'He can't stay here,' Concord said. 'First the Head-master doesn't phone. Now the new boy is ill. Something's going on.'

'We can't let one person bring something bad to all of us,' Justice agreed.

'The girls think so too,' added Merit. 'I know they're not allowed up here, but we should all have a say.'

'True. But all of us agree?' said Concord.

'No.'

The group looked at Dom.

'Dom, come on—' Concord started.

'But I don't agree! We don't know what's wrong with him. It could be a one-off. You know – he might be nervous about being somewhere new. Or he didn't eat much breakfast?'

'Dom, we were all there,' said Merit. 'He didn't just faint. He had some sort of fit or something.'

'What if he has a sickness and he gives it to us?' said Justice. He twisted the hem of his shirt agitatedly. 'What if we all get sick with an illness from the outside? What do we do then?'

'He won't make us sick,' Dom insisted. 'We don't know anything about him.' He appealed to Concord. If he won him over, Sol would be left alone. 'We don't know what the Headmaster wants with him. What if he comes back and finds out that we got rid of Sol? He might be angry.'

Concord hesitated. They all did.

'If it happens again, then we'll do something,' Dom insisted. 'But let's at least wait and see what Sol says when he wakes up.'

'Fine,' said Concord. 'Just until the Headmaster calls us. Which I'm sure will be tomorrow. Dom, when he wakes up, find out everything you can. If you think it might be something we can catch, you have to tell us.'

'I will.'

'Swear it!' said Justice, raising his voice.

'I do. I swear.'

They all stood behind Concord and nodded. Dom felt the weight of all their worries on his shoulders and itched with a feeling he'd tried to bury long ago: guilt.

'I'll make sure nothing bad happens to anyone,' he promised them.

When Sol opened his eyes, they locked on to Dom's, wide with fear. It was a moment before he licked his lips and spoke.

'You didn't call an ambulance, did you?' His voice was low and raw.

'Call a what?' Dom asked.

'Never mind.'

Sol tried to prop himself up on his elbows, then sank back down on to his thin pillow. 'I'm sorry,' he said.

Dom shuffled closer. Sol's brown skin had become almost grey. There were deep lines under his green eyes, and his palms were dirty and grazed from where he'd landed on the classroom floor.

'The others were here. They checked on you.'

Sol pulled a face. Dom could tell he didn't believe him.

'I stayed with you.'

'Thanks,' Sol said, but it didn't sound like he meant it. 'Can you not sit so close to me?'

Dom realized that he was leaning right over Sol, his face hovering inches from him. He sat back. 'Sorry. And I'm sorry about earlier too. We didn't mean to scare you.'

'Earlier?'

'When you fell.'

'That wasn't you. That was my back. I have . . . problems with it.'

'It's just you were looking at our names and when Concord said . . .'

Sol sat up. His skin took on a green tinge as the foliage in the dorm was reflected in his face. He dug his hands into the sides of the bed to steady himself.

'We didn't mean to scare you,' Dom said again. 'It's true we had to paint over . . . that name . . .'

'Clemency?'

'Don't say it!' Dom said urgently, holding up his hands. 'We're never supposed to say her name!'

'OK, OK, calm down . . . It's . . . it's not something you'd understand anyway.'

Even saying this looked like it was an effort. Splotches of pink appeared on Sol's cheeks. Dom went to press a cold cloth on to his forehead but Sol smacked his hand away.

'Leave me alone!' he snapped.

'I'm just trying to be nice,' said Dom.

'I don't need you to be nice to me.'

'You do. The Headmaster says nothing is more important than remembering our Niceness.'

'What is it with everyone here and Niceness?' Sol muttered as he swung his legs off the bed. He moved slowly, as if all his muscles were stiff. 'From what I've seen, no one's that nice. And your Headmaster didn't bring me here. I brought myself.'

'Niceness isn't just kindness. It's all the things we need to be and have.' Dom took a deep breath and started to sing the song they had all known since they were tiny. He knew that he wasn't a tuneful singer, so he tried to make up for this with enthusiasm, because it was the first time Sol had heard it and it was an important thing to get right. 'Theeeeere's AMITY and CALM and CHARITY and CONCORD and DILIGENCE—'

'Stop!' Sol held up his hands. 'Please shut up. I can't be dealing with . . . with whatever that was.' He rubbed his eyes.

'Sorry. I'll sing it to you another time. If nothing else, it's a good way to learn everyone's names. We can add your name to it now.'

'Concord said my name doesn't belong on the wall.'

'I think Concord might be wrong.' Dom bit his lip, feeling he had betrayed his friend. But Dom wasn't scared of Sol or what he might represent. He could see the Niceness in there, struggling to get out. Sol didn't want to be rude or unkind. Something was making him that way – he was like a toy that had been bent out of shape. Dom was determined to undo it.

He watched Sol move his arms in slow loops, clenching and unclenching his fists, wriggling his feet and bending his legs.

'What do you think I wouldn't understand?' he asked. 'You said the names didn't make you fall down. What did? I need to know, even if you think I won't understand.'

Sol stared at him, his face unreadable.

'Even if you understand, you can't help me.'

'I'm not going to hurt you either. Try telling me.'

Sol hesitated. Then he took a deep tremor of a breath and started to speak.

'They say it's some sort of pain syndrome. It started a while ago. It's this pain in my back and no one knows what's causing it. They say there's nothing wrong with me. But I get these sort of . . . episodes. Terrors. That's what you saw. First, everything gets blurry or hard to see. Next it's in my spine and then it's everywhere. I can't stay conscious most of the time. But they've done every test and asked me a million questions. Every foster parent I've ever had has dragged me about looking for a "miracle cure". Then they started saying that it's all in my head, but therapy didn't help at all.' He rubbed his sleeve angrily across his eyes. 'Anyway, the pain's been getting worse, so I went to hospital. They said I had to wait overnight to get my test results. Then this, this nurse – I don't know who she was, I'd never met her before – she woke me up in the middle of the night and said I was going somewhere else where they could help me. Here. But then you told me that your Headmaster has been gone for three years. I guess they thought this would be a good place to dump me. I don't even know what I'd do if I left.' He looked miserably up at the ivy and the dirty windows. 'I have nowhere to go.'

Episodes. Terrors.

Dom felt all the blood drain from his face. It took him a moment to clear his throat and find his voice.

'It sounds terrible.'

'It is,' Sol admitted. 'The worst part is not knowing anything. What if it is all in my head? But I don't know how I'm inventing it, so I can't stop. Then I think that can't be it. It's so real. Pain can't be imaginary. Can it?'

Dom coughed a few times. He looked down at the

50

mattress. 'I'm sure if you try really hard, it will stay under control.'

'No, the whole point is—'

'Sol, you *need* to keep it under control.' Dom tried to make sure every word he said lodged itself in Sol's brain. 'Maybe the Ash House will heal you, I don't know. But you have to keep this to yourself. When the Headmaster comes back, you mustn't tell him. This isn't a good place to get sick.'

'But I came here *because* I'm sick.'

'Nothing good happens when someone is sick!' Dom was on his feet. He grabbed Sol's shoulders and squeezed so hard that his fingers hurt. Sol tried to twist free, but Dom held him there. 'I'll help you hide the pain. I'll watch you. *All* the time. I promise, I'll never stop watching, I'll warn you and hide you if—'

'Get off. You're hurting me.'

'I'm trying to help you!'

'Just let go!'

Dom released him. 'The others can't find out. We'll keep it a secret until you're better. I'm good at keeping secrets.'

## 7: DOM

**D**om felt his guts turn to ice when he found out that Sol was sick. But he had a knack for finding silver linings in every situation. After all, hope was a very important Niceness.

After Sol fell back asleep, Dom stayed on the bed and thought the problem through. If he was going to hide Sol's illness from the others, he needed to trust that the Ash House would make him better with time. With a bit of luck (another Niceness), by the time the Headmaster came back, it would all be in the past, he told himself. Maybe that's why Sol was there in the first place: so he could protect him.

A second chance.

He was telling the truth when he said he was good at keeping secrets. But secrets sometimes involved lying, which wasn't something Dom did lightly or happily. The group would want to know what was wrong with Sol –

they had seen his pain episode with their own eyes. Dom turned the problem over and over in his mind, but each way he looked at it, he knew his friends would want to get rid of Sol.

He wasn't ready to let that happen.

A few days later, tired of watching Sol sulk, pick at his food and only grunt when spoken to, Dom took him to the place he went whenever he had a problem.

'I've sat in this classroom for days and never spotted this,' said Sol. 'What's in it?'

'The library,' said Dom. He couldn't suppress his smile.

'It looks like a cupboard.'

They were standing in the classroom on a gloomy day when the rain tapped on the ceiling and their shoes left dark, wet footprints across the floor.

'There's really a whole library in there?' Sol asked.

'There is. The Headmaster once told me that the answers to life's problems can always be found in books.'

Dom opened the door. The weak light from the classroom reached the shelves that were built into the back of the cupboard. The books' spines were so faded that they were all the same washed-out colour, like clouds reflected in a puddle. In the corner, a bucket caught a drip from the roof. The library smelt of mould, damp paper and soil. Dom breathed it in. Sol took a step back from the doorway.

'Isn't it great?' Dom stepped up to the shelves to read the time-bleached titles. 'We've got everything.'

'Have you?'

Dom thumbed through pages, releasing the smell of shoes that had been left out in the rain. Sol squinted at the books and read a few of the titles on the shelf that was at eye level. Then he scanned the two lower shelves. 'These are all fairy tales,' he told Dom.

'They're not.' Dom held up a copy of *Dracula*. 'This one is about a type of person called a "vampire".'

'That's a fairy tale.'

'How do you know?'

'It's made up.'

'All books are made up.'

'I mean vampires are made up. They're not real.'

'Whoever wrote this didn't think so.'

'Do you just believe anything anyone tells you about monsters?'

'Monsters are real, Sol,' said Dom firmly as he replaced *Dracula*. 'And if we meet one, I will be much better prepared than you because I have read every book here. More than once. One of these will be able to help us.'

'I was kind of hoping for a medical textbook or something.'

Dom felt a little cloud swoop over his good mood. 'I've never seen a book about medical text. But some of these are really very good.' He pulled a heavy book from the bottom shelf. 'I read this one about once a year. It's about wolves. Did you know you can train them to think you're a part of their family?'

'Really? I wish that worked for humans,' said Sol.

Dom ignored him. He was remembering winters in the dormitory, a blanket wrapped around every inch of him while rain sang on the roof and windows all day. Only he wasn't there: he was running through forests with wolves, running and running, free to go anywhere. The others told scary stories about wolves at night, but Dom always imagined the soft brown creatures from the book, who worried about feeding their family and protecting themselves from other wolves. It was part of the reason he'd felt drawn to the emblem on Sol's badge: the lone wolf.

Sol adjusted the bucket catching the leak.

'You don't study English or history. You only have fairy tales to read. And you've all lived here for ever. Dom?'

Dom, who was only half-listening to him, looked up

from the book.

'What happens when you grow up?' Sol asked.

'What do you mean?' he said.

'I mean, when you don't need the Headmaster any more and you're old enough to do whatever you like – what will you do? Where will you go?'

'We'll always need the Headmaster,' he told Sol. 'Learning about Niceness never ends. But he also told me . . . Hmm, no.' Dom shook his head. 'It's silly.'

'What?'

Dom passed the book between his hands, back and forth, and looked at the wall above Sol's head as he shared one of his most precious memories, quietly at first, and then louder and faster until all his words ran into each other.

'The Headmaster once told me that if our Nicenesses become complete enough . . . maybe one day we'll become Headmasters. He said it a long time ago, but I think about it sometimes. We could have our own Ash House and children to teach about Niceness. Wouldn't that be a thing? We could maybe run it together, you and me. I'd make my children lots of warm winter clothes and read them stories from my library every night, and swim in the lake every summer, and none of the names on my walls will be crossed out, and we'll have such a library, Sol – imagine it, *twice* as big as this maybe! And I'll never go away. I'll stay there for ever so my children always know where to find me, and I'll never leave them, never, never, *EVER!*'

Sol stared at him with his mouth open. Dom felt the warmth of embarrassment creep over him. He hadn't realized how loud his voice had got. They stood awkwardly and listened to the drips hitting the bucket for a moment, until Sol said quietly:

'It's OK to be angry with the Headmaster.'

'No, it isn't. And I'd never be angry at him.' Dom sniffed and rubbed a shoulder across his eye. He'd never told anyone about his dream to have his own Ash House one day. Now it had come pouring out, he realized how silly it sounded. He could never become a Headmaster.

'Sorry. I told you it was silly,' he said.

'I don't think it's silly,' Sol muttered. 'I don't think it's fair, either. You should be allowed to want more than that. Don't you ever think about leaving?'

'Leaving what?'

'The Ash House! Look, Dom . . .' Sol looked around the room as if searching for a point. 'You don't have to live like this!' He pointed at the bucket, but Dom wasn't sure what he meant.

Then what Sol was really saying began to sink in.

'You want to *leave*?' Dom asked.

'I think I might have to. And, not that it's any of my business, but I think the rest of you should think about it too. Go to the police, social services, whatever. They could help you. Why are you looking at me like that?'

'I – I'm not, I don't . . .' Dom shook his head, hoping it would get his expression under control.

'Dom, what is it? Why don't you leave?'

Dom chewed his lip. It was hard to know where to begin. 'When you cross the fence—'

'There's a fence?'

'When you cross it, you . . . die. But in a bad way.'

'I didn't know it was possible to die in a "good" way,' Sol joked.

'Don't make fun of it. I mean in the *worst* way.'

'What's the worst way?' Sol sighed with yet another question.

'You tell me.'

'I can't tell you, I just got here. I haven't been to the fence. What happens?'

'That's just it. Whatever the worst way to die is, that's how you die. You.' He prodded Sol's chest. 'What would be the worst for you?'

Sol thought about this for a moment. 'Sometimes I think . . . when my back's really bad . . . that it's going to break. But not just once or twice, not like slipping a disc or getting a fracture . . . like every tiny bone shatters and splinters and I bleed internally and . . . that's it. Did you know that you have thirty-three bones in your back?'

'That would be a lot of splinters.'

'Enough to kill you from the inside out.' Sol watched another drop hit the bucket. 'I know that can't really happen, though. What would be your worst?'

'Evaporation. As if one moment you're there, and the next you don't exist. So everybody forgets you.'

'And you think that happens if you cross the fence here?'

'There are stories. Being burnt alive, buried alive . . .'

'What if your Headmaster just made these stories up so you—'

Dom snapped the book about wolves shut and placed it back on the shelf. 'Sol, I'm trying to help you. I don't know if you've noticed, but some of the others don't like you very much.'

'I did notice, actually,' he said drily.

'Saying things like that isn't going to help. This is the most special place in the world if you just give it a chance.'

'How would you know? You've never been out into the world.'

'The Ash House is part of the world. Were you happy in the place you were before you came here?'

Sol looked down.

'Exactly. But I'm telling you that you could be happy here. Once the ash fixes your back.'

For a moment Dom was worried he'd made Sol cry. He stared and stared at the ground, but eventually he looked up and his eyes were clear and green.

'Fine. But fairy tales won't help us. Is there no one else we can ask? No grown-ups?'

'There were others when we were very little, but they left evenutally. Since then it's just been the Headmaster.'

'Doesn't the Headmaster have other books? If he's a teacher, he must have a different library somewhere.'

'I hadn't thought of that,' Dom said. He had to admit it was a possibility. The Headmaster must have read hundreds of books. 'If he does, they're not in his study, I'd have seen them.'

'Is his study in the Ash House?'

'Yes.'

'Then let's go and look together.'

'You're not allowed upstairs. Only I am. For chores.'

'What?' Sol's mouth fell open. 'No one else? That house is huge. It's a mansion. You're all living in a mouldy old greenhouse and having lessons in a barn, and you're telling me he only lets one person in there and it's for chores?'

'We're allowed in, just not upstairs.'

'What does he keep up there?'

'Statues mostly,' said Dom. He couldn't understand why Sol was so angry.

'What on earth does he have statues for?'

'I don't know.'

'What about the other rooms?'

'I don't *know*! Besides the study, I've only ever been in one of them.' The memory made his hands twitch.

## 8: SOL

Sol grew used to his clothes smelling of smoke, plants dripping on him in his sleep, taking notes when the man in the educational films told him to. Every morning he sat in the basement of the Ash House, which the others called the 'assembly room', and waited for the Headmaster to call. But day after day went by, and the phone didn't ring.

Despite the unsettled atmosphere, the children went about their chores as they were supposed to, only they spent more time whispering together, staring off into the distance when they were in the middle of a task, even wiping away tears when they thought nobody would notice.

They were divided into boy-girl pairs, and every pair had a task to keep the Ash House running smoothly. Once a week, Merit and Sincerity walked down the long drive, nearly a mile, to pick up a delivery – plain cardboard boxes filled with food, soap, sometimes even a piece of new clothing – and handed out the contents. No one was able to tell Sol who sent these packages – they simply materialized during the night.

Happiness and Temperance ran the big, cold kitchen at the back of the canteen, with quick smiles and strong arms. For breakfast they served porridge, toast with honey, and eggs from the few chickens they kept. The rest of the time it was vegetables, fruit, tinned food from the mysterious boxes, and bread Happiness made herself. Meat came occasionally and would be eaten that day. Libby caught them rabbits and squirrels, but the sight of the clumpy fur on the kitchen floor turned Sol's stomach and he never had an appetite when the game pies were served up.

Joy and Delight were in charge of cleaning the dorms, bathrooms, the canteen and assembly room with old rags and mops. Laundry was done in huge, ancient machines in a corner of the kitchen by Grace and Earnest, and Mercy and Wisdom, the two teams managing the never-ending cycle of washing, drying and folding.

Justice and Honesty had to keep the flaming torches outside the Ash House burning all day and all night. They were deeply superstitious about it, Sol noticed, which was perhaps why Justice was so jumpy all the time.

Their hands smelt of vegetable oil from soaking the wicks, and he found out that Honesty had cut her hair short because it was always getting singed.

Amity and Diligence were responsible for keeping the electrics in good working order and were often seen changing bulbs or pulling threads of wires out of ceilings and walls, caring for the generator behind the canteen like it was a prized racehorse. Sol often spotted Amity – a small girl with straight dark hair – fiddling with a leather pouch that contained shining spools of wire, pliers, tiny glass vials that Sol would never have known what to do with.

Patience and Persistence, who everybody called Persy, were always mud-stained because they were in charge of the enormous vegetable patch, which was nurtured so carefully that Sol felt confident they could survive for a while, even if the food packages stopped as suddenly as the Headmaster's calls.

Constance and Luck were called if someone hurt themselves, although it seemed to be a job they lived in fear of.

Charity and Reason kept the woods well tended; they moved with a quick, surefooted certainty and could name every type of tree, shrub and herb that grew there.

Resolve and Prudence guarded the old educational

video cassettes – they wiped them down after every lesson and kept them in tight plastic cases.

Love and Calm, a dreamy-eyed girl and a softly spoken boy, looked after the animals they kept. There were three goats, which Love tried to milk with little success, a dozen chickens, two elderly sheep and a rabbit Libby had snared the summer before, which Dom wouldn't let Happiness cook because he liked looking at the white tips of its ears waving as it listened to the world.

Since Sol didn't have a chore, Libby told him that he would help her.

'But I don't know how to hunt,' he said.

'You can help me with the other bit.'

'What other bit?'

He could tell his questions irritated her, and he couldn't understand why she was insisting that he helped her when she clearly didn't want him around. He followed her into the kitchen, where Temperance was whisking eggs while Happiness kneaded a smooth ball of dough. Libby picked up a bucket that was in the corner, near the ancient fridge.

'What's th— Oh!' Sol recoiled at the smell. It was something long-dead. He hoped more than anything they weren't expected to eat it for dinner.

'Come on,' said Libby.

He followed her across the courtyard and around the side of the house. The dorms and the canteen disappeared from view and soon they were on mossy tarmac, with brambles to the right of them and the grey walls of the Ash House to their left. It was the sort of place that never got direct sunlight.

The smell of burning was sharper there, and Sol was relieved that it masked the smell coming from the bucket.

Libby walked ahead of him in silence, her shoulders hunched.

'Who do you normally do your chore with?' Sol asked.

'Concord.'

'Why isn't he here?'

'He doesn't do this bit.'

A noise rumbled through the air towards them, like thunder rolling in from far away. Sol looked up. The day was overcast, but they didn't look like storm clouds.

Libby stopped walking. They were halfway along the path. She turned to him and held out the bucket. He took it reluctantly, breathing through his mouth the whole time. There was something furry sticking out of it.

'Now what?' he asked. 'What are we doing?'

'I told you, you're helping with my chore.'

She pointed at the ground to her left. Between them and the house was a ditch, where dead leaves gathered and bald, beige mushrooms grew on the bank. At the bottom, where the ditch met the walls of the house, there was a dark gap blocked by metal bars.

'Feeding time,' she said.

There was the thunder again, only this time, even though Sol knew it wasn't possible, it seemed to be coming from below the earth. Libby was looking at the metal grating, a serious frown on her face. Sol felt inexplicably drawn to the darkness. He didn't realize he'd moved towards it until he felt the damp grass through his trainers.

'Feeding . . .' Sol ran his tongue over the roof of his mouth. 'Feeding what?' he asked.

'Careful,' she warned, as he took a step towards the darkness.

'Does something live down there? Can it get out?'

'If it has to.'

'How?'

'There are ways of moving around the Ash House.'

'SOL!'

Startled, Sol dropped the bucket. Its contents slopped on to his shoes.

'Urgh!'

He turned to see Dom bouncing along the track behind them, glancing nervously at the house.

'Why did you do that?' Libby shouted at him.

Sol couldn't move and didn't dare look down at his shoes. Libby scooped up the bucket and its spilt contents, tossing them back in without even a grimace.

'Sorry,' said Sol. 'He made me jump.'

'What are you doing here?' Libby asked Dom. Once again, Sol was struck by how perfectly their grey eyes matched.

'Looking for Sol. Concord said he was with you.'

'He's helping me with my chore,' Libby said defensively.

'I know, it's just . . .' Dom looked from Libby to Sol and back again, the same nervous smile on his face. 'You already have a chore partner.'

'Con doesn't do feeding time, you know that.'

'Feeding what?' Sol asked again. His curiosity was wrestling with his urge to get away from the gloomy pathway as quickly as possible and wash his trainers. They ignored him.

'But I don't have a chore partner.' Dom picked up the binoculars hanging around his neck and waved them at Libby.

'So?'

'I was thinking Sol could be my chore partner.'

'No. He can't.' Libby put the bucket down and turned to face Dom, hands on hips.

'But chores are supposed to be done in pairs,' Dom complained. 'There's three of you.'

'You don't choose the pairs, the Headmaster does. And anyway, it's supposed to be boy-girl.'

'But the Headmaster's . . . We have to choose. Until he calls again. It's not like you get to choose.'

She glared at him.

'I don't need your permission,' Dom said boldly.

'Fine, then.'

'Fine.'

Dom continued to stand there awkwardly.

'Go on, then!' Libby snapped.

'We will. It's just . . . um . . .'

'What?'

'Well . . .' Dom took a deep breath and, looking at his feet, said, 'He'll need the spare pair of binoculars.'

Sol saw the blood rush to Libby's cheeks and her eyes fill with tears. She picked up the bucket and hurled its contents at Dom. The dead creature slapped on to his shirt and he shouted in disgust. She threw the bucket on the ground, pushed past Sol, and ran back towards the dorm.

Dom tried to wipe his shirt with a corner of his sleeve. The smell was overpowering.

'What on earth was that about?' Sol asked.

'Don't worry about it,' Dom muttered. 'It's my fault, really. I just didn't want her to be upset when she found out you took . . . Look, she just misses the Headmaster.'

The ground rumbled again, this time louder and clearer than before.

'We should go,' said Dom.

'What is your chore, anyway?' Sol asked. He took one last look at the grating as they walked away.

'Oh, I have the best one,' Dom said as he rubbed at his shirt. 'Birdwatching!'


Sol hadn't noticed the tiny wooden shed in the grounds. As he and Dom approached, he assumed it stored tools for gardening or working in the woods, but when they stepped inside, he saw a wall of boxy screens showing black-and-white images of different corners of the Ash House and its grounds. An old computer keyboard lay on a table in front of them. All around there were stacks and stacks of metal boxes, each one small enough to fit into the palm of his hand.

Several spiders skittered out of view when the boys closed the door behind them.

'So that's what the drones are for,' Sol said. 'They're filming us, aren't they?'

'Film-ing.' Dom over-enunciated it, like he did with each new word Sol produced. 'Drones.' He didn't ask Sol to explain the words – he just seemed to like new sounds. He settled down in the old office chair in front of the screens. Thin as he was, it sank slightly under his weight.

'Dom? Is that how the pictures appear on the screens?'

'It's just the birds.'

'You mean the drones?' Sol asked again. He had seen them every day he'd been at the Ash House, some static in the sky, others following them, watching them from above.

'The *birds*,' Dom insisted. 'That's what the Headmaster calls them. They see everything, and then they send the pictures here. The Headmaster says that these are their memories.' He pointed at the grey images. 'I watch them, and then I save them into these memory boxes and put them in the Ash House for the Headmaster.' He pointed at the nearest stack of hard drives. 'I press this button if I see something really bad.' He tapped a remote control that had five buttons on it. The 'bad' one was marked with a peeling bit of red tape.

'Bad like what?'

'People who shouldn't be here. One of us doing something we shouldn't.'

'What if *you* do something you shouldn't?'

'The birds will see that too.'

'But couldn't you just delete it and not give it to the Headmaster?'

'You can't delete a memory, Sol. And, even if you could, dishonesty is not—'

'A Niceness – yeah, I know. But these aren't memories. They're recordings.'

'Recordings?'

'They show what happened somewhere. Like the man in the lessons. He's a recording.'

'Well, that's what memories are.'

'No, they're not.'

'Whenever we remember something, aren't we just watching a recording in our brains?'

'That's the stupidest thing I've ever heard. Memories aren't the same as what really happened.'

Dom, as always, was unruffled by Sol's attempts to make him see sense, and gazed as the screens. Sol opened the shed door. He looked up at the swift-moving clouds, the deep green of the trees all around.

'I always thought there was something . . . I don't know, *quiet* here,' he told Dom. 'I can't believe I've only just noticed: there aren't any birds.'

There was no movement in the trees, no hopping shapes on the grass, no soaring wings in the sky – only the wind, and the drones.

'There are loads of birds,' Dom said dismissively.

Sol didn't have the energy to explain what he really meant.

'Does this mean that the Headmaster is watching us through the dro— I mean, the birds?' Sol asked.

Dom frowned. 'I suppose so. I definitely hope so.'

Sol didn't share this hope.

He watched Dom flick through the recordings. Soon he felt a tingle in his shoulder blades. It didn't hurt. It felt like static electricity being brushed through hair, but that's how the attacks started if he wasn't careful. He took a deep breath. One . . . two . . . three . . .

Dom interrupted his counting.

'I thought I saw it here a few days ago, but I wasn't sure. Now I'm certain – a pig.'

'What?' Sol stood behind the office chair, but he didn't know which screen Dom was looking at.

'Don't worry about it,' said Dom. 'I'll tell Charity and Reason to deal with it.'

'Aren't you supposed to be teaching me what to do?'

'I will. One thing at a time.'

'Where would it have come from?'

Dom didn't answer; he was flicking through recordings of the day before. Sol watched their blurred outlines appear now and then, but most of the birds – no, *drones*, he reminded himself – flew over fields or woodland that he didn't recognize. He couldn't even say confidently that they were part of the Ash House. Were they to stop people coming in or going out?

The tingle in his shoulder blades was growing, but he had to ignore it and focus on what he'd just been told.

'Pigs are big. If a pig can get in, that must mean we can get out.'

Dom pressed a button on the remote – and Sol pressed his point.

'Maybe there's a gap in the fence. What are Charity and Reason going to do with the pig? We could follow it and then—'

Out of nowhere, Dom smashed his fists on to the keyboards in front of him. Plastic crunched and snapped. Sol's arms flicked up to protect his face. Dom hung his head. The outburst had sucked all the noise out of the air.

Then Dom spoke quietly: 'I know where you're going with this, and I'm telling you: you're not crossing the fence. You're my friend and I won't let that happen to you.'

'But you have to admit that there's a chance—'

'I'm trying to look after you!' Dom shrieked. 'It's a Niceness! Nobody else is doing you a Niceness!'

Sol felt he was being backed into a corner, stuck between the impossible world of the Ash House and Dom's impossible demands on him. 'Dom, what if the Headmaster never calls again? Or never comes back?'

'Don't say that.'

'Are we going to live here for ever? Slowly starve if the deliveries stop? We're totally helpless.'

'He won't let that happen to us, and we definitely won't let that happen to each other. You say you came here to get help for your pain. But you can't see when someone's trying to help you!'

'That's different!' Sol raised his voice in return. 'You don't know about my pain. You don't know what it feels like waiting for it every day. To have nothing ahead of you but . . . but . . .'

Sol gritted his teeth. He couldn't stop the tears dripping down his face, but he wasn't going to let yet another person write off his pain as something he could fix with a new attitude.

Dom stood up and let out a long, tired sigh that made him sound much older than he was.

'I have other things to worry about.' He headed to the

door. 'When you let go of this Nastiness – this silly fence idea – I'll let you help more with birdwatching. And maybe we'll help you.'

'I don't want your help. I'm fine on my own.'

Dom looked at him with moon-grey eyes. 'Sure.'

He left.

Sol stared at the screens glowing in the gloom. The black-and-white images were blurry until he wiped his eyes enough times and they came back into focus. There it was: his new world. He could see Dom hurrying back towards the dorm. He could see Patience and Persy in the vegetable patch. He could see a corner of the wood-land with nobody in it, and then, in a blink, there was Libby. As if she'd appeared out of nowhere. She glanced at the bird – and her eyes were right on Sol.

## 9: DOM

The dormitory at the Ash House sometimes felt like a living thing. Perhaps it was the vegetation slowly taking over, reclaiming it for the earth. Perhaps it was all the sleeping bodies, snoring gently alongside each other. Perhaps it was all the dreams swirling in the air every night, brushing against each other, being breathed in and out by all of them. They all had their theories.

It was difficult to keep secrets and opinions private. Every night, Dom heard thoughts whisper down the room towards him – quiet, cautious conversations that moved from bed to bed, the same thought Sol had been bold enough to say aloud:

*Maybe the Headmaster was gone for ever.*

The morning after his argument with Sol, Dom took the memory boxes up to the Ash House. He walked the familiar length of the Headmaster's study, pausing to admire the statues, but careful not to touch anything other than the cool metal boxes tucked under his arm. He reached the door of the vast vault and punched in the code that only he knew.

He liked the vault. He knew he was lucky just to be allowed upstairs and into the study, but it was even more special to have a place at the Ash House that was only his. Racks and racks of memory boxes, carefully sorted by Niceness and then chronologically, gleamed in front of him. There was a shelf for each Niceness, decorated with the same emblem as their badges. He walked into the darkness and placed each memory box in the correct place.

Part of his mind was replaying the argument with Sol, over and over. Dom had thought he'd like having someone to share his chore with again, someone to share the burden of always watching, always protecting everybody. But Sol didn't care about that. He only thought about leaving.

Dom put the last memory box in place, then turned to go. He paused by one shelf and looked at the emblem: a heart on fire.

He wasn't going to let another person leave him.

When he came downstairs, he found Concord in the hall staring at the phone. Without a phone call from the

Headmaster, they didn't know who was on duty after Concord, so he had stayed in the position.

'I've been waiting ages,' said Concord when he saw Dom. He was kneeling next to the small table, frowning and picking at an old sticker on the side of the phone.

Dom gently moved his fingers away to make him stop. The sticker had the Headmaster's handwriting on it – he'd only written a series of random numbers, but it was still a part of him, and Dom didn't want it to get damaged.

'And?' Dom asked, even though he knew the answer.

'And nothing. Come on. Assembly.'

'Another minute,' said Dom. He squinted at the phone, willing it to generate the voice he loved.

Concord crossed his arms and waited next to his friend. When the minute passed uninterrupted, he put his hand on Dom's shoulder.

'They're waiting for us.'

'Fine.'

They went down the passageway into the assembly room. No one asked about the phone – they knew from their faces.

Concord stood on stage and went through the various chores for the week ahead. He then stood aside, and it was Dom's turn to speak.

'Um, yes, nothing about the Headmaster, I'm afraid,' he said, taking the spot where Concord had been standing. 'But yesterday I spotted an unwanted visitor in the grounds. I've followed the rules and Reason and Charity took care of it. It's down by the lake. I think it will take all of us, so . . .'

Concord moved back to Dom's side.

'Libby and I are in charge,' he barked. 'Everyone do what we tell you. Wash your hands afterwards. We'll start after chores. That's everything.'

The room was filled once more with murmurs and chairs scraping as they got ready to leave. Dom and Concord sat down on the edge of the stage and tapped the floor with their toes. Merit squeezed out of the crowd and approached them, his dark eyes full of concern.

'So that's it?' His voice was soft as ever, but Dom could hear the worry in it. 'Nothing from the Headmaster?'

'We would have said,' said Dom.

A few of the children started to gather around them, while others headed towards the stairs.

Concord got to his feet and stretched his arms, taking up as much space as he could. 'Maybe he's staying away because he doesn't want to look at *Nastinesses*.'

He flicked his hand as Sol went past and tried to

smack him in the face.

Sol jerked out of reach.

'Takes one to know one,' he said pointedly to Concord.

Dom felt torn. Concord being mean to Sol didn't feel like a Niceness, but the argument in the shed was hard to let go of. Forgiveness was a Niceness that felt out of reach. He looked down at his feet until Sol passed.

'Spending less time with your new best friend?' Concord asked him.

Dom ignored the sarcasm. 'I took Sol to the shed with me yesterday. He's going to do birdwatching with me. But he keeps talking about trying to cross the fence and leaving. I've told him everything, but he won't listen. He said he doesn't want my help.'

'Everything?' asked Concord. 'You even told him about—?'

'We'll need to find some tarpaulin for this afternoon,' Justice interrupted. His pale brows were set in a worried frown. 'It's going to rain.'

After chores they went to the dormitories and put on their oldest shirts and trousers. Dom dug out one of his favourites from when he was younger, a cream shirt with a green pattern, but it was worn through at the elbows and collar. As he put it on, he noticed that it now felt too tight across his shoulders.

The boys clanged down the staircase to meet the girls, who had changed into old jeans that were too large for them. They used old scarves and strips of silk for belts. Sol was also standing in the courtyard, looking lost.

'It's this way, *Nastiness*,' Concord growled at Sol. Some of the others sniggered.

Dom knew that his friends still didn't trust Sol. They hadn't forgotten his fainting spell, even though Dom had kept his promise and not told them about Sol's pains.

They went around the dormitories and walked down the sloping, tangled lawn towards the lake. Dom didn't check to see if Sol was following them.

The lake was in the small forest that wrapped itself around the Ash House's grounds. On the nearer side of the ancient trees, not far from the vegetable patch, was an area where Love and Calm kept the animals.

Charity and Reason led the way. The blossoms and fruits on the trees were long gone. Only a few blackberries remained on the dense brambles, and the occasional mushy apple on the ground. Fat clouds stayed still in the sky, threatening the rain that Justice had warned them about.

Everyone clustered around something on the grass, a few yards from the edge of the forest. Dom was relieved it had strayed this far into the Ash House grounds. He didn't want to have to go near the fence. The group stood on tiptoe and craned their necks to see over each other.

'What are you looking at?' asked Sol. None of them answered him.

Concord moved easily through the crowd and Dom followed in his wake.

A dead pig lay at the centre of their circle.

It was twice, if not triple, their size and weight. It had been dead for a day. Its pink skin was greying, puffy, soft and marshmallowy, but its limbs were stiff. Its dead, frozen eyes stared at the children. The corpse stank.

'Oh, my god . . .' Sol held his sleeve to his mouth and tried to back away, but the wall of children blocked him, forcing him to look at the dead animal.

'We need it buried by nightfall,' said Concord to the group matter-of-factly. 'Spades are over there. We don't have enough, so we'll take turns. I think we need to go deep. It will take most of us to lift it.'

'Oink, oink,' said Happiness sadly. She had scooped up some of the least rotten apples for supper and was holding them in the outstretched fabric of her jumper.

Some of them went to fetch the spades.

Concord marked the grave with sticks stabbed into the ground.

'Are we going to have to touch it?' asked Sol. He was standing as far away as he could, breathing through his dirty shirtsleeve.

'It's not going to float into the hole,' said Merit.

'You've done this before?' Sol asked with horror.

'Just go get a spade,' said Dom. It was the first time they had spoken since their argument in the shed.

'Slacking is a Nastiness,' Merit added.

## 10: SOL

It was exhausting. Digging, sweating, hauling earth into tumbling, crumbly piles. The shovels gave them yellow blisters on their hands. The rain soaked them and the wind chilled them, until they were grateful to be the ones digging because at least they were warm. Two drones, which the others insisted on calling 'birds', whirred overhead while they worked. Sol did his first shift early. He didn't haul nearly as much soil as Concord or Justice, whose white-blond hair had gone completely dark from running his muddy hands through it. But he helped widen and deepen the hole. When he couldn't dig any more, Sincerity pulled the shovel from his hand and took over.

The hole was finished at twilight. By that time they all had their jeans rolled up above the knee and their feet were bare. Every inch of skin was smeared with mud. The rain had passed and now the sky was turning pink and purple over the trees.

'Time to move it,' Concord called. Even the ones who weren't needed gathered around to watch this part. 'Solitude, take the head.'

Sol had just finished his second shift. He was breathing heavily, reluctantly gasping the stinking air. While everyone had struggled with the size of the task, it had taken more out of Sol. He wasn't used to this sort of labour.

'What?'

'Grab it.' Concord was directing people to the limbs, the bulky back, a few others to make sure that the walls were reinforced so the hole wouldn't cave in as they dropped the pig. Black and red earth was piled next to the hole, ready to fill it back in.

'I – I – don't want—'

'Solitude, take its head. Now.'

Before he could say anything, Dom was next to him, trying to help.

'Like this,' he said. 'See?' He cupped his hands under the squelching flesh without a grimace.

'Don't do it for him, Dom,' Concord snapped.

Sol gagged. He bent over and leant on his knees. He worried that the work would ignite his back pains, but the real problem was his stomach.

He counted to five.

Slowly, Sol reached out and tried to take a hold of the head. It was heavier than he thought. It slipped through his hands and thumped on to the ground.

'Not like that!' Concord shouted. The others were organized at their stations.

'He's going to cry,' said Justice. 'He's scared of the piggy-wiggy.'

'Why are you scared?' demanded Concord. 'Look!' He picked up a stick and stabbed the corpse with it. 'It's dead! Dead!'

Sol didn't reply. He just cringed, bent down and scooped up the head again, lacing his fingers together the way Dom had showed him.

Some girls behind them made snorting noises. Sol cried out as the flesh slipped in his fingers.

'It's just a pig, Sol!' snapped Concord.

'Shut up! Just shut up, shut up, shut up!'

The laughing and snorting noises stopped. The others lowered the rest of the pig to the ground, then Concord brought his face close to Sol's.

'You. Don't. Shout. At. Me.' He enunciated each word, full of menace. 'That is not a Niceness.'

Every pair of eyes glared at Sol in the fading light. Even the pig's.

'I'm sorry,' he whispered. He felt empty and full at the same time. It was like he needed to be sick, but he couldn't, because there was nothing inside him.

They turned wordlessly back to the task.

The corpse landed in its fresh grave with a sickening thump. Sol was glad there was no more digging with clay walls looming over his head and the last of the sun slipping away.

There was no prayer or pause for thought. They were all hungry and light-headed.

Dom picked up a spade and approached the mound of earth that would fill the hole. But Concord stepped into his path and took it from him.

'Con—'

'Solitude will fill it in.'

Sol was standing on the edge of the grave, staring solemnly down at the pig. Now he turned around to look at Concord and Dom, startled.

'What?'

'You complained about the first bit. Now you do this bit.'

'He can't do it on his own,' said Dom.

'I'll be here all night,' said Sol with a shiver. 'I don't want—'

But he didn't get a chance to explain that he was

scared to be there in the dark, the real dark, when the sun was so far below the horizon it couldn't do anything to help him.

Concord swung the full weight of the spade's metal blade into Sol's stomach. Air left him. Sol crumpled in half, staggered back, and slipped smoothly into the hole.

No one laughed. Concord's face was contracted into a suppressed smile.

'You've been here long enough to know that laziness is a Nastiness. You know what else is a Nastiness?'

Sol could only wheeze in response.

'Wanting to cross the fence.' Gasps whispered around the group. 'Dom told me,' Concord said to their shocked faces. 'And Nastiness needs to be punished. Doesn't it?'

Nobody said anything.

Even when he was gasping for air, even with Concord standing above him, spade raised, Sol scrambled to climb the walls of the grave, trying to put as much space between himself and the pig as possible.

His black fingernails reached the grass. Concord stabbed the edge of the spade down dangerously close.

'Pl-please . . .' The words came choking out, coated with terror. 'Help me out. I'm sorry. Get me out, get me out.'

Concord swung the spade away and Sol thought he

was done. He wasn't. He scooped up some of the dark earth and flung it in his face. Sol fell back, spitting the damp dirt out of his mouth. He tried to say something, but he had earth in his hair, his eyes and ears, down his neck.

Finally, he heard Dom's voice.

'Con, that's enough. Leave him alone.'

Silence. Above ground, eyes reluctantly looked away from Sol and focused on the battle of wills between the two boys.

'We're all tired,' Dom was saying. 'Let's finish and then we can eat something and rest.'

'Not everyone has worked hard enough,' Concord replied. 'And working hard together is a Niceness, Dom. So is not complaining. So is respecting the fence. We all know what happens when we forget our Niceness.'

Sol couldn't see their faces, but he heard Dom say, 'There are other Nicenesses too. Others that we all forget sometimes.'

'What's that supposed to mean? Where are you going?' Sol heard Concord yell. 'Dom, come back! Dom! Fine . . . fine . . .' he muttered, but failed to convince anyone that he didn't care about Dom storming off.

Then he reappeared above Sol.

'You don't like being here?' demanded Concord. He towered at the edge of the hole. His outline clutched a spade. 'You don't like working here, eating here and sleeping here? Then sleep with the pig. Sleep in a hole. Sleep *on your own*.'

He scooped up some loose earth and started to fill in the hole.

## 11: DOM

Dom couldn't sleep. It took him a while to work it out. He had helped dig a big hole. He had stood under the steaming shower for longer than usual. He was tired. Sleep should be easy.

He guessed it was close to midnight. He sat up and absentmindedly rubbed an ivy leaf between his thumb and forefinger. He looked at Sol's untouched pillow on the bed next to him. He looked over at Concord's still, sleeping form on the other side of the room. Concord had been in charge of getting rid of the pig. He'd done what he thought was right. But Dom couldn't remember the last time he and Concord had argued.

Dom snapped the leaf free and made a decision.

He put his filthy jeans and shirt back on, then crept barefoot down the centre of the dormitory, lifting a coat from a lopsided hook by the door. It smelt musty. It hadn't been worn in months, but now he needed it.

His feet whispered down the metal stairs. He paused at the bottom and listened. He couldn't hear anything from the girls' dormitory. He couldn't resist peering in at the glass panes, but beyond the round, pale shape of his face, he couldn't see anyone, only the shadowy outlines of plants and flowers. He couldn't explain the strange feeling of missing the girls, especially Libby, even though he saw them every day.

Dom knew his way in the dark because sometimes, in the summer, he, Concord, Merit and Justice went on expeditions at night to swim in the lake. They didn't do it much, only when the seasons changed and they felt they really needed to, otherwise they'd go mad from missing the Headmaster. They never would have dared when he was around.

The grass was wet and sharp with cold. The trees made a pleasant murmur and the scent of burning was light and crisp in the air. A perfect night, Dom thought to himself as he walked away from the dorms.

Down by the forest, Sol was sitting next to the dark hump of dirt that marked the grave. He was shivering, his arms wrapped tightly around his knees, and his white shirt was now so dark he blended in with the grass.

Dom stopped a few paces behind him. Sol must have heard him, but he didn't turn around.

'You got out,' said Dom.

'No thanks to you.' Sol's words jumped through chattering teeth.

Dom stared at the trees. They were green and navy in the dark. When he turned back, Sol was scowling at him.

'He tried to bury me alive and you didn't stop him.'

'He wouldn't have really buried you alive.'

Sol raised his voice: 'You just walked away!'

'Shh!' Dom looked over his shoulder. He could just make out the outlines of the buildings: the glass dormitory crystalline, the house smoky and insubstantial. He knew where they were more from instinct than sight.

He sat down next to Sol. The mud was cold and soft and he couldn't smell the pig at all.

'Why did he do that?' asked Sol.

'I mentioned our argument in the shed,' Dom admitted. 'But that's not why. Not really.'

'Is it because I'm new? Or does he think I'm taking you away from him? Because if you want, you can tell him you and I aren't friends any more.'

Dom thought about this option. 'No, thank you.'

Sol sniffed.

Dom felt helpless. Where Concord led, the other boys would always follow. Dom was the only one with influence over him. He'd tried to stop him, but that evening he'd discovered that influence wasn't enough. He couldn't protect Sol. But there was a chance Sol could protect himself.

'It's because you're ill,' Dom told him. 'I haven't told them about your pain thing, so they don't know what you're ill with, but they sense it. Ever since you passed out in the classroom, they've been able to tell.'

Sol rested his cheek on his folded arm and looked at Dom. 'I shouldn't have said anything.'

'You're my friend,' said Dom. 'I'm glad you told me. It's just . . .' Fear rushed up his gullet like vomit. He looked back at the house and its reassuring, murky shape.

'Are you all right?' Sol looked at Dom with concern.

'I need to tell you something.'

'What?'

'I really, really, really need you to believe me.'

'Is this going to be about the fence again?'

'Sol, promise!'

'OK, OK, I promise.'

Dom sucked air in and out. He needed to say something they rarely said aloud. They didn't need to. They had seen it and felt it, but Sol hadn't. Dom knew he had to say it. The burning, sickening feeling in his throat didn't go away.

'Sol, we're not allowed to be ill here. Ever.'

Sol laughed, but it was high-pitched and nervous. Dom pressed on.

'Bad, *bad* things happen if someone gets ill. Nothing can stop it.'

'What happens? Dom? Whoa, OK, calm down.'

Dom felt panic flood through his veins. His breaths came out juddery and wet. Sol put his arm awkwardly around him and patted his shoulder. The arm was still trembling, but Dom found it reassuring.

'Sorry,' he gasped.

'It's OK,' said Sol. He removed his arm and they gazed into the dark. Dom's breathing and Sol's chattering teeth were the only things they could hear.

Dom fought to get control of his body again. He gripped the earth with his hands, feeling the ground beneath him. The ash would protect him, he reminded himself. The terror faded.

'Are you all right?' Sol asked again, after a few minutes.

Dom nodded. 'It's just scary, that's all.'

'I get that.' Sol's face was unreadable in the darkness. 'So that's why they don't like me?'

'That's part of it,' Dom admitted. He couldn't bring himself to explain the other part of it – the reason they didn't like the idea of Sol sitting in the spare chair in the shed, or adding his name to the list on the classroom wall. 'Con is usually very kind and wise and—'

'Yeah, OK,' Sol scoffed.

'He is!'

'I'm sorry for being mean to you when I first arrived,' said Sol out of the blue. 'I thought . . . I thought it would help me – you know, show I wasn't going to be messed about.' He gestured at his muddy shirt. 'But I suppose I get what I give.'

Dom nodded. 'I'm sorry too. I shouldn't have walked away when Con knocked you into the grave.'

'No. You shouldn't have,' said Sol.

Then Dom whispered to himself, 'He'll do it again.' It was more of a realization than a warning. 'If you're sick, there's nothing Concord won't do to protect us.'

Sol scrambled to his feet, flicking mud everywhere. 'You're supposed to be helping me!'

'Yesterday in the shed you said you didn't want help.'

'I don't.'

'I can't protect you from Concord if he finds out.'

'Is this why you told me to keep my pains a secret? You think if he finds out, he'll – what? Kill me?' Sol's eyes widened. 'He – he wouldn't *literally* kill me. Would he? Dom, would he?'

Dom gazed at Sol's outline against the dark house. It looked like the smoke was coming off him, as if he was made of a fire no one could see. Then Dom looked down at his own hands, buried comfortably in the earth. He didn't know what Concord was capable of any more.

## 12: SOL

Sol dreamt of being buried that night. He woke up with the taste of dirt on his tongue and the pain in his back worse than ever. He listened to the dorm creaking and dripping; he wished it wasn't being taken over by plants.

In the shower, the mud that had been washed off by others was grainy on the damp floor and stuck to the soles of his feet. His stomach was cherry red where Concord had hit him with the spade. At breakfast, nobody spoke to him, but he felt their eyes on him all the time, especially Concord's. It was a relief when lessons were over, and he and Dom could go to the shed.

They walked in silence. As they approached the trees, Sol realized that the shed wasn't where he thought it was. It was further east, nearer the forest. Its walls and door and roof looked exactly the same. Nothing had moved inside.

But the next day, the shed had moved again. It was even further away now, tucked under a horse-chestnut tree nearer the drive.

'How does it . . .?'

'Move?' said Dom. 'I'm never sure.'

'Does someone do it while we sleep?'

'I doubt it,' said Dom. 'That would be very strange.'

'Yeah, and nothing strange ever happens here,' said Sol. A drone followed them, watching as they made their way to the shed.

Sol's pain was shaping up to be a full episode. He squeezed his fists and buried them in his coat pockets, the same coat Dom had worn when he came to find him at the pig's grave. His teeth and jaw hurt from clenching them. Sometimes the pain would stroke a tentacle up his back, into his neck and skull. He imagined it rootling in his brain, pressing the buttons that made him scared, tired and furious all at once.

When they reached the shed, he shoved the door open and quickly lay down on the wooden floor, not caring about splinters, and tucked his fists under his lower back. It was the only position that didn't make him want to scream. He could feel the sweat on his forehead, on his arms, in his hair. The tentacles were curling tighter and tighter around his shoulder blades.

Dom had seen him like this a couple of times, so Sol no longer felt the dull ache of embarrassment. But he wanted someone to help him, even if it was one of the useless doctors he used to go to who just gave him painkillers that did nothing at all.

During the episode, he retreated into the back of his mind. He was dimly aware of Dom moving around him and placing something cold on his forehead.

When it began to pass, there was a sharp pain that writhed all over him – just in case he forgot what it could do – and then it curled up and left a tense ache behind. By the time he got to that stage, the ache felt like the most blissful thing in the world.

His attention came back to the room. He was able to notice the rough floor, the spiders on the beams above him, Dom tapping at a keyboard. Sol sat up. A damp cloth slid down his face and flopped on to his lap.

'It's getting worse.' Dom said this as casually as if he was commenting on the weather.

'It is,' said Sol. Even his voice was raw. Had he been making noises?

'We won't be able to hide it much longer.'

'I can feel when it's about to happen.'

'Even then.'

'How are the birds?' It had become easier to use

Dom's word for the drones – Sol even found himself forgetting that they were machines and not creatures.

'Fine.' Dom stared at the screens, his chin resting on his fist. Sol could see his reflection; his round face was lined with worry. 'No more pigs, anyway,' Dom continued. 'Which is a good thing.'

Sol nodded, then stopped immediately because it made his neck feel like it might crack. He peeled the damp cloth off his lap.

'Thank you.'

'That's OK.'

'Not just for this,' said Sol. 'For coming to find me after the thing with the pig. No one else did. It was . . .' He wracked his brain to explain to Dom what it meant to him to have a friend in this strange, dark place. 'It was a real Niceness, Dom.'

Dom's eyes widened as he turned around. His face was split by the purest smile Sol had ever seen. '*Thank you*,' he breathed. He scrambled off his chair and on to the floor next to Sol. For a moment Sol was worried that Dom might hug him, but he just crouched there, swaying on the balls of his feet.

'Usually if I don't know what to do, I just remember my Niceness. But recently, it's like they get all tangled in my head. Like with the pig – Concord was right about some things . . . But it didn't *feel* right. It was like we were doing a Niceness and a Nastiness at the same time. That probably doesn't make any sense.'

'It does,' said Sol. Guilt seeped in where the pain had been as a plan formed in his head.

Dom smiled again and then returned to the screens.

Sol waited until he felt stronger. He slowly stretched out each limb and bent his back, checking every muscle. The pain had retreated to the tingly feeling he had when he woke up. He let his plan take shape in his mind.

'Speaking of Niceness,' he said, when he finally felt able to stand and walk about. 'I was wondering if you'd do another one for me.'

'Yes,' said Dom. 'Anything.'

'I want you to show me the fence.'

Dom spun around in the chair. 'Sol, no. The fence is not a Niceness.'

'But helping a friend is,' he reminded him. 'And I need to see it. Just to look at it. To know where it is. After that, I swear I'll never mention it again.'

'No. I told you. No way.'

Sol felt both giddy and guilty at the power the language of the Ash House held over Dom. 'But it would be a real Niceness. To me.'

*

The forest was so ancient and tangled that it was easy to believe they were the first ones to ever walk into it. A few steps in, the trees wound together and blocked off any view of the house and grounds, but the smell of the burning torches and the soft haze in the air never left them. Sol was reminded of the dorm. Every plant was deep green, burgundy or gold, gleaming and shifting, making him aware that everything around him was alive. The ground swallowed the sound of their footsteps, yet all around them was rustling and creaking. It was as if every time he turned his head, the trees stopped moving, only to pick up their roots and follow them when he turned away again.

They crossed a shallow stream that ran through the forest, balancing on rocks to keep their shoes dry. Dom said that this was the narrowest point of the forest, and so the shortest walk to the fence. He walked quickly but paused often, as if torn between hurrying and not wanting to be there are all. It was comforting to know that the shed was behind them, just beyond the trees, no matter how dense they became.

After they had been walking for a few minutes, Dom stopped. Sol wasn't sure how far they'd come, or how much further the forest stretched ahead. It seemed impossible that nearby there would be villages and houses and cars, the old phone box he'd seen on the drive in, and places where people went about their ordinary lives with no flavour of smoke on their tongues.

'Here,' said Dom.

'What's here?' Sol went a few paces ahead of him and then he stopped too. There was no sign of a fence. The trees looked identical to all the others.

'Have we gone in a circle?' he asked.

'You wanted to see the fence. We've seen it. Let's go.' Dom was already turning back.

Sol grabbed his arm.

'Wait! There's nothing here. This can't be it. We need to go further.'

Dom was more impatient and snappier than Sol had ever seen him. He paced and wrung his hands and picked at the skin around his nails, his eyes darting all around as if he was on the lookout for monsters. He jabbed his finger over Sol's head.

'There!'

Sol turned and looked up.

Dom was pointing at a wire. It was a single strand of bright silver, so clean and shining that it could have been new that day. It was more than two metres off the ground and threaded its way through branches in a straight line that began and ended out of view.

'That's not a fence,' said Sol. He looked at the ground beneath it. There was no sign of more fencing or traps.

'Get away from it,' Dom insisted, dragging Sol back.

'But, Dom, it's just a wire! We could walk right under it.'

'We can't. And we're not going to try.'

'Is it some sort of electric boundary? I've heard of those. Dom?'

Dom was staring straight ahead beyond the boundary, shaking his head. Sol couldn't see anything other than the twisted wall of trees and undergrowth.

'Dom!'

Dom's attention snapped back to him.

'What?'

'What happens if we cross the boundary? Is there something there we can't see?'

'I-I told you . . . No, shh! I told you what happens if you cross it.'

Dom's focus was split again. He still had a tight hold of Sol's shirt, but his eyes were pinned on the trees – as if he could see something.

Someone.

He was talking to someone. His words were getting muddled in his agitation. He was trying to warn Sol, but was having fragments of another conversation at the same time.

'It's very – just wait – we have to – No, not now. Go away! I said, *go away*!'

'Dom, no one's there!' Sol wrenched himself out of Dom's grip. 'Look, I'm sorry. But we can't stay trapped here because of some story.'

That got his attention. The worst part was seeing Dom's face fill with horror as he realized what Sol meant.

'You said you just wanted to see it. You liar!'

Sol gave Dom a rough, awkward hug. 'I'll send people to come and get you all, OK?'

'Sol, *NO*!'

Sol broke free and tried to run. Dom wasn't following him, but the trees now seemed to be working against him, clawing at his face and tripping him up. He didn't care. He was going somewhere that didn't smell of ash.

Dom screamed his name again. The fence was there, within reach, but before Sol could run under it, it felt like a giant elastic band had been wrapped around his middle and was gradually pulling him back.

'No!' he choked. The wire was just above him. He was so nearly through. Dom was far to behind him and he refused to believe the trees could really reach out and stop him.

The pull was coming from himself.

Hesitation.

He had stopped running.

He looked up through the branches at the wire and the grey clouds above.

Buried alive, burnt alive, evaporated . . . Sol looked down. A stick had fallen and started to decay – its bark was flaking off to expose the spongy fibres inside. He was afraid. Tears of frustration ran down his cheeks, but he couldn't make himself take one more step. He didn't have a name for the force that was pulling him back. It was more than the scary stories Dom had told. It was the glass dorm, the moving shed, the comforting weight of the binoculars around his neck, his seat in the canteen . . .

'Sol?' Dom had come closer. He was holding out a hand.

'I can't cross,' Sol whispered. 'I don't have anywhere to go.'

'You have the Ash House,' Dom insisted.

'I can't cross,' he said again.

'I know. But do you really need to cross?'

'I can't live like this,' said Sol, turning to face Dom. 'The pain . . . I just can't bear it.'

'The ash will heal you. We'll find a way.'

'But there's no one to help. No doctor.'

Something flickered over Dom's face, like a cloud drifting in front of the moon for a second, so fast Sol wasn't entirely sure he saw it.

'We'll work something out,' Dom said. 'Anything's a better idea than this.' His eyes moved beyond Sol again, like he was speaking to someone over his shoulder. 'We're going back. Come on.'

He held out his hand. Sol wiped his face and took it. He didn't let go until the torches burning near the Ash House came into sight.

## 13: DOM

Sol's situation was more desperate than Dom imagined.

He lay awake that night, and when everyone was asleep, he called a meeting: going from bed to bed, gently shaking the boys awake. They followed him outside, moving carefully so that they didn't wake Sol. Rain hammered on the glass roof and on the metal staircase. As they got further away from the dorms the din faded and the world became softer and quieter.

They walked towards the lake and the spot where they had buried the pig. Familiar tracks were worn into the grass, showing where they often walked or played. The sun-drenched, dusty days when they'd played chase-the-tail were now a distant memory. They walked past the pig's grave and on towards the forest. They couldn't see the house through the dark screen of rain.

Dom thought of Sol, fast asleep with his mouth open,

curled up on his side so that his back didn't touch the mattress, and he felt certain that he was doing the right thing for him. A real Niceness. The new friendship made him feel more anxious than he'd ever felt before, but it also gave him a purpose that he took pride in; it made him stand a little taller and speak a little louder.

The boys gathered under a large ash tree that stood slightly apart from the forest. Justice pulled back his hood. His hair was slicked on to his forehead and fluffed up at the back. It was bright white against the rain-streaked tree trunk.

'The girls might not come,' he told Dom. 'Libby's still angry you took Sol to the shed. She said you're trying to replace – you know . . .'

'I asked her,' said Dom. 'They'll come.'

'What if Sol wakes up and sees that the dorm is empty?'

'He'd probably quite like that.'

'I dreamt that once,' said Justice. 'I was here on my own, all day. I dreamt it the day after the Headmaster stopped calling.'

'That's what you get for sleeping in Merit's bed until you were eight,' grumbled Concord. He held the only torch they owned, but it was just a precaution. They all knew their way in the dark. 'Dom, just say what you want to say so we can all go back to bed.'

'We've hardly seen you since Sol arrived,' moaned Reason, joining the conversation.

'That's not because of him,' said Dom defensively. 'I have to spend more time with the birds because the Headmaster's gone.'

'He's not *gone*. Don't say it like that,' said Persy, who was wearing the muddy jacket he wore in the vegetable patch.

'While he's unable to call, I mean,' said Dom.

'Did you hear something?' Merit whipped around. All of them fell silent. Somewhere beyond the dorms, there was a deep, low growling noise. It rumbled towards them before fusing with the sound of the rain hitting the leaves.

'It could be thunder?' Dom suggested.

'Right,' snapped Concord, who turned to address the group: 'Dom, start talking, because I'm not hanging around here if the house is going to open its doors tonight.'

Then Wisdom pointed back towards the dorms. 'Concord, look!'

'Don't tell me what to do,' said Concord.

The girls were walking towards them. Their pale outlines looked like ghosts. Dom felt a wave of relief swell in his stomach.

Love reached them first, the dreamy-eyed girl who looked after the animals with Calm. She gently touched her chore partner's elbow when she got near.

'Did you hear it?' she asked nervously.

'We thought it was thunder,' said Dom.

'*You* thought it was thunder,' said Concord. 'I know a Shuck when I hear one.'

'Where are Libby and Sincerity?' Dom asked, noticing that they weren't all there. For a moment, his heart sank; he hoped Libby hadn't refused to come.

'We're here.'

Dom jumped and turned around. Libby wore her wax jacket open so it flapped around her nightie. Her legs were bone white. They had come from the wrong way, as if they had walked out of the forest.

'How did you—?'

'We should start,' said Sincerity. She wore a heavy wool coat over checked pyjamas that had once belonged to the boys. 'We heard Shucks.'

The girls formed a wide circle and the boys followed their lead. Dom felt nostalgic about being all together again during the night.

When they were children, they'd all slept on the top floor of the dorm, girls and boys. Dom used to have Concord on his right, Libby on his left. Then there was

Justice and Honesty, Merit and Sincerity, all of them together and thick as thieves. How many times had he helped Justice and Honesty scrub the smell of vegetable oil off their hands? How many afternoons had he and Concord waited at the golden gate for Merit and Sincerity to come back with the delivery? He'd spent many years whispering to them after dark, watching moonlight shape their faces, listening to them talk about their dreams before they were fully awake. They had shared everything: clothes, secrets, nightmares.

Then, not long before he left, the Headmaster had said that things at the Ash House had to change. The girls were taken out of the upstairs dorm and banished to the ground floor, where the shadows were deeper, and moonlight never really reached. In the month that followed, Dom often thought he heard Libby's voice in his sleep, but it was just the wind. From then on, when they played games, it was boys versus girls. The girls sat in secretive groups at the breakfast table, laughing or whispering. The boys made up codes and games and wouldn't tell them the rules. Dom found no joy in it and he knew Libby didn't either.

There were things he wanted to tell Libby, especially since the Headmaster had left and she was angry at him all the time, but she seemed so far away. Watching her in the dark now, with purple under her eyes, he missed her desperately.

A night like this could change all that, he thought. It could be like old times, all together again in the night. Only he didn't have time to suggest this, because Concord yanked his arm, made him stand in the middle of the circle and told him to start talking.

The word 'Shuck' was still echoing around the group, but whenever Dom focused on a face, the person's lips weren't moving. The hum of a bird swooped overhead, but Dom couldn't spot it in the dark.

'I've been spending some time with Solitude,' Dom began.

'Your new best friend,' Merit sneered.

Dom ignored him. He raised his voice to be heard over the rain. 'He's told me, in secret, that what we thought when he first arrived is right: he's sick.'

At that moment, the noise that sounded a lot like thunder erupted from the direction of the Ash House.

Everyone turned to look. Dom cursed it in his head. If everyone thought a Shuck was loose, they'd be even less likely to help him.

'Should we go back?' asked Libby. Dom detected a rare note of hesitation in her voice.

'Listen to me,' he insisted.

'It's coming from the house,' said Concord.

'Listen!' Dom stamped his foot. 'About Sol. I think the Headmaster wants us to look after him.'

'Just because you look at the birds, that doesn't mean you know what the Headmaster wants,' Libby said.

'Well, I don't *know* – none of us do. He's away.'

'Don't say that like it's *our* fault.' Libby gestured at the girls.

'I didn't – I wasn't!'

'Then stop trying to guess what the Headmaster wants,' said Honesty. She ran her fingers through her short hair, then flicked the rainwater off her hand.

'If Sol's sick, he has to go,' said Libby. 'He's not staying here.'

'Hey, I already tried to put him in with the pig,' said Concord. 'I did my part.'

There was a snuffle of laughter from the circle.

'That was not a Niceness.' Dom threw every ounce of fake confidence he could muster behind his words.

The laughter stopped. They all looked nervously from Dom to Concord.

'And the answer isn't to get rid of Sol,' Dom pressed on. 'We have to give him a chance. Con, what about when you got your scar? Did we try to bury you?'

Concord glared at him, his eyes glowing, even the one

from under his scar.

'We helped you and you got better,' said Dom. 'I've thought of a way we can help Sol and make him better too.'

'You can't compare Sol's situation to what happened to Con,' Libby said doubtfully.

'Sol came here because he really believed the Ash House could cure him when no one else can,' said Dom. 'He doesn't know what the ash can do. Tomorrow is a full moon. It's the perfect time. I think if we help, it will heal him. We've seen it before.'

There was a long-drawn-out silence as they looked from one to another. Weight shifted from foot to foot.

'This is a lot of fuss for someone who isn't one of us,' said Concord.

## 14: SOL

Sol thought it was strange that there were puddles on the floor in the morning. That day everyone kept a cool distance from him, even Dom. At breakfast, he felt he was being watched, but whenever he looked up from his porridge, no one was paying any attention to him. Dom had gone back to hanging out with Concord, Merit and Justice. Sol passed the day on his own and tried to draw as little attention to himself as possible.

His back ached and when he went to bed, he was exhausted. He lay flat on his front, hoping he could sleep.

His mind dipped into a twisted dream where he was walking through the forest with Dom, who was just out of sight. It was the height of summer, the trees sun-drenched and vivid, the way Sol had never seen them. Then he couldn't hear Dom's footsteps any more. He tried to find him, but the ground was muddy and sticking to his feet. He lurched and nearly fell. He called Dom's name. Then again. Again. He heard another voice behind him, a girl's voice. He turned around, and a giant hand pressed an enormous lump of clay into his face, covering his eyes, nose and mouth. He tasted dirt.

He jerked awake just as his back electrified him.

Impossibly strong fingers were clamped over his face. They smelt of sweat and dust. Concord's unsmiling face appeared in the darkness. Sol's stomach sank and twisted into some terrible shape. The others were standing behind Concord wearing coats over their pyjamas.

They were going to dig up the pig and throw him back in. He was going to be given a whole new grave. He was going to be locked in the creepy, cold house on his own all night. Every horrifying thing they could do to him ran through his mind.

Concord lifted his hand off Sol's face a fraction.

'We're going out,' he hissed.

'Even me?' Sol asked with dread.

'Yes. Coat and shoes. Now.'

Sol got out of bed and stumbled to the wall near the bathroom. The only coat left was musty and made him cough as he slung it around his shoulders. When he went to put on his grubby trainers, Merit stopped him.

'Just carry them,' he said. 'Until we get down the stairs.'

Sol saw all of them were holding their shoes, ready to leave.

'W-where's Dom?' Sol asked nervously.

Concord shushed him and pushed him out of the door.

At the top of the stairs Sol looked over at the Ash House. The windows were blacker than the sky. The night was cold and clear. The full moon had a neat, vivid outline and its silver light made the world feel even colder. Looking out over the grounds, Sol saw a dark trail in the grass. Someone was ahead of them.

They trod carefully around fat leaves that had fallen and were starting to crisp. They were heading towards the pig. Sol's stomach twisted at the memory of it. He hoped more than anything they wouldn't put him back into that grave. But they peeled off and headed for the wall of trees.

Then Sol worked out where they were taking him.

'Are we going to the lake?'

'I won't tell you to shut up again,' snapped Concord.

The others often spoke about the lake with reverence and affection, and while Sol knew where it was from watching the birds, he'd never been allowed to go there. On another day, he might have been pleased that they were all going there together. But it was the middle of the night, Dom was nowhere in sight, and his warning of bad things happening to them when they got ill was heavy on his mind. All he could do was put one foot in front of the other as the forest enveloped them.

It wasn't long before they emerged from the trees again. The lake was in a quiet clearing, smooth as glass and dark as the night sky above them. The bank they stood on was a soft mixture of mud and sand. They weren't alone. Sol was flooded with relief to see Dom waiting there, and the girls standing by the water's edge.

Their coats were thrown in a pile on the ground, and they wrapped their goosebumped arms around their white nightgowns. The moon threw a white stripe down the centre of the water.

Sol saw Dom and Concord exchange looks, and it made him feel excruciatingly alone. They all knew the way in the dark. They knew what each other felt without speaking. Every single one of them was a planet in each other's solar systems, while Sol felt as insignificant as dust.

The boys moved away in small groups, following the edge of the lake, bending their heads under low-hanging branches and sidestepping wet tangles of weeds. Coats and shoes were left on dry land as they joined the girls.

There wasn't so much as a gasp as they entered the water.

Sol was starting to see the outer reaches of his breath in the cold. He wasn't sure if he was supposed to join them, so he watched, shivering in his coat, until he was the only one left. Then he felt a tap on his shoulder. Concord had stayed behind too. He gestured for him to follow.

'This way.'

'Where are we going?'

'To the Lookout.'

They went around the water's edge and through the trees. Sol was reluctant to follow. Concord had tried to bury him alive, in daylight, with an audience. He didn't think he'd hold back in the pitch black in the under-growth where no one could find them.

The far side of the lake was more rugged than the smooth beach where the others had entered the water. The Lookout was at the furthest point – a heap of rocks piled together, the biggest towering over the water. From the top, Sol thought he'd be able to see the roof of the Ash House and their dorm.

Concord began to scramble up the rocks, and Sol followed.

Stones slipped and rolled under his feet and his palms became sore from grabbing sharp edges and gritty surfaces. He pictured all the terrible things Concord could have in mind. Perhaps he'd be thrown off the Lookout and then his back would finally break into a thousand pieces as it clearly wanted to. If anything, it would be a relief. Sol climbed as fast as the pain in his back would allow.

When he reached the top, Concord was waiting for him. Sol had been right: he could see the glinting rooftop of their glass dorm and the grey shape of the house behind it. He could also see the dark heads and pale bodies of the others in the water beneath them.

Concord stood watching them, then he said, 'They're everything to me. Especially now that the Headmaster is gone.'

'I thought he was meant to be coming back soon?'

'I don't know about that.' It was the first time Concord had sounded less than certain about anything. 'And ever since you turned up . . .' He glanced at Sol. 'It's a strange time. For all of us.'

'I guess so,' Sol muttered. He hadn't really thought about how strange his arrival had been for anybody else.

A moment passed in silence and Sol couldn't wait any longer.

'Whatever it is, I want to get it over with,' he blurted out.

Concord glanced at him. In the dark, his scar was

almost invisible.

'What?'

'Whatever you're going to do to me – bury me again, drown me, lead me out into the forest, then leave me . . .'

'I've got something much bigger than that planned for you.'

Sol tensed, readying himself. 'Let's hear it, then.'

'I'm going to cure you. Here, sit down.'

'What? H-how do you . . .?' Sol spluttered. He thought he'd hidden his pains. And even if Concord had noticed, there was no way he would offer to help him.

Concord sat with his legs dangling over the edge. His face wasn't curled into a frown or a snarl. He looked thoughtful, maybe even sad. Sol distrusted him, but he was curious, so he sat down cautiously and placed his hands behind him, gripping the rock in case Concord tried to push him.

'Dom is my best friend,' said Concord. 'I always try to take his advice. He's very wise.'

Sol thought of Dom's dopey grin. 'OK.'

'He made me see that we didn't really give you a chance. That maybe you're here for a reason.'

Concord stared at him as if the pause meant something, but Sol didn't know how he was supposed to fill it. Concord helped him.

'I need you to tell me about this pain you have.'

'Oh. Dom told you.'

'He had to. You can trust me,' said Concord. 'I look after everyone here.'

'It's a long story,' said Sol. 'And since coming here my memories have become all . . . faded.'

Concord nodded. 'Try anyway.'

'Well . . .' Sol tried to find the clearest memory in his mind to start with. 'There was a hospital . . . and a car. Someone told me I'd get better – you know, the pain would go away. I guess they meant the Headmaster would cure me. They must not have known that he's away.'

'But why do you hurt in the first place?' Concord asked.

'If they knew that, I wouldn't have been dumped here,' said Sol. 'Maybe no one can fix me, and this is just a way of getting rid of me.'

'Maybe it is a way of bringing you to where you are meant to be.' It was the kindest thing Concord had ever said to him. He was clearly uncomfortable saying it. He coughed to clear the air and continued: 'The Head-master hasn't called for so long I don't know what we're meant to do. But Dom had this idea and if it doesn't work, then I'll know there's no reason for you to stay here and put everyone else in danger.'

Sol shivered again and this time it wasn't the wind.

'The Headmaster wants the Ash House to be as self-sufficient as possible,' Concord continued. 'We grow most of our food. Sew lots of our own clothes. And all our water comes from right here. Did you know that?'

'This whole time, I've been drinking and showering in lake water?'

'It's filtered, but yes,' said Concord. 'You know, I was sick once. My friends saved me. Dom, Clem . . .' His face twitched as her name escaped his mouth.

'Who's Clem? Oh! From the wall.' Sol remembered the painted-over name. 'Dom told me we're not meant to talk about her.'

'That's just Dom.'

'Were they really good friends?'

Concord nodded once. Then he climbed to his feet, so Sol did the same.

'What happened to her?'

'She's not here any more.'

'Where is she?'

Concord turned and jutted out his chin, indicating the far side of the grounds, beyond the vegetable patch and the forest. Towards the fence.

He started to climb back down the rocks. He clearly

wasn't going to elaborate.

'Dom has done you a Niceness by asking us to bring you here,' he said. 'But if the ash can't heal you, nothing can. And you'll have to leave.'

Sol stayed where he was, looking down at the black water. 'If the ash does heal me . . . can't I go home?' he asked, but even as he said it, he didn't know where home was. He remembered the impossible force at the fence, pulling him back, persuading him to stay.

'I doubt it,' said Concord's voice from behind him. 'But you could be happy here, like us. Do you want to be happy? Do you want to belong somewhere?'

Sol turned to face Concord and nodded. Of course he did. That's all anyone wanted, as far as he could tell. Trying to see beyond the day when he stopped being in pain was difficult. But he hoped there was something there. A Niceness.

'Hold your breath,' said Concord.

'What?'

Concord's fist pummelled into Sol's chest, and he fell.

The water slapped his back and he was pulled down, down, water rushing around his scalp, into his ears, under the thin trousers he was wearing. He could taste it, though he was certain that he hadn't opened his mouth. He hadn't even called out when he fell.

The downward tug of the water ceased. He was suspended, unborn. He opened his eyes. The ceiling of the water looked like the start of a thunderstorm.

Now it was pulling him up. How could the moon have gravity from down here, he wondered? Every muscle in his body relaxed, and it took a moment to realize why it was such a pleasant experience.

The lake was warm. It was the temperature of a bath that had been left to cool the right amount of time. No wonder the others had walked into it so easily.

For the first time in the longest while, his back didn't even ache. The feeling made his heart soar in his ribcage. He wanted to stay there for ever, but too soon he felt hands wrap around his wrists. He was pulled to the surface.

Sol gasped for air when he came up, only then noticing the burn in his chest. A trickle of water slipped into his mouth. It tasted metallic, closer to blood than pennies. Dom was holding one hand, Libby the other. They were smiling. All the others surrounded them.

'Freedom is a Niceness,' Dom said quietly, echoing the words he'd said when he first showed Sol the house and pressed his hand against it.

'Liberty is a Niceness,' Libby said next.

They went around in a circle, each repeating their

name and the phrase softly. Finally, when the last name was said, there was silence. They all looked at Sol.

'Solitude is a Niceness,' he whispered.

As soon as he said it, he spotted a tiny fragment of light floating down from the sky. It settled in the water in front of him and slowly turned grey.

Ash.

It was falling, quieter than snow, thicker and thicker, settling on the surface of the lake as if carried on the wind from a nearby fire. Sol gasped and looked around. All around him the ash glowed. Each atom of it was a tiny firefly, burning orange and yellow. It lit the water all the way up to the shore.

He tipped his head back and laughed, feeling like every day he had spent in fear of the pain was pouring out of him, losing its power to hurt him. The others laughed with him.

Concord was still standing on the top of the Lookout. His arms were folded across his chest.

'Do you see the ash?' he called down to Sol.

Sol nodded, unable to speak. He stretched out his hands and saw that the ash speckled his skin as if he were an egg. Somewhere overhead, the whirring of a bird swooped past, but everyone ignored it.

'Good.'

Concord took a run up and launched himself into the lake. The water exploded when he hit the surface, tossing droplet-sized lamps into the air. Sol laughed.

Concord reappeared, tossing more light aside as he wiped the water from his face, and started swimming towards them. A dark wake of water trailed behind him.

The rest of the group whooped and shouted and patted Sol on the shoulders. Dom let out an animal howl and dunked Sol under the water. They cheered for him to do it over and over. The ash got into his eyes, but it wasn't hot enough to hurt. It was warm and washed the world with gold and silver. Sol was ready to lie and say that his eyes were streaming from the water, but nobody asked.

'It's going to make you better,' Dom told him. 'The ash.'

'How do you know?'

'We found out when Concord got ill a long time ago.' Dom slurped up a big gulp of lake water and swallowed it, ash and all. 'It's good for you.'

Sol hesitated, then followed suit. The ash was bitter at the back of his throat. He thought of it lighting up his insides, turning his stomach into a calm, golden lake like the one he was floating in.

'Why didn't you tell me?'

'We weren't sure you were one of us yet,' said Libby. She floated next to Dom, the glowing spirals of her wet hair framing her face. 'But Dom said that you deserved a chance.'

Before Sol could reply, the children nearest the shore hushed them urgently.

Sol's toes touched the sandy floor to steady himself. All eyes were fixed on the beach where they had first waded in.

Sol couldn't see it at first. When he did, he wanted to vomit up the water that had settled in his stomach.

It looked like two candles – perhaps someone holding one in each hand. But the lights were too green for candles. Those were its eyes. They were the colour of a leaf when it first bursts from its bud.

Around the eyes, he was able to make out the shape of night-sky-black fur. The light from the ash in the lake should have been illuminating its face and jaws, but it was like the fur could absorb anything luminous, making the creature darker than any darkness Sol had ever seen. The ash in the water near it had turned grey. Mist appeared from nowhere – no, from its paws – and crystallized on the surface of the water.

Dom was very still next to him, staring at the beast.

'Dom, what is that?'

'That's a Shuck.' Dom spoke so quietly it was like the word was formed from his breath. 'Remember when Libby took you to—'

'Sshhhhh.'

The Shuck stared. The children stared back.

Slowly, one by one, they extended their arms in front of them and held out their palms facing up. Dom was nodding at Sol, urging him to do the same. Sol made the gesture, touching his little fingers together like Dom did.

The inside of his chest felt cold. One of the tests they'd given him in hospital pumped salt water through his veins, and that was how it felt, only it was pouring directly into his heart before being pumped around his body. His breath came out in thick, white clouds as if it was deepest winter.

The Shuck sniffed the air and grunted. Despite the complete absence of light or colour on its fur, Sol could see how gracefully it moved. It finally turned away and padded into the trees. There was no rustle of leaves or snap of twigs as it went.

The group relaxed. Their hands dipped back into the water. Sol didn't feel it was safe to speak until someone else did. He was relieved to hear Concord's voice as the temperature of his heart started to return to normal.

'Is everybody OK?'

Dumb, slow nods.

'Sol?'

'I'm . . . I think I'm OK. My chest . . .'

'It passes,' said Dom, rubbing his own ribcage with the heel of his hand.

'Has it definitely gone?'

'Back to the house. Yes.'

Sol felt his jaw drop. 'It lives in the Ash House? Wait, Libby's chore . . .'

'She feeds the Shucks. Three of them,' said Dom.

'There are three of them?' Sol shuddered at the thought of six of those green eyes, the strange feeling he'd had looking at the darkness beyond the metal grating. 'How did it escape?'

'It didn't escape,' Concord explained. 'The Headmaster lets them out.'

'But he's not here.'

'The birds see for him,' said Dom. 'Even when he's away, he controls the Shucks. We're not supposed to be out of bed . . . but it's gone now, so he must have decided it's OK for tonight.'

'As long as you stay still and do this –' Concord repeated the hand gesture – 'it shouldn't hurt you. If you give it no reason to.'

Sol hesitated to ask his next question, but he knew

he'd never sleep again if he didn't. 'Has it ever hurt anyone?'

Concord and Dom glanced at each other. Then Concord nodded.

'Yes.'

'Can we go now?' Justice asked. 'He's drunk the ash.'

Sol suddenly felt vulnerable and less trusting of the water than he did before. 'What's it going to do to me?'

'Make everything here go back to how it was before you arrived.' The edge was returning to Concord's voice. Sol felt the moment with him on the Lookout slipping away.

'And it makes you a part of the Ash House,' said Dom with a smile. 'Like us.'

The rest of the group waded towards the shore and began the uncomfortable task of pulling on their shoes and coats over wet limbs.

Sol trailed his fingers in the water, leaving patterns of light on either side of him as he moved. Everything about the lake seemed unbelievable to him, but nothing more so than the moment when he pulled his body from the water.

The pain in his back was gone.

## 15: DOM

Dom kept his eyes closed and listened to the *plink plonk* of the dormitory. He felt like the ash was still on him, a warm dust that would look after him all day long. He would shower in the evening, he decided. The Headmaster always said that cleanliness was a Niceness, but surely one day wouldn't matter much.

Leaves were rotting on the glass roof, dappling the morning light. It was cold enough that they needed to fetch the thicker blankets and push the beds closer together. In summer Dom liked sleeping on the floor, but in winter they often shared beds and kept their clothes under the blankets at night so they weren't damp in the morning.

When he couldn't ignore the morning any longer, Dom sat up and saw that Sol wasn't in bed. He was standing at the end of the dorm, looking out through a gap in the vines. He'd wrapped his blanket tightly around his shoulders.

'Sol?' Dom whispered. He climbed out of bed and went to join him. 'How do you feel?'

He gave Dom a twitch of a smile. 'Weird.'

'Oh.'

'My back . . .'

'Are you—'

'Better. I feel *so* much better.'

'Really?'

'I can't tell you . . . So long looking for answers. I had test after test. For a while I really thought I might be making it up, somehow. But every time the pain started again, I knew there was just no way. I could never imagine my life without it. Until now . . .'

Dom felt impossibly happy. Sol continued gazing ahead, his eyes shining in the sunlight.

'The house . . .' he began.

'What about it?' Dom asked.

'The ash. Dom, it's made of the ash.'

The Ash House stood magnificent in the frosty morning.

'It's so beautiful,' Sol whispered, so quietly Dom barely heard him.

'Does that mean you don't want to leave any more?' he asked.

Sol gave him his rare, thin smile. His eyes were the exact colour of the ivy knotting itself all around dorm. 'This place is starting to feel like home.'

Dom threw his arms around Sol. He had done it. He had turned a perfect stranger into a person bursting with Niceness.

The lake was all anyone talked about at breakfast. Sol's good mood was infectious. Even Concord was pleasant and kind, passing food left and right. Sol chatted to the people either side of him. Dom thought back to that first day and the withdrawn, angry boy who had emerged from the car. He hoped that by helping Sol, he had done what the Headmaster wished. Perhaps even done enough to make him come back.

The sun shone recklessly over the Ash House. The others started to go inside for assembly, but Dom and Sol hung back, clutching cold cups of tea, looking at the grey, hazy walls and enjoying the warmth a little longer.

'We should go to the lake every night,' said Sol. 'I've never known Niceness like it.'

Dom felt he could glow from Sol's happiness. Then, from somewhere inside the house, they heard a panicked yell.

'DOM? *DOM!*'

Footsteps slapped the stone floor and the back door burst open. It was Concord, pink-faced, breathing heavily.

'Dom!'

'What? What's wrong?'

Dom put his mug down on the concrete and rushed to the door. Concord looked deranged. He didn't answer. When he reached the steps, Dom realized why. A sound was coming from inside the house.

The telephone was ringing.

Dom covered his face with his hands and started to cry.

'Sit still,' Dom told Sol, who kept wriggling in his chair and jogging him. 'If the Headmaster's coming back, you don't want to make a bad impression.'

The chill gradually left the underground room as the children filled it with their excited chatter. Dom squeezed his hands together between his knees. It had been so long that he struggled to picture the Headmaster's face. It only came to him if he closed his eyes and started with the facts: hair colour, eye colour, the shape of his smile.

Concord came downstairs. He moved slowly, placing his full weight on each step. He then trudged on to the stage. In the few minutes he had been upstairs, he had changed. His skin was grey and lined; Dom half expected it to crackle like paper when he talked. He looked sick. He looked tired. He looked, Dom realized, like someone about to deliver bad news.

When Concord didn't speak, Libby prompted him.

'So? Did you speak to him?'

'Is he coming back?' Justice asked.

'It, um, wasn't him. It was . . . Apparently, he said he's sorry. And he won't be able to call again for some time. A very long time.'

All the joy Dom had felt just moments before drained from his heart, through his knees, into his feet, and seeped into the floor.

'If it wasn't the Headmaster, who was it?' Sol asked. 'Who else has this number?'

'Someone else,' said Concord.

Sol was leaning forward in his chair, oblivious to the rising tension in the room. Dom tried his best to push worried thoughts from his mind. The lake fixed everything, he told himself. But they hadn't had visitors at the Ash House since they were very small, and the Headmaster was always there. The few they'd met since those days were not welcomed with open arms.

'Who?' demanded Sol.

'The Doctor.' Concord licked his lips. 'I just spoke to him. He's back. He said he's been watching through the birds and he thinks we need some check-ups.' He looked at the floor and took a moment to gather himself. They waited in an aching silence. 'He'll be here tomorrow. Sol has the first appointment. He said that the Headmaster, as always, would like us to remember our Niceness.'

Concord then talked about the usual things: chores, maintenance the grounds needed, Niceness. Dom couldn't hear him. His hands were cold and numb between his knees. When he raised his head and looked around, everyone else was looking down, lost in their own dark thoughts. Everyone except Sol.

Dom didn't understand. They had taken him to the lake. They had immersed him in the ash. Trust is a Niceness and Dom had done it with all his heart and now it was letting him down. Anger bubbled up inside him. He swallowed. His hands were slippery.

When he finished the announcements, Concord didn't wait for his friends. He left straight away.

'What's going on?' asked Sol when Concord had disappeared. He was the only one speaking.

'The Doctor's coming,' said Dom.

'Well, I'm glad. To be honest, when I first got here, I thought you didn't get any kind of medicine at all. Dom?

I'm sorry the Headmaster is going to be away a bit longer. But at least you know he's safe. Just . . . look, don't cry.'

'I'm not.'

Dom didn't dare bring his sleeve to his eyes. He knew what the others would say if they saw him burst into tears: courage is a Niceness too.

## 16: SOL

Nobody saw the Doctor arrive. His car was black and shining and didn't have number plates. The children gathered around it and looked at their stretched, alien faces reflected in its glossy metal. Stray flakes of ash were already settling on its roof.

'Will he know what happened to my back?' Sol asked.

'It's just a check-up,' Dom replied in a lifeless voice.

'He might check you over, then leave again,' said Libby flatly.

'That's true.' Justice nodded, as if this was what he was hoping for.

'Whether he can or not, I guess I have Dom to thank,' said Sol.

Dom whipped around. His expression looked as if Sol had just slapped him.

'What!'

'Because of the lake,' said Sol. 'You said that if I drank

the ash, the house would look after me and everything would be OK. I guess the house summoned a doctor!' Then he slapped his arms against his sides and laughed, unable to control the fizzy mix of joy, relief and disbelief he felt.

'Well, as long as Dom's looking after *you*,' Libby muttered.

'I didn't do it,' Dom insisted. 'I didn't call the Doctor. I just wanted you to get better.'

'He didn't mean it like that,' said Concord, putting an arm around Dom. He had been quiet since the assembly, not even snapping at Sol when he got the chance.

'He'll know what happened,' said Sol, gazing up at the windows of the Ash House. 'He'll be able to explain everything.'

Libby ran her hand lightly over Sol's back, skimming the fabric of his shirt.

'Let's see,' she said softly.

'You go in, up the stairs, around the corner, then up the stairs again,' said Justice. 'That's where his office is.'

'We're allowed upstairs for a doctor's appointment?' Sol asked.

They nodded.

'It's the only time any of us are allowed up there. You should go,' said Libby, guiding him towards the front steps. They all watched him walk up the steps. He glanced back to smile at them. Dom was chewing his lip. Libby's eyes were wide with worry. Sol felt a moment of hesitation, then pushed it from his mind, and went inside.

The Ash House was silent and dark, a place made of shadows. Sol was used to being surrounded by the noise of the others. He touched the badge on his chest and found that the cool feeling of metal helped clear his mind.

He went past the telephone and the bowl, and, for the first time, approached the grand staircase. The steps looked like stone, but they felt soft as carpet under his trainers.

The staircase was wide and had a smooth wooden bannister. The only sound was Sol's palm sweeping along it. As he went higher, he was delighted to find framed photos lining the walls. He paused to look at them and saw the faces of his friends staring back, years younger than they were now.

There was one that looked like any other class photo. The taller kids were at the back, the smaller ones seated with their hands in neat fists on their knees. Sol squinted at it. He quickly found Dom's round, smiling face under the most disastrous haircut he'd ever seen. Then there was another photo of Concord holding hands with a freckled, wild-haired girl Sol didn't recognize. Concord was smiling a wide, beaming smile that Sol had never seen, and there was no C-shaped scar across his face.

The further Sol went up the stairs, the older the photos became. He spotted Libby as a little girl with her arms around Patience and Charity. It was like turning the pages of a family photo album. He half-expected to see a photo of himself amongst them, perhaps his younger self standing on his bed in the dormitory or peering around a tree in the grounds on a snowy day.

His memories from before the Ash House were becoming more faded and blurred with each passing day. He felt a pang in his chest. He had nothing, while his friends would always have these happy moments they had shared.

He wanted to see what the Headmaster looked like, but as he went on, he only saw pictures of the children. Yet in places he could have sworn the ash walls had dark, rectangular patches the same size as a photo frame, as if some had been lifted off the wall.

He reached a landing. A corridor was on his left, leading to a closed door on the first floor. A small window let in a square of light.

According to Justice's directions, the Doctor's office was higher up. Sol took a few steps up the next flight of stairs. There weren't as many photos here. There was a black-and-white picture of three enormous black dogs standing in front of the Ash House. Sol stopped to peer at it. There was something in the dogs' eyes that didn't look right.

He was standing there looking at it when the Doctor found him.

First, Sol saw his shoes, as black and shiny as his car, as he came down the stairs. Then long legs, a shirt tucked into belted trousers, and a smiling face.

'Solitude?'

'That's me.' Sol wiped sweat from his forehead with his shirt cuff.

'This way, please.'

The Doctor spoke with a clipped, confident accent that Sol had only ever heard from people on television. He was handsome in a way that made it difficult to tell how old he was. His grey hair was short, his skin was tanned, and he had light-blue eyes. He didn't wear a white coat or stethoscope. He carried a closed laptop, kept a biro behind his ear, and had something pinned to his chest that surprised Sol: one of the metal badges. The

Doctor's was dark and had a beautifully detailed bird engraved on it. It had long plumes of feathers with flames underneath.

He didn't seem like any of the doctors Sol had met before.

They went into a small office, which was old and uncared for, like most of the house. It smelt like the windows hadn't been opened for years. Despite that, Sol was glad to be there. Being in a real room – not a greenhouse or a shed – was a luxury. There was a squishy chair for him to sit in and a battered desk for the Doctor. Stacks of folders were on the floor, pushed against the wall out of the way. Sol read the labels: medical notes, conditions and histories.

'I thought I'd introduce myself,' said the Doctor as they settled into their seats. 'I've been the Doctor at the Ash House since it first opened.'

'When was that?' asked Sol. He struggled to imagine a time when the Ash House didn't exist.

'Long ago,' he replied with a smile. 'I remember when all your friends here were taking their first steps.'

Thinking of Dom, Libby and all the others as babies growing up at the Ash House made Sol feel strange, the same way the photographs had. He wished he had been one of them. They were so strong and self-sufficient, but they can't have always been like that.

'Of course, things were much more hands-on back then,' the Doctor continued. 'I'm not needed half as much. But the Headmaster told me that you might need my services.'

'I've never met the Headmaster.'

'I understand that. His being away like this must be hard for you all. But before he left, he told me all about the new boy who was joining our family here.'

'Really? He knows about me?'

'Of course. He knows everything that happens here.' He pulled the biro from behind his ear and tapped it decisively on the desk. 'So. What brings you to me, Solitude?'

Suddenly all Dom's warnings about talking about his back gripped his tongue. Sol trusted Dom. Dom had tried to keep him safe, even if he hadn't always succeeded. So when the Doctor asked the question, Sol's mouth went dry.

The Doctor held up his hands.

'I've been told I have an interesting case here,' he said. 'But I wasn't given any specifics. I assure you that one of the reasons the Headmaster relies on me is because I am an excellent diagnostician.'

Then Sol felt something that brought to mind his

journey up the twisting drive, the rain tapping on the roof of the car, the driver gripping the wheel too tightly, and the bolt of shyness he felt when he saw Dom hunched on the top of the gate.

Hope.

He came to the Ash House hoping that someone would have answers. Instead, he'd been given mysteries that had slowly been woven into a new life – one he was starting to like. If there was only a one in a thousand chance that this doctor could explain everything, Sol had to take it. Besides, he was better. It hardly mattered any more.

'It was my back,' he said.

'OK.' The Doctor smiled encouragingly and opened his notebook.

'I had these pains. Not regular back ache. These awful, awful, really just . . . very, very bad pains.'

'I see.' He looked genuinely concerned. 'Have you seen a doctor about this before?'

'Yes, loads and loads.'

'Did they do any tests?'

'Any test you can think of, I bet I've had it.'

'And the diagnosis?'

'Central Pain Syndrome. Complex Regional Pain Syndrome. Chronic Fatigue Syndrome.' Sol felt the old resentment and frustration building in him as he listed all the dead ends that had been thrown in his face. 'Fibromyalgia. Anxiety. Attention-seeking.' He shrugged. 'Depending on who you speak to.'

'In other words, you're still undiagnosed.'

'I guess so.'

'When did all this begin?'

'Over two years ago.' He had lost track of the date since he'd been at the Ash House, but he knew that it had started in the autumn.

'Was there some sort of illness or accident preceding the symptoms?'

'Some doctors said it was because . . . Well, there was a fire. My parents didn't get out. Most doctors focused on that. After they died, I was moved around – foster care, you know, and most of them took me to the hospital a bunch of times and . . . Sorry, I can't remember much of that since I got here.'

The Doctor nodded. 'Emotional trauma and physical pain have been known to manifest in—'

'No! It's not that!' Sol insisted. 'This isn't in my head. It's real. It's the most real thing I've ever felt. You should see me when it happens. It makes me think I'm going to die.'

'We're all going to die.'

'From the pain, I mean.'

'That sounds dreadful.'

'It is,' Sol admitted, relief blooming inside him. 'It's the worst. Then the hospital where I was staying sent me here one night. I guess they thought the Headmaster might be able to help.'

The Doctor's face was blank. 'And the people at this hospital know the Headmaster?'

Sol shrugged. 'I suppose so.'

'Do you know which hospital it was?'

'No.'

'Think very carefully, Solitude.' The Doctor leant forward, his grey hair catching the light. 'Do you remember anything more about how you got here?'

Sol's mind became murky with the feelings of panic he'd had when he first arrived at the Ash House, and felt his memories turn grey.

'I really can't. I'm sorry.'

The Doctor folded his hands and nodded. Sol's answer seemed to please him.

'That's all right.' He wrote something down. Sol craned his neck, but the Doctor held the notebook with its spine against the table, its pages tilted away.

'And how are you finding life here at the Ash House? Nowhere else like it, is there?'

'No. Definitely not.'

'Have these pains continued since you've been here?'

'Yes. For a while. But now . . .'

'Now?'

'This morning I feel better.'

'Do you?'

'Yeah. Loads.'

'Why do you think that is?'

'I don't know.' Some instinct told Sol not to mention the lake. He didn't want to get the others in trouble by saying they had gone swimming there at night.

'So, this pain has been getting worse over a period of two years, but today you feel better,' the Doctor clarified. 'Do your friends look after you? When you have these attacks?' His eyes were pale and fixed on him.

Sol glanced out of the window behind the Doctor. All he could see was grey.

'They don't know anything about it,' he said automatically. He sensed the Doctor sitting back slightly in his seat, as though this answer reassured him.

'That must be lonely.'

'I'm OK.'

'Even so, I think we should get to the bottom of this, don't you?' The Doctor smiled, his eyes creasing as his white teeth appeared, and Sol felt a sensation like warmth hitting his skin the second after the sun shows itself.

The Doctor asked the questions nobody else had asked. That's how he became enchanting.

Soon Sol was telling him about the few memories he had hung on to. Black smoke enveloping a house. A woman shouting – he thought she was his mother, but he couldn't picture her face. Trying on new, black clothes. The first time the pain came, and being so sure that he would die because his body couldn't take it. Red and blue lights. And then all the times it came after that. Lying on a bath mat, moving between warm cotton and cold tiles. Peeling off his pyjamas after wetting himself from the pain. Different bedrooms, some he shared, others where he was alone. And through it all: pain – a lightning-storm pain – a wildfire pain – a tsunami pain – that could swallow the world.

Then he got to the parts that were clearer to him, including the Ash House.

After he finished explaining, the Doctor listened to his heart and his breathing, took his blood pressure, measured and weighed him. He asked him to take off his shirt and move his arms and back in several ways.

'Do you think it's really gone?' asked Sol as he showed he could raise his arms above his head. 'Just because I'm here?'

The Doctor rubbed his palm over his chin as he considered this question. He stood behind him and looked at the muscles move under Sol's skin like he was considering a particularly difficult puzzle.

'No.'

'What?'

'I think you're experiencing a reprieve.'

'But I feel so much better.'

'That's what a reprieve is. But things like this do not simply disappear, Solitude.'

'I don't think so. The Ash House—'

The Doctor reached out a cold thumb and pressed it into the middle of Sol's spine.

The electricity, the fire, the ice, the earthquake in his nerves shot through his entire body.

He screamed. His jaw couldn't stretch wide enough.

The world went black in a blink, then he was on one knee, as if swearing fealty to his pain. He was panting.

'What was . . . How did you . . .?'

The pain was gone again. It had only lasted a moment, but it was a moment of soul-wrenching agony that Sol would rather die than face ever again.

'As I said –' the Doctor calmly handed him his shirt back – 'a reprieve. It is still inside you.'

'But – no, I can't . . . It has to—'

'Calm down, son.'

The horror of it was too much. Sol wanted to jump out of his own body and become a spirit, a thought, a will-o-the-wisp that burnt on the Ash House grounds for the rest of time, and never have flesh to call his own.

'I can't go back to how it was before!'

'I know. I won't let that happen.'

'What?'

'I can make these pains leave you. For good.'

'You can?' Sol asked as he sat down, trembling, in the chair. 'You don't think it's all in my head?'

'Many doctors treat the mind and body as if they're separate,' the Doctor told him. 'As if the brain is just a machine inside another, more powerful machine: the body.'

'But you don't think that?' Sol asked.

'Not at all. I think the brain is the most powerful machine of all. With it we can create entire galaxies, entire lives, just with our imaginations. But I'll need you to trust me.'

Sol decided long ago not to trust any doctors, but he found himself torn over this offer. The Doctor was warm, friendly and calm. It felt nice to be around an adult who was in charge. But he had also brought the pain back with just the touch of his finger. Like he could control it . . . He wasn't just kind and understanding. He was powerful too.

'OK.'

The Doctor looked up from his notebook and smiled. Sol felt the wave of warmth wash over him again. Reassurance. He couldn't remember the last time he'd felt it.

'You carry a little extra hope around with you just in case. That's wise. But you'll need more than hope. It will be a long recovery process. Things may get worse before they get better.'

'But I will get better? For ever?'

'Yes.'

'What will I need to do?'

'We'll have to schedule an operation.'

Sol's heart sank. More hospital gowns, more doctors. He didn't know if he could take it, and it would probably mean leaving the Ash House for a while.

'Do I have to?' he asked. 'If my back's starting to feel better—'

'Yes. Experience tells me these pains will return, and worse than before, as we just saw. You don't need to look so nervous. I'll do the surgery myself, right here at the Ash House. You'll be in safe hands.'

'Have you done this before?'

'Similar procedures, yes. Experimental medicine is a particular interest of mine, and boundary-pushing operations come with that. Solitude, I wouldn't do it unless I was totally confident I could heal you.' There was that smile again. 'Do you want that? Do you, Solitude? Do you want the pain to end?'

Tears stung Sol's eyes. He didn't blink. He barely even breathed as he said: 'Yes.'

'Then I'll have you as good as new by the time the Headmaster returns. Won't that be wonderful? You'll be able to meet him, whole and healthy, and thank him yourself for letting you come here.' The Doctor clicked the lid back on his pen.

'Is he coming back soon?'

'In a little while, I think. Time enough for us to get started. I don't want to waste time.'

'When do we start?'

'Soon.'

At the end of the appointment, Sol moved dreamily to the door, reluctant to leave the Doctor's presence. He floated down the stairs and didn't even glance at the picture of the black dogs as he passed it.

## 17: DOM

While Sol had his appointment, Dom was supposed to go to the shed and check what the birds had seen, but he couldn't bring himself to stray from the house. He'd promised himself he'd watch over Sol, and that was what he was going to do. He sat on the front steps, watched the drive trail away from him and avoided looking at the black car.

He didn't hear Sol coming down the stairs. He only knew the appointment was over when his friend nearly tripped over him on his way out of the house.

Dom leapt to his feet.

'Are you all right?' Everything inside him felt tense, ready for a fight.

Sol turned around, beaming. 'I'm better than all right. Better than I've ever been!'

'Oh. Really?'

'He's going to make the pain stay gone, for ever,' Sol

told him. 'That's what he said.'

Dom stared at him.

'And he said the Headmaster will come back soon,' added Sol. 'Did you know that the Doctor is also a surgeon?'

Dom didn't like the way Sol was smiling, the way he talked about the Doctor's promise. He tried to change the subject.

'We have to go and watch the birds.' He climbed down the steps and started heading towards where he thought the shed would be that day.

'Why didn't you tell me about him?' Sol asked as he kept pace with him. 'He's actually really nice. You lot were acting like he's – I don't know. And I got to see loads of photos from when you were little. They're hung on the walls.'

'Oh, yeah.' Dom tried to ignore the photos whenever he went upstairs – he felt he shouldn't look at them directly, in his mind or in real life, as if they were tiny suns. His childhood memories were precious, and he didn't like to linger on them in case they lost some of their magic. He rationed himself carefully. He didn't want them to fade as his memories of the Headmaster were starting to with the passing years.

Sol continued chatting as they strode over the field

with the tree-lined drive to their right. He asked a question that Dom missed.

'What?' said Dom.

'Who called him? You said it wasn't you.'

'It really wasn't. I swear.'

'So who did?'

'He must have found out somehow. Sometimes I wonder . . .' Dom thought about the birds and instinctively reached for his binoculars. Had the birds seen something? Had he not been careful enough?

Sol had stopped walking.

'Look. Either you're not listening to me, or you're admitting it's your fault. Which is it?'

'What's my fault? The Doctor? No! Sol, I would never . . . *Never* bring him here.'

'Exactly. You watched me in pain every day. You're the only one who knew how bad it was. And you didn't do anything!'

Dom realized two things at once. First, Sol's joy had evaporated as they'd walked. Second, he was somehow angry with Dom.

'I didn't do anything?' Dom repeated. He clenched his hair in his hands and shouted: 'I did *everything*! When everyone figured out your secret, I convinced them to let you stay. I convinced them to take you to the lake. I sat with you, I watched over you, I held you up, I-I-I—'

'But you didn't do the one thing that would actually make me better – calling a doctor!'

Dom held up his hands to ward off Sol's anger. 'You're angry because I *didn't* call the Doctor?'

'You did nothing – just like that day with the pig!'

'You hate doctors just as much as we do,' Dom reminded him. 'You said that before you came here they only made things worse.'

'None of my doctors were like him.'

'Of course they weren't. No one's worse than him!' Dom snarled.

'What's wrong with you?' Sol asked. 'You're supposed to be my friend.'

'I am your friend – I'm trying to look after you! And anyway, the lake made you better – you don't need his help. Whatever he says, don't do it. Just wait until the Headmaster—'

'NO!' Sol shouted. 'I've had enough of waiting. I've waited for years. The pain could come back any minute – he showed me. The Doctor says he knows a simple operation that—'

'NO!' Dom shouted back at him. 'You mustn't let him help you!'

Sol narrowed his eyes and lowered his voice: 'I thought you were my friend, but I guess not. The Doctor's going to make me better, and then I'm leaving this place. For good.'

Dom carried on to his shed – this time it was on the edge of the forest, so close that a branch tapped on the window – and spent the rest of the day staring at the screens, not taking in anything they showed. He thought he saw something flicker in the trees but didn't have the energy to rewind and take a closer look. He wanted to cry, but his throat and eyes felt dry and raw. The ash that he hadn't showered off in the morning was powdery and itchy under his clothes. He didn't turn the light on when it became dark, and he missed supper. He was quietly furious that nobody came to find him and check that he was OK.

The Niceness song churned through his head, as it did whenever he was sad or angry.

'Luck . . . Mercy . . . yes, Mercy.' He felt that apologizing to Sol would be a Niceness. But it wasn't enough. He needed to make Sol see sense about the Doctor. He needed to win back his trust. The right Nicenesses would help him do that. He continued: 'Patience . . . Peace . . . Persistence . . . Yes. Mercy and Persistence.'

He focused on these Nicenesses, and when he felt they were clearly fixed in his mind, he turned his attention to the screens. Everyone was in bed, except Concord, who was in the doorway of the dorm, talking to someone outside, possibly one of the girls.

And, with an awful lurch, Dom saw that Sol's bed was empty.

Dom ran up the stairs two at a time and shoved the door open with his shoulder. He walked down the dorm and counted the still lumps in their beds. Everyone was there, except for Sol. Dom imagined finding out that Sol's arrival had been a dream, telling Concord over breakfast that he'd dreamt a green-eyed new boy had joined them at the Ash House, and all of them would laugh and tease him about such a ridiculous idea.

He selfishly hoped it was true.

No Sol meant no visit from the Doctor.

Dom put his head around the partition separating the dorm from the bathroom. No one was there.

Dom thought very seriously about going to bed. He hadn't eaten, and he was exhausted from feeling tense and angry all day. He wanted to put on his thickest socks and drift off under his blanket. But he knew he wasn't going to. He put on his shoes, his coat and some spare gloves that were lying on the floor. He left, closing the door quietly behind him.

He went down the stairs and headed towards the Ash House. He had only taken a few steps when a voice came from the shadows behind him, making him jump out of his skin.

'What are you doing?'

Dom whipped around. Libby was sitting on the concrete outside the dormitory. The glass behind her was dark, concealing the outlines of the girls in their beds.

'Libby. You scared me.'

She wore a heavy coat over her nightie and her skinny ankles stuck out underneath it. Her cheeks and forehead shone in the moonlight.

'I said, what are you doing?' Her breath materialized around her in clouds.

'None of your business.' Dom turned his back on her and set off again, a new determination in his step.

'You can't go in there,' she called after him. 'It's night-time.'

He hesitated. 'I know that.' Then he turned. 'Did you see Sol leave?'

She nodded.

'When?'

'Not long ago. He didn't see me. He was with the Doctor.'

'Who is that?' a voice called from the top of the stairs.

Dom looked up and saw the outline of Concord's coat.

'Me and Libby. We're just talking, go back inside,' said Dom.

'He wants to go and get Sol.' Libby betrayed him without even a blink.

Dom scowled at her and pulled his coat tighter around himself. It was too cold to be standing still.

Concord hurried down the steps, each one ringing with his weight, not caring who he woke up.

'He's with the Doctor,' he said. 'You can't go in there.'

'Maybe his appointment hasn't started yet.'

'You have to leave it, Dom,' said Libby.

'You can't do anything,' said Concord firmly. 'He brought all this on himself. He doesn't listen to us, so he doesn't get our help.'

The three friends stared up at the Ash House as they had so many times throughout their childhood. The windows were dark.

'I'm just going to check,' Dom said, with all the casual confidence he could muster.

Before he could move, Concord grabbed him roughly

by the wrist.

'You're coming back upstairs with me.' His fingers squeezed hard, twisting his skin.

'He's right, Dom,' said Libby. 'There's nothing we can do right now.'

'No! He doesn't get to do this again!' Dom cried.

'What exactly does that mean?' Libby spat, as Dom twisted his wrist in Concord's grasp.

'You know what!'

'Oh, I get it. Sol's special, is he?' she demanded. 'You're unbelievable. Con, take him back upstairs.'

'Let go of me!'

Dom tugged and turned, but Concord, still holding his wrist, flung his arm across Dom's shoulders to restrain him. He could barely turn his head. He struggled, but Concord had always been bigger, stronger, more certain in what he wanted.

'Get off!'

'You're not going.'

'You can't stop me.'

'That's exactly what I'm doing. Dom, you're acting with pure Nastiness right now!'

'I'm not, I'm Niceness! I'm Mercy and Persistence, Mercy and Persistence!'

'What?'

'Mercy—'

'Your name's Freedom!'

Dom tried to sink his teeth into Concord's hand. Concord squeezed harder, pushing the air out of him, making the grey outline of the building swim.

'It's for your own good.' Concord was straining with the effort and his voice came out as a whisper. A wet whisper. 'I'm looking after you.'

'I – don't – need—'

'Dom, stop being so *Nasty*!' Libby snapped.

There was a bang. They froze.

A door had slammed somewhere.

They looked up at the house. Concord loosened his grip on Dom. No one appeared. No lights turned on.

Dom used the distraction to wrench free, his determination to prove them wrong eclipsing any fear. He ran towards the house. He ran, ignoring his name – the warm, comforting Niceness of his name – drifting after him as Libby and Concord begged him to come back.

He knew they wouldn't dare follow him.

It wasn't clear where the night ended and the house began. Dom wished the ash would light up and show him the way, but if it did, he would be spotted. He found the back door they used every day was shut. His fingers felt for the handle, but when he tugged it didn't budge.

Then he heard the machines.

There was a cranking, a clanking, a low buzz that he wouldn't have heard by the dorm. It was coming from the classroom.

Dom had no idea if the classroom was open. None of them ever locked it, and none of them went in there after bedtime. Why would they? There was nothing there but desks and decaying books.

As he drew nearer, the machine noises grew louder. There was a line of light under the door, like a parade of glowing ants. Dom knew that sliding the door open even a crack would make a din. If the Doctor was inside, he'd hear it. But Sol must be in there too.

Whatever was happening, Dom knew he had to stop it. He also knew another way into the classroom.

Brambles clutched at his trousers and he had to avoid thick clumps of nettles. There was no path round the back of the building – not that he would have been able to see one in the dark. He found his way by keeping his right hand on the rough breeze-block wall. When he thought he was close to the point he was looking for, he trampled down the brambles and patted the wall until he touched a concrete corner and then cold, cobwebbed glass. The window opened on to the library; Dom had often propped it open to clear the musty smell of the books.

After putting his fist into a nest of nettles, sucking his teeth at the stings, Dom found a stick that felt long and sturdy enough. It took a few awkward attempts at scaling the rough breeze blocks before he could dig his finger-nails into the wooden ledge, pull the window open and put the stick in place. He pulled himself up and on to the sill, breathing in the smell of damp paper.

Dom's body swayed as if on a seesaw; there was noth-ing for him to grab to steady himself. The mechanical hum was definitely louder now his head was inside. The window ledge dug into his hips as he wriggled forward and tried to curl his knees through the gap. He tried to cling on to the metal window frame, but his weight carried him forward and he fell, muffling a grunt, on to the concrete floor.

He lay there, listening. When he was certain no one had heard, he picked himself up.

Dom pressed his ear to the door and heard metallic clinking. He placed a trembling hand on the doorknob and started to turn it. He paused. He decided to kneel down. He felt safer nearer the floor, making himself smaller. He stretched his hand, smarting from the stinging nettles, above his head and wrapped it around the doorknob. He felt sick with fear of what would happen if he opened the door, and sicker at the thought of not opening it.

He pulled the door open. A line of light exploded at its edges.

He couldn't see the desks – only a corner of a blue sheet. Its smell seeped into the library. Footsteps rustled on it. Dom heard a noise that sounded like air pumping through a rusty machine.

Another inch. More sheet and a table leg.

Another. Tubes tracing and lacing over each other, running from the floor up on to the table.

One more. A dark, curly head lying on the table.

He was too late.

## 18: SOL

When Sol first woke up from the operation, he thought that he was in the woods and the trees were speaking to him. The room was damp and green and thin light worked its way past the leaves. Then his sight focused on the murky glass. He was in the dormitory. And the whispering came from the other boys.

Sol was in his bed at the far end of the room, looking out towards the Ash House. He was lying on his left side and wanted to turn on to his back, but he knew it would hurt. He was still thinking about moving when sleep pressed itself back on to him.

He didn't know how many days he spent swimming to the surface of consciousness only to sink again. His world consisted of a strange taste in his mouth, heaviness in his arms and whispers that came and went.

When he finally woke properly, his head aching but clearer than it had been for days, the dorm was quiet and mid-afternoon light fell over his legs. Sol lifted his head. He paused, waiting for a shooting pain or burning in his back, but nothing came.

Dom was sitting at the foot of a bed on the other side of the aisle.

'Hi,' Sol murmured.

'Hello.'

'I saw you,' he told Dom. It was the last thing he remembered clearly: a moon-sliver of Dom's face, his grey eye pressed against the gap of the library door.

'I know.'

'You were coming to stop the operation?'

Dom opened his mouth to speak, then closed it again. He nodded.

Sol reached behind him. It felt like a brick was tied to his wrist. He wasn't wearing a shirt, only pyjama bottoms. His fingers brushed a thick wad of bandages that covered his back.

'I think it feels better. He said it would get better.'

'He says a lot of things.' It was as if Dom couldn't settle on being either sad or angry. 'Slow down. Don't move too much.'

Sol propped himself up on his elbows. There was a deep bruise on his arm – as if he'd been linked up to a cannula, like when he'd visited hospital for all the tests, only it hadn't been put in very well.

'Does it hurt?' asked Dom.

'It feels weird.' Sol rolled over, sat up and squinted at his feet.

'I can get you food when you're hungry,' Dom told him.

'Thanks. I . . .'

'Then when you're better, I'll take you downstairs. You probably want some air. Maybe some milk.'

'Dom, I—'

'What? You don't want milk?'

Terror threatened to overwhelm Sol, far worse than any pain episode he had known.

'I can't move my legs,' he whispered.

Then he screamed it so loudly it was impossible for anyone near the dorms not to hear.

'DOM, WHAT HAS HE DONE TO MY LEGS?'


The worst part was how kind they were to him, as if they'd seen it coming all along and were taking the high road by not saying, 'I told you so.' The Niceness wasn't because they liked him. It was because they felt sorry for him.

Concord brought Sol his lunch on the second day. He sat on one of the beds and made small talk about how

173

high the lake was and how the chores were changing as the weather got colder. The Doctor had locked himself away in the Ash House – no one had seen him since the night of the operation, but his car was still there, its shiny paintwork becoming speckled with ash.

Sol burnt his mouth on the soup and wished Concord would leave, then felt guilty as soon as he wished it.

Dom helped him to and from the bathroom. He lifted Sol on to a blanket and then dragged it down the length of the dormitory. Sol always refused when any of the others offered to take him.

The following day it was Justice's turn to bring him lunch. Everyone else was in the canteen. Sol imagined it full of its usual clamour, not knowing that nowadays the children sat in morose quiet.

'Do you need help . . . um . . .?' Justice mimed putting food into his mouth.

'My arms work fine,' Sol snapped.

He balanced the tray on his useless legs. He had some feeling, a vague tingling sensation sometimes, but they couldn't so much as twitch. He spread butter on his bread and started working his way through the tinned soup.

'I thought Dom was bringing me lunch,' he said to

Justice, steam slipping out of his mouth as he spoke.

'He said he'd come later. He's with Libby.' Justice was sitting at the end of the opposite bed, where Dom had been when Sol woke up. He looked so pale Sol thought he could trace every vein in his neck if he wanted to.

'Doing what?'

'Trying to cheer her up, I think. She's pretty upset.'

'She hasn't even seen me.'

'I know,' he replied, speaking mostly to his socks. 'But after everything that happened with Clem . . .'

'Clem? Oh.' Sol remembered his conversation with Concord at the Lookout. 'Clemency. Concord told me about her.'

'Really?' Justice blinked. 'And you wanted an operation anyway?'

'I – what?'

'Dom said you wanted the operation.'

Sol thought of the gap in the names on the classroom wall, the letters visible under the white paint. His knife and spoon clattered on to his plate. He opened his mouth then closed it again. It had never occurred to him that something like this had happened before.

'Hello you two.'

Justice had left the door propped open, so neither of them heard Dom come in.

They didn't reply. Sol stared at his soup.

'I brought you an apple,' Dom said. Then he looked from Justice to Sol, and back again. 'What's wrong?'

'Nothing,' Justice said quickly.

'I'll take the tray down if you want,' Dom offered.

'OK.'

Justice jumped up and hurried out of the dorm, clearly relieved to be out of Sol's company, and Dom took his place.

'What was all that about?' Dom asked.

Sol pushed his food away. 'Everybody here knew about the Doctor except me. No one warned me.'

'We did.'

'No. You didn't. No one did! I thought he would heal me. I went *to* him.'

Dom threw up his hands. 'What do you want me to say? I tried to tell you!'

'You didn't try very hard!'

'He doesn't like it when we talk about the bad things he does,' Dom whispered. 'Even if I had, you would have thought I was lying. The Headmaster watches through the birds, but so does the Doctor sometimes. If we're sick, he comes to see us. I was trying to protect you. I *have* protected you. A little bit, anyway.' His gaze settled on Sol's legs.

They sat in silence until Sol picked up his spoon again.

'Look, I'm sorry I left you after your appointment,' said Dom. 'Anger is a Nastiness. I let it take over.'

'Me too,' Sol admitted. 'Do you think—?'

Sol stopped mid-question. Dom had raised his hand and was staring at the doorway. Sol heard it too. The ring of expensive shoes on the metal stairs.

'Give me that.'

Dom grabbed the tray with Sol's lunch and cast about for somewhere to hide. He slid the tray underneath the bed he had been sitting on, then crawled in after it, just as the Doctor entered the dorm.

'Solitude! You're awake.'

His smart shirt and shining shoes looked out of place in the mouldering dormitory. He walked down the aisle with a spring in his step, the tendrils of ivy brushing the top of his head.

'I've never done an appointment in here,' he called out, swinging his black doctor's bag in one hand before setting it down on the floor next to Sol's bed.

'What?'

'The Headmaster always said that you all needed your space, so I've always done my work in the house.' The Doctor looked around for a chair. When he realized that there were no such luxuries, he sat on the end of Sol's bed.

'How are you feeling?'

It was the smile, Sol realized. It had sucked him in, made him doubt everything Dom had said, and now here it was, at the end of his sickbed, trying to do it again.

Questions buzzed in Sol's head like flies. What had happened to his legs? And, most importantly, was he healed? He hadn't felt a single twinge in his back since the operation. He ached, but he never once felt that oncoming wave of mind-blowing pain. It occurred to him that his legs might be the price he had to pay for this, but surely the Doctor would have told him if that was the case. It wasn't a trade he would have made lightly.

'How – how do you think I'm feeling?' Sol was careful to sound curious, not aggressive. He needed to see how much the Doctor understood of what had happened.

'A little tired and sore, I'm sure. Have the back pains gone?'

'Yes.'

The Doctor's eyes widened, and he leant towards Sol. 'Have they really?' It was like he couldn't believe the results of his own work. Like he'd had no idea what was going to happen.

'Um. Yup.' He couldn't hold the Doctor's gaze. His eyes fell back to his blanket. He didn't dare glance at where Dom was hiding.

'How extraordinary.'

The Doctor began opening his bag and rummaging inside it. Something about him was different, Sol noticed. He'd lost some of the smooth calmness he'd had before the operation.

'I knew I could do it, of course – *of course* I could do it, but sometimes these things . . . Well, that shows something, doesn't it? Just a helpless little boy with these mystery pains, and who fixes it? Who fixes it, Solitude? Me. All on my own. None of those other doctors you saw.'

He was speaking to himself; every word was frantic and muttered. He only stopped when he pulled out a needle.

Sol recoiled, gripping the edge of the bed.

'What's that?'

'It's for the pain.'

'I told you, I don't get the pain any more.'

The Doctor lowered the syringe, clearly confused. 'I meant the pain from the operation. It will help get you moving about sooner. Is something wrong, Solitude?'

Sol was sweating and feeling more trapped than he

ever had in his life.

'I don't want an injection.'

The Doctor stared at him. For a second, Sol thought he was going to ignore him and force the needle into him. Those blue eyes were unreadable.

Then slowly, calmly, the Doctor put the syringe back in its plastic case. It clicked shut.

'Something's wrong,' he said matter-of-factly. 'And if you don't tell me, then I can't help you, can I? Is it the other children? Have they been saying things to you?'

'No,' said Sol, a bit too quickly. 'No, it's, er . . . it's my legs.'

'You have pain in your legs?'

'No. I can't move them. Ever since I woke up from the operation.'

A crease appeared between the Doctor's eyes.

'Ah.'

'Is that normal? For the operation I had?'

'I have no idea.' The Doctor rubbed his chin. Then he moved Sol's blankets off his legs. He touched a toe. 'Can you feel that?'

'No.'

'This?'

'No.'

'Anything?'

'Yesterday that one itched.' Sol pointed at his right leg. 'Like a tingling.'

'I see.'

'Is that good? Does it mean the feeling will come back?'

'I have no idea,' he said again.

'How can you have no idea? You're a doctor!' Sol paused. 'Aren't you?'

The change in the Doctor's demeanour was so sudden it was like he was possessed. His attention snapped from Sol's legs to his face.

'Of course I'm a doctor, you wretched brat!' Spit flicked on to Sol's face.

'Sorry, sorry, I know . . .' Sol grabbed the blanket, as if it could protect him.

And, just like that, the Doctor changed back. He wiped his mouth and smoothed his hair with a trembling hand.

'Not even doctors have all the answers, Solitude. We're only human.' His gentle, logical voice had returned.

'Yeah. I know. Sorry.'

'That's quite all right. But this is a mystery that needs to be solved. I think the best thing to do is to give you another day's rest. Then we'll open you up again and see what we can find.'

'Open – open me up?'

The Doctor had shoved the box with the syringe back into the bag and pulled out the notebook and pen. He slashed and jabbed at the paper as he made furious notes.

'Do you mean another operation?' asked Sol.

'Yes, yes, yes. I'll get in there and see what I can fix.'

'I'm not a car.'

The Doctor chuckled, as if they were making pleasant small talk. Sol did his best to shuffle closer and hold his attention.

'Doctor. I don't want another operation. I really, *really* don't.'

'It will be fine,' he muttered to the notebook.

'Isn't it dangerous? So soon? Especially if you don't really know . . .' Sol trailed off as the cold blue eyes found his.

'Know what?'

'Nothing.'

'Leave it with me, Solitude. I'll get you all shipshape again, which is more than any of those other doctors can say.'

He finished his notes and clapped the book shut.

Sol couldn't believe it had taken him so long to work it out. This man wasn't a doctor. He saw Sol as nothing more than a guinea pig. Sol had no idea how far the experiments could go, but one thing was for certain – he didn't want to find out.

After the Doctor left, Dom appeared from under the bed, with a smear of soup on his cheek.

'Are you OK?' he asked.

'I can't have another operation, Dom, I *can't*. He doesn't know what he's doing. Anything could go wrong! Is he even a real doctor?'

'The Headmaster thinks so,' said Dom, as he dusted himself off. 'I don't like to think the Headmaster is wrong about anything . . . but maybe he's wrong about the Doctor. It isn't the Headmaster's fault,' he added quickly. 'But that's why we avoid him when he comes here.'

Sol felt trapped like a bug under a microscope. Dom gathered up the tray to take it downstairs. Before he left, he put his hand on Sol's shoulder.

'We won't let him do another operation.'

'We can't stop him. I can't run away. I can't even walk!'

'I have an idea.'

'I don't think the ash can really save anyone, Dom.'

'It can – it can do amazing things! I know someone who can prove it.'

'Please don't bring Concord into this.'

Dom's cheeks flushed scarlet. 'Oh, don't worry, it's not him. It's . . . well, it's someone else.'

## 19: DOM

Dom marched past the vegetable patch on his way to the woods. The light was going, and mist spread over the grass, like the whole world was getting ready to go to sleep. Dom set out with determination, muttering Nicenesses under his breath, but as he went past the animals, the spot where they buried the pig, and then the lake, he slowed down.

By the time he reached the trees, he was already chickening out, trying to think of other ways to help Sol – hiding places, traps for the Doctor, or even offering to take his place. None of those things would work. Dom knew that, despite everything he had done, he would never be brave enough to attack or hurt the Doctor. There was no escape.

This churning wheel of thoughts kept his feet moving until he reached the fence. That and the memory of the Shuck's eyes reflecting off the lake at night. He didn't like the idea of one being released while he was out in the forest in the dark on his own.

High above him, the wire shone like spider's silk. *Buried alive, burnt alive, evaporated.* Dom tried not to think about how easy it would be to step over and not exist any more – never to have existed, never to have had a problem, because his entirety had been undone.

He stopped a few metres from the fence.

'Hello?' he called. There was no sound, not even a breeze to make the leaves murmur to him.

'Hello?' he called again, and wrapped his arms around himself. 'I know you're there.'

Far off to his right, he heard something snap, and a rustling that started and stopped suddenly.

'I can't stay long,' he called out.

The quiet stretched on. He was ready to turn back when he heard the rustling again, this time so close that he couldn't write it off as the woods.

A face appeared through the tangle of branches. A smile.

Wild hair. Freckles.

'Clem,' he breathed.

It was nearly dark in the woods by the time Dom finished his story. He was sitting on the damp ground, leaning against a tree, pulling off bits of bark and watching them curl like parchment.

'Now the Doctor wants to operate again. I can't let him. Sol's my best friend.'

'What about Con?'

Clem had climbed a thick, low branch and was draped over it like a cat. Leaves and twigs were caught in her hair. Her fingernails were entirely black, and every inch of her was smeared with soot and ash. Occasionally she yawned and then coughed out a dark puff of smoke. To Dom, she was comforting and terrifying at the same time.

'Oh yes, Con too!' Dom ripped a shred of bark in two. 'So much has changed, you wouldn't believe it.'

'What does he say?'

'He says Sol shouldn't be here. That he'll put us all in danger. That he *has* put us all in danger. The Doctor's here now.' Dom paused. 'Do you think Con's right?'

Clem wrinkled her nose. 'You know what I think about the Doctor. The question is, what do *you* think?'

She was difficult to look at. Sometimes she was solid and vivid, more alive than anything, yet there were moments when, out of the corner of Dom's eye, she looked as if she was made of smoke and ash like the house – one moment sharper than life, the next, hazier than memory.

'I think . . .' Dom stared hard at the ground as the answer formed in his mind. 'I think there's Niceness here. Somewhere. I feel it. But I can't find it.'

'Sol's the Niceness.'

'Yes.'

'You must save him.'

'*Yes.*'

'Because he will save you all, when the time comes.'

'What time?'

Clem was on her back, gazing dreamily at the canopy above her. Her eyelids dipped as if she was fighting sleep. She twirled a finger through the smoky air, creating patterns in the darkness.

'Is the Headmaster back?' she asked.

'No.'

'Didn't think so.'

'I need help. How do I save Sol?'

'The birds might help.'

Dom hadn't considered this. He chewed his lip. 'The birds? Maybe. How?'

'Because they remember everything.' She sat up and dangled her legs under the branch. Her hair glowed like there was fire within each strand. 'We need to remember. And others need to see. They need to believe.'

'Believe what?'

'Believe what happened. To me. To all of us. You know what I'm talking about. An old memory box, from long ago.'

'Those are kept in the house.'

'Those memories will be the Doctor's undoing.'

'But they're *in the house*,' Dom stressed. 'I can't—'

'You can.' Clem glowered. The dark pupils grew and grew until her eyes were nothing but black. Dom felt cold to his centre, like a Shuck had brushed right past him. 'But you don't.'

'Don't be angry with me!' Dom yelped. 'You don't understand. Seeing things isn't easy! I never wanted to see – the Headmaster made me. It's my chore, only mine, so no one else understands what it's like to see everything! I should be able to protect everybody, but I don't think I can!'

Clem's face softened. The darkest wisps of smoke drifted away.

'Poor Dom. It's a lot.' As she spoke, Clem ran her thumb over her badge. It was covered in soot, but Dom knew she was feeling the symbol etched on it. It was a heart, like Love's badge, only with flames around it. 'But it's not only you now. Someone else does your chore with you.'

'Sol.'

From beyond the boundary, Clem sometimes saw things in a way he couldn't, but what she was suggesting was impossible. That particular memory box was locked away in the heart of the Ash House. And what on earth was Sol supposed to do with it, even if Dom could get his hands on it?

A tendril of smoke reached out and touched Dom's shoe. It made him look up sharply. The smoke was enveloping Clem.

'Please don't go yet,' he begged.

'I don't get to decide.'

'But I don't know what to do!'

'You do so, Freedom.'

'Wait!'

The smoke made Dom cough, and the second he closed his eyes was long enough for the smoke to contort and engulf the outline of her. It hung motionless in the air until a slight breeze, so gentle it was like the wood sighing, let it flow away. The branch Clem had been lying on was empty.

'I miss you,' Dom whispered to the soot-stained trees. 'We all do.'

'This was your idea, Dom. If you're not going to help, then why are we bothering?' Justice clapped his gloved hands together to keep his blood moving. They were on the lawn outside the dorm. Its glass was dark green and shining under the pale clouds.

'Someone has to watch for when he leaves . . .' said Dom. The Doctor had gone up the stairs into the dorm to visit Sol.

'Stop whingeing and get on with it,' Concord snapped at Justice.

The Doctor had visited Sol to discuss the next operation, while Justice, Concord, Libby and Dom had a project of their own.

In front of them stood an ancient pram, a dismantled bike and one of the chairs from the canteen. Libby and Justice sat on a damp log; she was tackling a wheel with a rusty old spanner that left orange flakes on her sleeves, while he stitched a new cover on to an old cushion, sighing often to let his friends know what he thought of the task. Concord knelt on a sheet of plastic and held the wheel steady for Libby while she worked.

'Should we go in?' Justice asked them.

'No,' said Concord. 'Don't be stupid.'

'I'm not the one going to all this effort for someone with a Doctor's appointment.'

'Right.' Concord stood up and held a blackened screwdriver dangerously close to Justice's eye. 'You've done nothing helpful since you got here, so if you've been waiting for the day you and I have matching scars, you're in for a—'

Justice tried to twist away but fell into the long grass. Libby's laugh sang through the air, the first time anybody had heard it in days.

'Can you two stop it?' said Dom. Concord threw down the screwdriver and helped Justice to his feet. 'The sooner we finish this, the sooner we can go back inside and get warm.'

'This bit's nearly done,' Libby told them. 'Justice, give me the cushion, we need to put it all together.'

'I think it's good,' said Justice, holding out the lumpy cushion by its corner. 'Not much use on the stairs . . .'

'Someone can help him with that bit,' said Dom. 'At least this way he can still do things.'

'What things?' asked Concord.

'You know, chores and meals and stuff.'

The others exchanged looks over his head.

Concord went over and patted Dom on the back.

'Dom, when the Doctor really wants to treat some-one, then . . . Well.'

'What?' Dom demanded. 'Then what?'

'Then there's not much we can do.'

'We don't want you blaming yourself if things go

badly,' said Libby.

'You've tried to be a real Niceness to him,' Justice added.

'You did warn him,' Concord said firmly.

Dom took in their pale, concerned faces, and then glanced down at the smudge of soot still on his shoe.

Suddenly Justice said: 'The door's opening.'

When they were sure the Doctor was back inside the Ash House, Dom, Concord and Justice carried their project up the stairs. Sol was in bed – he hadn't left the dorm since he'd woken up from the anaesthetic. Dom saw that his blanket was twisted around him. Sol stared at them as they clattered through the door, dropped the chair on to its wheels and pushed it towards him.

'What's that?' Sol asked.

'It's a gift,' Dom told him. 'We all helped. Libby did most of it – she's good at building stuff. I know it's a bit clunky. I'm going to work on making it less heavy.'

Dom parked the chair next to the bed proudly. Sol looked past him at Concord and Justice.

'You helped?' he asked them.

They nodded.

Sol took in the wheels, the bright seat, the sturdy handles. He looked at them all. Then his face crumpled like leaves.

'Thank you,' he muttered.

'Yeah, well . . . You can't lay about in bed all day,' said Concord.

The boys stood awkwardly as Sol buried his face in his hands and started to hiccup. Concord gazed determinedly at the ivy on the ceiling. Dom patted Sol on the shoulder.

'Does this mean you'll use it?'

Sol nodded, wiping at tears and snot.

'Come on,' said Dom. 'Try it.'

He pulled Sol's arm around his neck and was startled at how cold he felt. Then he slid an arm under his knees and lifted him. He placed his friend gently in the chair.

'How is it?' Concord asked stiffly.

'I can't believe you made it,' said Sol. He ran his hands over the dirty wheels. 'Thank you.'

'Libby said she'd make you some gloves too,' said Justice.

'We'll help you get up and down the stairs,' Dom told him. 'Let's take it downstairs and try it out.'

Dom carried Sol and Justice followed them with the chair. He let it clatter on each step and Dom worried about the frame. Concord came last. His hands were in his pockets and he didn't offer to help. Libby was waiting for them, shivering in her blue woollen coat and rocking back and forth on her heels.

'You like it?' she asked.

'Yeah.'

'Now you don't have to spend all day stuck up there with those Nasty-Nasty boys,' she said. 'I also got you . . .' She rummaged in her coat pocket, paused, and then pulled out a pair of binoculars. She handed them to Sol. 'Here.'

'Really?' he asked. He turned them over and gently wiped a lens with his sleeve.

'You do birdwatching. You should have them,' Libby said, though her eyes were on Dom.

'Thank you,' he murmured.

'We have chores now,' Concord said abruptly. 'Can't be late for feeding time.' He pushed past them roughly and headed towards the house.

'I thought you said he never feeds the Shucks,' Sol asked.

'He doesn't,' said Libby.

'Why not?'

'I'll go and check the torches,' said Justice. He hurried after Concord.

Dom placed Sol carefully in the chair. He noticed him wince as it pressed against his wound dressings.

'Look after them,' Libby told Sol, nodding at the binoculars. 'They're delicate.'

'I will.' He hung them around his neck and smiled up at Dom. 'Look! Now we match.'

Dom felt his heart could burst with joy.

## 20: DOM

Dom did his best to explain how things were different when the Doctor was visiting. They had to watch the birds as much as possible to keep track of where everybody was. If somebody suddenly got called in for a Doctor's appointment, they had to let everybody know. If the Doctor went wandering around unexpectedly, they had to alert them too. No one was allowed out alone. Concord and Libby gave them updates in their dorms each evening. They were in charge of keeping an eye on his car and telling them the second he drove away.

Dom told Sol all this in the shed. Sol practised rolling and turning his chair next to Dom's as they watched the black-and-white images. The wind whistled through the plank walls.

'I can't decide if he's a crazy person pretending to be a doctor, learning it all on his own,' Sol told Dom, 'or if he's a real doctor who's gone crazy.'

'I never understood why the Headmaster lets him come here,' said Dom. 'We barely saw him when we were little. But then he started coming more and more. Then Con's eye . . .'

Sol wheeled himself closer.

'Yes?'

'That's when we realized: he wasn't really good at healing people at all. Con nearly went blind.'

'What happened?' Sol couldn't hide his curiosity. 'How did he get his scar?'

'It was years ago. In the summer. You'll love the summer here, Sol. Everything goes all warm and yellow and slow. Con was feeding the Shucks, but there was a mistake. You've seen the bars that keep them under the Ash House?'

Sol nodded. Dom felt a knot of anxiety grow in his stomach just at the thought of what happened.

'Well, the grating opened. It wasn't meant to, but it did. One of them jumped out and attacked him. Libby was there, but she couldn't stop them, of course. The Doctor heard and came running, forced them back into their kennel, but Con's face had been scratched. He was really hurt.'

'*That*'s why he doesn't help Libby with feeding time,' Sol realized.

'He almost never goes back there,' said Dom. 'The Doctor stitched up the wound. But it got infected and took too long to heal. Con got a fever. Every time the Doctor tried to help, he got worse and worse. So we hid him and told the Doctor he was fine. Libby brought him food, and water from the lake. He got better, but the scar . . .' Dom pointed at his eye. 'Constance and Luck know how to heal people – just little things like cuts and fevers. The Headmaster taught them; it's always been their chore. They say the Doctor doesn't do any of the things you're supposed to do. He's not so good at healing people. Sort of the opposite.'

'You know when I was talking to Justice? He, um . . . he said something like that happened to Clem too.'

'What!' Dom yelped at the mention of her name. 'You're not supposed to say her name!'

'Concord told me you made that rule up. What happened to her? Did the Doctor do something to her too?'

Dom's heart was beating hard in his chest. He managed to nod, just once.

He wasn't sure if anybody else knew that Clem was still there, wandering the boundary of the Ash House; if they did, nobody said anything. She was his secret. He had often thought that he should tell someone about it, maybe Libby or Concord, but he always found an excuse not to. To him, Clem was fragile, insubstantial. He had a strange feeling, like one wrong move could make her disappear for good.

'These are hers, aren't they?' Sol held up his binoculars. 'She used to do birdwatching with you.'

Dom swallowed. He was holding a memory box in his lap, running his hands over the perfect grey metal. For nearly all his life, everything Dom had seen Clem had seen too. Every Niceness and Nastiness, every secret shown to them by the birds. He had always had someone to talk to about them. He had never had to make a decision without her. Then all the secrets were his alone. Now he had Sol to share them with, but there was too much that he'd seen on his own. The urge to tell Sol everything was so strong. Sol had trusted him with his secrets, yet Dom couldn't bring himself to do the same. Silence stretched painfully between them.

'You said you would speak to someone who would know what to do about the Doctor,' Sol said. 'Any luck?'

'No.'

'Who was it?'

'I shouldn't say,' Dom muttered.

'You can tell me. Is it one of the girls?'

'No, none of us.' Dom found it difficult to look Sol in

the eye, so he focused on the screens.

'What do you . . . ? Dom, is there someone else here?'

'Not here exactly . . .'

'Outside!' Sol bounced as if he wanted to leap out of his chair. 'I can't believe it – you can speak to somebody *outside*? Who is it? Can they get us out of here?'

'No! She had this idea . . .'

'She!'

'But it's impossible. We'll have to think of something else.' They spent a moment in silence – Dom trying to pretend the conversation wasn't happening, Sol too stunned to speak.

'Look, the leaves are nearly all down,' Dom said eventually.

'Something else? Dom, there isn't anything else! If you know someone who can get rid of the Doctor, we have to take their help. Where is she? Who is she? Is she someone you can phone?'

Dom picked at the badge that sat over his heart. 'Not really. She's beyond the fence.'

'The *fence*?' Sol stared at Dom, who didn't explain what he meant. 'You hate the fence. You said you never go near it.'

Dom felt his cheeks turn pink. He knew what Sol would say about his secret chats with Clem: that he was mad, silly, seeing things, dreaming of the impossible.

'This is a miracle,' Sol whispered to himself. 'Someone out there knows we're here! And you were just not going to tell me! Argh, this is too much.' He buried his hands in his hair.

Every word from Sol's mouth made Dom more and more nervous.

'Sol, please, *please*, don't tell the others.'

'But she can go to the police!'

'I don't know what that is,' Dom said quietly. He hated it when Sol used his words from the outside, reminding him that he hadn't grown up at the Ash House, that he wasn't really one of them.

'They're people who can help us!' Sol was nearly yelling now. 'People who should know we're here!'

'But we'd have to do the impossible,' Dom muttered. 'It's not fair.'

Sol wobbled nearer to him, still getting to grips with his chair.

'Dom,' he said sternly. 'Look. You don't have to tell me who it is. But what exactly did she say?'

When Dom didn't reply, Sol grabbed his shoulder. 'Please remember what happens to me if we sit around and do nothing.'

Dom swallowed. This is why secrets are not a

Niceness, he reminded himself.

'There's a memory box. That's the problem. We'd have to steal it.'

'That's not hard. We have all the memory boxes.'

'No, an old one. It's in the Headmaster's study.'

'You're allowed in the Headmaster's study.'

'But I'm not allowed to take the memory boxes. That's stealing.'

'Yeah, but . . .' Sol sat back in his chair, winced, then sat up straight again. 'But he's not here. He wouldn't know.'

'He will when he comes back and sees a memory box missing,' Dom insisted.

'What's in it?'

'I don't know.'

'Dom!'

'The Doctor . . .'

'Memories of the Doctor . . .' Sol was lost in thought for a moment. 'Why would that help us?'

'Exactly. It won't,' said Dom, starting to relax.

'Unless . . . Well, it depends what's on it.' Sol looked at the screens. 'Dom?'

'Yes?'

'What if the birds know something?'

'What?'

'What if they know about some of the bad things the Doctor has done?' Sol was getting more and more animated. 'What if they remember? What if those memories are saved on a hard drive somewhere?'

'It's a memory box,' Dom mumbled.

'It's *proof*! Dom, we have to find it and take it to the police!'

'We can't do that!' Dom shrieked at him. 'We can't do any of that! It's locked away in the Ash House. The Doctor will stop us. The fence will kill us. We'll never come back! Clem's wrong!'

Dom bit his tongue and tasted blood.

'Clem?' Sol frowned in confusion. 'What's Clem got to do with it?'

'We're supposed to be watching the screens, OK?' Dom snapped. 'Chores are an important Niceness. No more questions.'

Dom tried to give him what he hoped was an encouraging smile, but Sol was scowling at his hands.

'I promise we'll think of something else, Sol. We'll find an answer.'

## 21: SOL

Sol found staying awake easy. The other boys went to bed with the tension of the last few days visible in their lined faces, the purple under their eyes. But eventually all of them drifted into twitching, fitful sleep. Sol watched the spaces between the vines turn from blue to black as night set in.

When he felt certain that everyone around him was dreaming, he pushed himself upright. His chair was by the door, where Dom had left it. That was his first challenge.

The afternoon had made his head spin. Sol didn't know what to believe. Did Dom really know somebody beyond the fence? Was it something Clem had told him before she left? It seemed impossible – they would have sent for help years ago. But still, Dom seemed to know some things for sure; he knew about the memory boxes and how the birds worked. It was a possibility. The only one Sol had for the time being. The Ash House was a web of habits and rules that his friends had spent their lives obeying. But he wasn't like them. He wasn't scared of the Headmaster.

Dom could have his secrets, but Sol would have his own.

He was going to find that memory box.

He struggled to lower himself from the bed to the floor, landing on his bum with thump. He then pulled his blankets off the bed and on to his lap. He started to shuffle backwards towards the door, with his legs in front of him.

He tried to be as quiet as possible, but his trousers dragged against the floorboards and the heels of his hands padded one-two as he hauled himself along. The dirt, hair and skin of the dorm floor stuck to his hands. He tried not to think about it.

He reached the chair and felt a surge of affection for the crudely assembled thing, made by the first real friends he'd had in years.

He yanked a few of the coats down, wincing when the buttons pinged against the floor. He then tucked the coats and his blankets around the chair. He padded the wheels, folded fabric over the metal frame and wrapped up the jutting handles. When he was done, his chair looked like an oddly wrapped Christmas present. He swung the door open, praying that the gust of cold air wouldn't disturb anyone, and pulled the chair after him.

He shuffled down the freezing metal stairs, dragging the chair with him. It was bulky but not too heavy, and the fabric stopped the frame from ringing on the staircase. By the time he reached the bottom, the heels of his hands were dented from the stairs' treads. He paused there, spraying clouds of his breath into the air as he rested in the freezing cold. His back was still sore from the operation and the house was intimidatingly far away. His feet tingled. He hoped that was a good sign.

When he got his breath back, Sol undid the blankets and attempted something he hadn't tried before: to climb into the chair on his own. His arms and back protested with every awkward movement. He prayed that none of the girls would wake up and look out of their window.

After a final heave with his arms, he succeeded. He pulled one of the blankets back on to his lap and began to wheel himself towards the Ash House.

Opening the door on his own was harder than he'd expected. There was a lot of wheeling forward and back, forward and back, trying to move the door slowly so that it didn't creak. Eventually he tied one of the blankets around the handle and tugged it open. Once he was inside, Sol decided it was safer to climb the stairs without the chair, no matter how useless he thought his limbs were. Dragging it up with him would make too much noise and, as far as he knew, the Doctor was sleeping somewhere up there.

He looked up at the blackness of the staircase. His feet tingled some more.

Getting out of the chair was trickier than he'd thought. He slid forward, but lost his balance and hit the floor hard.

'Idiot,' he muttered to himself. He'd hurt his hip and hands. Despite the cold, he was sweating from the effort.

Only a few days ago he'd climbed these stairs without thinking about it. His head had been filled with the Doctor and what he might say. Now they seemed like a daunting mountain he had to climb. A wave of anger surged through him. It pumped new strength into his arms.

He placed an elbow on the bottom step and started climbing.

After an initial struggle, he found a technique. Elbow, elbow, pull up, reach back, drag leg, reach back, drag other leg, rest. He thought it would be easier to do it with his back to the stairs, but he didn't want to take his eyes off the landing above him, in case a light was turned on.

When he was halfway he paused for a longer rest. He rubbed the sweat on his face away with his sleeve. Then he started the cycle over again.

Elbow, elbow, pull up, reach back, *creak*.

Sol froze.

He wasn't certain what he had heard. It sounded too far away to be the stairs below him. He looked up but there was no light, no other noises.

He dragged himself on, agonizingly slowly.

Reaching the landing at the top felt as blissful as floating in the water of the lake. The others had told him that the Doctor stayed on the top floor of the Ash House; Sol listened carefully, but there was no sign that he'd heard him. To Sol's right was the flight of stairs that went up to the Doctor's office. To his left, there was the short corridor that led to the closed door. The Headmaster's study.

He dragged himself across the floor, and crossed the square of moonlight that came through the window. Once he reached the end of the short corridor, he pushed the door open and entered the study.

It spanned the full width of the house. The moon's silver light weaved its way in strange tendrils around the room, gleaming on the wood-panelled walls and a cobwebbed chandelier. The study was arranged like a fascinating library, with endless shelves and cabinets and display tables – only they were filled not with books but with birds. Real birds, not drones. So that was what Dom had meant when he said the Headmaster collected statues.

The stuffed birds lined the walls and shelves and caught Sol's eye every way he turned: a snowy owl with a mouse in its beak; a flock of starlings suspended overhead so their wings nearly touched and turned the ceiling dark; three blue tits side by side on a shelf, their flat heads smudged with cobalt. From tiny sparrows and wrens to sleek ravens and crows, they were all arranged on their spindly legs, frozen in time. A tawny owl glared down at Sol from a high shelf. He wanted to run his fingers over the feathers.

Further down the room there were peacock feathers, creamy flamingos and dead-eyed parrots, as well as mounds of paper with sketches of birds and buildings. There were vases as big as Sol's torso filled with murky water and sealed with glass stoppers.

He dragged himself across the dusty carpet. At the far end of the room there was a workbench. It smelt of metal. Sol sat up and craned his neck and saw carving tools – a chisel, some pliers and a variety of knives – as well as blank, metal disks just like the badge that was pinned to his shirt. He touched the wolf's head that was etched on his own badge. He had come to feel a strange affection for it. Like the other children, he didn't even take the badge off when he slept.

Over by the windows the shadows became more vivid, like pieces of black card held up to a lamp. In front of the windows, looking out of the grounds, was an enormous desk and a swivel chair with a cracked, green leather seat. The Headmaster's chair. Sol reached out to touch it. Dust came away on his fingertips. How long had it been since someone had sat there?

And where was the hard drive in this huge room? Then he remembered that Dom had said the memory box was locked away. Sol peered around and at far end of the room made out a sheet of dull metal set into the wood panelling, where there might once have been a set of double doors.

Sol crawled over to it. He looked for a lock or a handle. It had neither, but etched into the metal door were over a hundred names. All of them Nicenesses.

It reminded Sol of the bowl by the front door that Dom had pulled his name from, only here there were more, far more. The Headmaster must have had much bigger dreams for the Ash House than he'd realized. There were names he hadn't had a chance to give out yet.

Next to each name was a tiny metal notch, like a button. Sol reached up and pressed one – Zeal. It made a satisfying click, just like a combination lock. It must be a vault, Sol thought. And to open it, you needed a code – a code of Nicenesses.

But how to break it? What combination of Nicenesses would the Headmaster have chosen? Sol had no idea how to begin figuring out the mind of a man he had never met.

There was a button at the top with no name next to it. Sol stretched up and clicked it, and the button next to Zeal's name sprang back, resetting the puzzle.

He crawled back to the desk and dragged the leather chair over to the vault. It squeaked horribly as he pulled himself into it. He set to work.

Sol wriggled his fingers and wracked his brain. Click by click, he tried all the girls' names, all the boys' names, then everybody's names together. He tried various combinations of people who could have been the Headmaster's favourites. He tried all the names that hadn't been given out yet. He closed his eyes and tried to remember the names that were painted on the wall in the classroom, but that didn't work either.

He slapped the metal with frustration. It was impossible. The potential combinations might as well have been infinite.

*Think*, he told himself, *think*. You're in his study. Get to know the man.

He slid off the chair, pulled it back to the desk and hauled himself into it again. There were drawers on either side, some small shelves and neat piles of dusty paper everywhere. The top drawers contained empty pens, paper clips, some unused stationery. In others there were stacks of drawings and paintings made by the children. Sol flicked through the indecipherable shapes until he found one labelled 'Freedom – aged 6'. He found himself smiling at it and laid it carefully on the desk in front of him.

Among the papers he found some building plans for the Ash House. It seemed at one point the Headmaster had planned to build a proper dorm, a classroom block and even a playground. There were invoices, lesson plans and letters – the Headmaster clearly hadn't been on his own the whole time, Sol realized. People must have helped him create the Ash House. He wondered where those people were now, and what they thought had happened to everybody left there.

He uncovered several maps of the house and grounds,

which he unrolled on the desk. He could see the lake, the woods going on and on until they fell off the page. One of the maps was covered in green lines. Sol squinted at it. They connected everything: the dorm, the Ash House itself, the vegetable patch, various points in the grounds. He couldn't think what the lines represented.

At the bottom of one drawer, he discovered a list of names – proper names, not the Nicenesses they had been given. Sol didn't recognize any of them. He puffed out his cheeks and worried that the whole adventure had been a waste of time.

Then his gaze fell on a photograph laying on the far corner of the desk. It was one of the children when they were very young, clustered on the grass with their arms around each other. The Doctor stood behind them, beaming. It made Sol shudder.

Then he realized: that had to be it. He must have done it wrong the first time. The Headmaster loved everybody and loved them all equally. Dom was always telling him things like that. Dom would know who the Headmaster would choose, Sol thought.

Then he realized: Dom might have already given him the answer.

He made his aching way back to the vault and sang slowly under his breath the song Dom had been trying to teach him since he arrived to learn everybody's names and Nicenesses.

'There's Amity and Calm and Charity . . .' He clicked each button in turn. He hoped he wasn't imagining that they all clicked into place more easily than before.

When he pressed the last one – Wisdom – he stopped and listened. There was no sound from the thick door. He tried to wedge his fingers into the gap around the edge, but it didn't budge.

Sol swore.

He looked at the photo again. What could he be missing? There was no button for the Doctor, so it couldn't be him. Then he slapped his hand to his head. Of course. He was the new boy. He knew the new version of the song. But the Headmaster had left three years ago. When Clemency was still at the Ash House.

His hands trembled with excitement as he repeated the song, this time carefully slotting in Clemency after Charity.

Nothing.

Sol gazed at the names in despair. Heavy with defeat, he pressed the blank reset button. He'd have to go back to the dorm, pretend to sleep for the rest of the night while he played out the horror of his next operation in his mind. He couldn't bear it. He looked at his own name bitterly. Solitude. He certainly felt on his own.

Then, not quite knowing why he did it, he reached out a finger and clicked the notch next to his name.

A noise came from within the door. It was followed by lots of clicking and whirring sounds and then a deep, mournful groan. A thread of darkness appeared where the door met the wall.

Sol, numb with disbelief, reached out to open it wider.

Then a hand clamped over his eyes, another over his mouth, and he was yanked from the chair.

Sol tried to scream, but the hand pressed his mouth so hard that it seemed to push the air back inside him, inflating his chest until he thought he would burst.

He scrabbled with all his strength at the hands and arms holding him.

Just as he thought he was going to pass out from the pressure, he was released. He hit the floor hard – and heard the vault door slam shut. Even in the gloom he could see dark dots swim across his vision.

The attacker pushed him down so that his face was pressed into the floor and a knee dug into his back, making his surgery wound sing with agony.

'C–Concord?' Sol was able to splutter into the carpet.

'No, it's me.' It was a voice Sol knew well.

'Dom? Dom! Get off. Let me go.'

'You're not allowed to steal from the Headmaster.'

'Are you crying?'

'I can't let you,' said Dom, his voice close to Sol's ear. 'You're going to ruin everything.'

Sol managed to twist from underneath Dom, who was loosening his grip. 'Ruin everything? I'm the one trying to end this nightmare! This is the only hope we have.'

'I can't believe you would do this. I can't believe I have to break every rule to come in here and stop you!'

'Dom, we have to get the hard drive,' Sol hissed.

'It's a *memory box*! And you can't have it, so shut up with your Nasty outside words.'

'You're the one being a Nastiness right now!'

The scuffle was fast and vicious. Dom seized Sol by his hair, but Sol was ready this time, pushing Dom's chest with one hand and scratching his face with the other. The fight wasn't fair – Dom used his knees and his feet as weapons, while Sol needed his arms both to fight and to move. In their fury they forgot all about the Doctor upstairs; Dom gabbled loudly about Nicenesses and Sol swore at him.

Sol finally got enough leverage to throw Dom off him

– sending him rolling across the carpet and into one of the cabinets. It wobbled. A stuffed magpie thudded to the floor.

'This is ridiculous.'

Sol seized the swivel chair and hauled himself up with a groan of pain.

'Take me to the desk over there.'

'Why?'

'Just do it.'

'This is the Headmaster's desk,' Dom said quietly, more to himself than to Sol, but he dragged the chair with Sol on it. 'The Headmaster sits here.'

'I found this,' said Sol, holding out Dom's drawing.

Dom's lips parted and he swallowed a cry. His trembling hands took the picture.

'He kept it. It's mine and he kept it!'

'I know the Doctor is messed up. But the Headmaster does seem to really love you all,' said Sol. 'Look at this photo I found. I know I've never met him, but I really don't think he'd want you to stay here with the Doctor.'

Dom took the photo from him. The moonlight turned half of his face silver. Still clutching his drawing and the photo, he examined the other pieces of paper: the maps, the bank statements, the list of names.

'I don't know this language,' he said.

'It's not a language. They're names,' Sol said.

'I've never seen names like this.'

'They're common on the outside. Dominic. Elizabeth. Connor . . . I think . . .' Sol stared at the list, feeling some memory stirring at the back of his mind, but whenever he tried to watch it, it disappeared.

'Dom, did you have a different name before you came here?'

'Before I came here?' he repeated the question like it didn't make sense. 'I've always been here.'

'But have you? What if these are our names?'

'I don't see Freedom.' He squinted at the paper.

'What I mean is—'

The window brightened.

It was as if someone had lit a small light outside and it was reflecting into the room.

'What's that?' Sol whispered.

'The light upstairs,' said Dom, looking out of the window. 'I can see it on the grass. We need to go, right now.'

'But—'

They heard footsteps above their heads.

'Go-go-go-go!' Dom hissed. He slid the papers back into the drawers and then he scooped Sol up. He staggered slightly under his weight, shifted his arms, then ran to the door. On the threshold of the study, they saw a faint yellow glow on the stairs above them.

If they didn't leave now, they might not get out at all. Dom crept down the stairs with Sol in his arms, towards the waiting wheelchair, which cast a strange-shaped shadow on the wall.

## 22: DOM

The children trudged from breakfast to assembly, sticking close together, as they always did when the Doctor was around. Dom felt even more nervous than usual. He rubbed the bruise on his chest made by Sol's elbow. He'd been aching all morning. And worrying.

He had decided to ignore Clem and never return to the fence again. Nothing good came from her advice. He should never have told Sol what she'd said. He was lucky he'd got to the Headmaster's study in time and got them out before the Doctor found them.

As the others took their seats, Dom looked around. Was he the only one who had ever gone upstairs? Or did they all break the rules sometimes, and just didn't tell each other because they were scared of the repercussions? Maybe when the Headmaster came back, he could speak to him about changing some things. No more Doctor's visits. No more memory boxes. Perhaps even a trip to the outside. See the police, those nice people Sol said he wanted to find.

'Ow,' Sol exclaimed as Dom jammed Sol's chair into a row near the back.

'Sorry.'

'My shoulder still hurts,' said Sol.

'Shh!' Dom leant down to whisper to him. 'I already said I was sorry.'

'And I already said that you're an idiot.'

'And we *both* said that we wouldn't tell anyone, so keep your voice down.'

Dom took the seat next to Sol. Merit and Justice sat in front of them. They tried to include Dom in their conversation about keeping the dorm warm for the rest of winter, but he was too tired to concentrate, and knew it was only a distraction anyway. No one wanted to think about how much longer the Doctor would stay.

They waited for the phone to ring upstairs without much hope. When it didn't, Concord came down and talked them through plans for winter and minor chores that needed doing. It was like any other day. Until they heard the click of smart shoes coming down the stairs.

The Doctor watched the assembly with interest. Concord didn't rush. He went through each item. The only sign that he felt nervous was a pink glow on his ears.

When he was finished, he nodded to the Doctor, and returned to his seat.

All noise drained from the room. Sol stiffened in his chair next to Dom.

'Children, I have some unfortunate news,' the Doctor began, as he stepped on to the stage. His cold blue eyes rested on each face in turn, lingering uncomfortably on Sol in his new chair. When they reached Dom, he felt the hairs stand up on the back of his neck.

'I have reason to believe that there has been a serious breach of conduct here at the Ash House.'

Dom saw that Sol was trying to catch his eye, but he and the others had years of experience keeping their faces blank when the Doctor spoke to them.

'And as our Headmaster is still absent, it falls to me to get to the bottom of it.' The Doctor had his hands behind his back and was bouncing on the balls of his feet. 'This morning I happened to go into the Head-master's study. And I have reason to believe somebody tried to steal something from there recently.'

'What!' Concord's voice burst over their heads. There was a sharp intake of breath. No one ever spoke when the Doctor was speaking.

The Doctor's gaze gripped Concord and silence fell. Dom regretted sitting behind Concord and found himself shrinking into his seat. Sol nudged him, so Dom risked shooting him a furious warning look that made Sol cower in his chair.

'Someone went into the study and meddled with the Headmaster's desk,' the Doctor continued. 'But who? And why? There are a few possibilities. Perhaps our Headmaster returned briefly and left in the night.'

The hope that lit up his friends' faces was more than Dom could bear.

'Or possibly someone sitting in this room right now decided to go in there themselves. Children, I happen to know for certain that the Headmaster hasn't returned.'

The Doctor's gaze was as cold and slow-moving as a glacier. Sol's arm pressed Dom's very gently.

'I would like whoever is responsible to come forward,' said the Doctor. 'Now.'

The children knew better than to look at each other. They stared at the front of the room, hiding any curiosity or fear they might be feeling.

*Don't cry*, Dom told himself. Crying will only draw attention.

'Freedom.' His name floated into the sickening silence. Dom lifted his head. The Doctor was magnetic. 'Come here.'

Dom felt he was a puppet and somebody else was

moving his limbs. Someone else made him subtly shake Sol's hand off his sleeve, get to his feet, shuffle sideways and approach the stage.

'Freedom.' The Doctor towered over him.

'Yes?'

'You are the only one allowed to enter the Headmaster's study.'

Dom was too paralysed by fear to even nod. It was the closest he had been to the Doctor in years. Every 'medicine' that could be given to him raced through his mind. If he moved or opened his mouth, he was certain that he would be sick.

'You know why I'm angry, don't you, Freedom? Everything in that study belongs to the Headmaster – you are only allowed there to deliver memory boxes, which go in the vault, which is nowhere near his desk. But you crept in at night which you know is forbidden and looked through his papers – Nasty, Nasty, Nasty!' He paused to wipe a fleck of saliva from his chin. 'Was it you, Freedom? You alone?'

Dom wanted to answer him without a crack in his voice. He stood a little straighter and – eventually – said: 'Yes.'

Something near the edges of the Doctor's eyes twitched.

'You had no help?'

'No.'

'I find that unlikely.'

The Doctor's eyes pierced him; every second was like the pain of touching dry ice to dry skin. Dom tried to keep his mind as blank as possible, as if the Doctor would hear Sol's name if it slipped into his thoughts.

'I think you had accomplices.'

'I didn't. I swear.'

'Well, well, well. Let's see if that's true, shall we?'

'W-what?'

'Sit down.' His voice whipped through the room.

Dom longed to run for a chair at the back, or even to make a break for the stairs, but he didn't trust his legs. He stepped down from the stage and wobbled towards the front row.

'It would seem Freedom is lying to protect his friends,' the Doctor told them. 'He has already proven himself to be utterly dishonest, untrustworthy, a pure Nastiness. We cannot trust a word he says. But that does not matter. The Ash House will discover the truth for itself.'

Dom felt shame burn through every cell of his body. He never wanted to be a Nastiness. Nastiness didn't belong at the Ash House. He always tried so hard to remember his Niceness, but lately he'd got them all wrong. For a moment he thought the Doctor was going to force him to leave the Ash House and banish him for ever.

'Usually, I would leave this for your Headmaster. But this is not something that can wait for his return. If people are breaking rules, then they should be punished immediately. I have no way of knowing who Freedom is protecting.'

Dom felt a wave of panic. What if the Doctor turned his attention back to Sol?

'A terrible crime deserves a terrible punishment. It will have to involve the Shucks.'

'What!' Concord burst out with indignation and terror. A few of the boys and girls uttered strange, suppressed cries, a sound like water clogged in a gutter.

'You will not question my decisions!' the Doctor thundered over the outcry. Silence fell again and he continued at a normal volume: 'How dare you come into the Ash House at night? How dare any of you go upstairs into the Headmaster's study, and tamper with his documents? No punishment is enough. But I must try to make you all understand the severity of what you've done. You'll face the Shucks, all of you, one by one. And we all know who will go first.' He looked at Dom.

It took a moment for what he'd said to sink in.

'Think of it as a race,' said the Doctor, smiling at their confusion.

'W-we're racing against Shucks?' Libby asked tentatively.

'That's right. Whoever completes the route around the forest before the Shucks will be forgiven.' The dread-filled silence kept them frozen in their places, staring at the Doctor in disbelief. They waited for something to let them know that it was a joke, or at least not as dangerous as they thought, but he simply stood in front of them grinning.

Then there was a loud scrape and a clatter as a chair fell over. Concord had sprung to his feet.

'No,' he said.

'No?' The Doctor took a small step back in surprise.

'Dom admitted that he did it. He said no one else was involved. Punish the person who broke the rules, not everybody else.'

The Doctor watched Concord with an expression that was more intrigued than angry. When he didn't reply, Concord pressed his point, his voice getting louder and more confident.

'It's not fair. And anyway, a race doesn't make sense.'

'Is that right?' The Doctor smirked as if he was in on

some wonderful joke that the rest of them couldn't possibly understand.

'Yeah. There's no way we can outrun a Shuck. What's the point of a race no one can win? Shucks are dangerous. People will get hurt. They'll be punished whether they've broken the rules or not.'

The Doctor's face changed, like shutters snapping over a window. He snarled and shouted at the same time, so what he said sounded like one shapeless word:

'Someone broke one of the most fundamental rules of this place—'

'You know what?' Concord threw up his arms and shouted back: 'You're not the Headmaster! You aren't in charge of us! And you can't sentence us to some death race without his say-so.'

The Doctor stepped off the stage and moved towards them. The children huddled further into their chairs. Only Concord stood, drawing himself to his full height, unblinking, unapologetic, his chin raised and his scar gruesome in the light of the assembly room. Dom's shame was now fused with guilt. It was his fault – he should be the one being brave, not Concord.

'I am in charge of welfare and discipline here.' The Doctor brought his face very close to Concord's. 'If one of you strays, forgets your *Niceness*, then that endangers everybody who lives here. I won't let that happen.' Then he softened. 'But thank you for your honesty and outspokenness, Concord. These are Nicenesses in their own ways. So, out of respect, I will rethink the races.'

'Really?'

'Oh, yes. I'm a man who can admit his mistakes. Dom can forget about his Shuck race.'

Dom groaned and put his head in his hands with relief. Libby's hand trembled over her mouth. But the Doctor wasn't finished.

'He can forget about it for the time being. Because you, Concord, will be going first.'

## 23: DOM

They waited their turn in the dorm. The light outside had the pale, watery quality that meant that winter was deepening. No ash floated through the air. It felt still, like in the hours before a storm. The Doctor had told them to wait in silence on their beds until they were called. No one lay down. They sat cross-legged or with their legs dangling off the end of their beds, hair clutched in hands, eyes closed. Dom kept glancing at Concord's empty bed near the door. He longed to speak to Libby, but she was downstairs with the girls, no doubt sitting in the same tense silence.

After the assembly, Dom had avoided Sol and didn't help to bring him up the stairs. Dom knew that Sol couldn't understand fully what a race with the Shucks would mean. He had only ever seen a Shuck from a distance. But he had to understand the most important part: in his chair, he wouldn't stand a chance. Dom saw him out of the corner of his eye, poking his legs hopefully, pinching the skin and shaking his dwindling muscles.

The only person disturbing the peace was Merit. He had an old yellow ball that he bounced on the floor, sometimes rustling the leaves overhead. As the wait got longer, the ball got louder. Finally, it thumped on to Dom's blanket.

'Merit, please don't,' he said, tossing it on to the floor where no one could reach it.

'You're not in charge just because Con's gone.'

'I didn't say I was.'

'If he doesn't come back, it's your fault,' said Merit.

'He'll come back. He's fast and strong,' said Dom.

'He hates the Shucks,' Justice chimed in. 'Think how scared he'll be.'

At that moment they heard a low rumble like thunder. They all lifted their heads. It got louder and louder, like a machine scraping right past the dorm. It was the sound of Shucks leaving the Ash House, and it was too loud to be just one Shuck.

Dom went to the glass wall at the back of the dorm, the one with a view of the house if he pushed aside enough foliage. He saw that all the lights were on in the Ash House. The Doctor's shape was a sharp silhouette in one of the top windows, looking down over the court-yard. Dom peered closer, hoping to see Concord. A massive black shape streaked across the cracked concrete. Dom recoiled and let the leaves spring back into position.

'Well?' Wisdom was nearest to him. He was twisting a leaf round and round his little finger. 'Did you see anything?'

'Shuck,' said Dom.

'Not Concord?'

'No.'

Silence fell over the room again.

'Listen, Dom . . .' Wisdom began. His blond fringe fell over his eyes as he concentrated on twisting the leaf faster and faster. 'I know it's none of my business, but why – why would you . . . I mean, what were you even doing in there?'

Dom hesitated. None of the other boys were looking at them, but he could tell they were listening closely. Sol had gone very still on his bed. Dom thought about just telling them the truth about Clem. He could explain everything she'd said and why Sol went into the Head-master's study . . . But they'd never believe him. Or they'd hate him for keeping it from them. He had already made so many mistakes. He didn't have the courage to risk another.

'I was looking for an old memory box,' Dom said quickly. 'I just wanted to see it. Make sure it was safe.'

'But the desk—'

'I didn't go near his desk!'

Sol looked at him, but Dom avoided his eyes and returned to his bed on the floor.

Hours passed and they only heard one sign that there was any sort of struggle as they waited. A blood-wet howl ripped through the room. It came from the direction of the lake. They all turned their heads as if they could see what was going on.

'Con or Shuck?' Merit asked.

'Shuck,' said Justice. He sounded confident, but he was paler than any of them.

'Yeah, Shuck,' said Merit.

Wisdom started to cry. He was trying to suppress it, but a few blubs managed to escape. Nobody made fun of him.

Hours passed before the silence was broken again. There was a heavy *thump* at the bottom of the staircase, echoing all the way up into the dorm.

'What was that?' Sol's voice trembled.

'Concord!' Merit was on his feet and racing for the door.

'No!' Justice threw himself at his friend to hold him

234

back. 'It could be a Shuck.'

'It's not!'

'It could be.'

Most of the boys shrank away from the entrance, some of them creeping on to beds further down the dorm. Dom did the opposite. He joined Justice and Merit, who were now wrestling as Merit tried to reach the door.

'I'll look,' said Dom.

'Don't,' Justice pleaded.

Dom reached for the door handle. Then there was another thump. It sounded like something dragging itself up the staircase.

'It's definitely a Shuck.' Justice was hysterical, pinning Merit down. 'Dom, don't open the door!'

Dom was frozen by fear and doubt as more thumps and bangs came from the metal stairs.

The next thump was so close to the door it couldn't have been more than one step down. But this time it was accompanied by a groan.

'It *is* him,' Dom insisted.

Ignoring the yells of his friends, he yanked open the door.

Concord was sprawled on his front, his elbows on the top step, ready to pull himself up. He was soaking wet and his back was drenched in blood. A shiny black wound seeped scarlet, which turned pink as it mixed with the water. It wasn't raining, Dom realized. He must have come from the lake.

The rest of him was streaked with blood and dirt. He had a split lip and his teeth where edged with red when he spoke, looking up at Dom.

'Is anyone going to bother giving me a hand?'

Dom, Merit and Justice put Concord under the shower and poured cold water over his back while the others watched. He had four cuts that pumped out an impressive amount of blood. It turned the tiles, their hands and the water around them pink. His body was covered in many more cuts, including one on the top of his head that made his hair sticky and red. He trembled uncontrollably.

Dom handed Justice a clean towel, which he pressed against Concord's back to try to stop the bleeding. Justice followed instructions silently, no doubt feeling guilty about leaving Concord out on the stairs on his own.

Between gasps and grunts, Concord tried to tell them what had happened.

He had to run from the back of the house, around the

boundary and back again, while countless birds flew overhead, watching him. He was given a head start. At first, he couldn't even see the Shucks. He ran fast, and just when he thought maybe it was some sort of twisted trick and there were no Shucks at all, he saw one in the distance.

He got into trouble near the lake. All three had been released and they were herding him, drawing just close enough so he could feel the coldness in his chest, but then they'd hang back, as if they were playing with him. He splashed knee-deep into the water and tried his luck. He turned around and did the hand gesture that they had been taught. They paused on the shore. Two of them stepped back, but the third one leapt snarling into the lake. Concord turned to run, but it got his back with its claws.

The rest was a blur. He made it back to the house, not knowing if the Shucks were on his trail or if they'd stayed at the lake. He collapsed in the courtyard. The Doctor had been there waiting for him, timing him with a stopwatch.

'I saw the Doctor go into the girls' dorm. One of them is next,' he finished.

'You're one of the fastest,' said Merit. 'The rest of us don't stand a chance.'

'At least you know what you're going into,' Concord snapped. 'Ow!'

'Sorry,' said Dom, peeling the towel away from the cuts. 'I don't think these are too deep, but Luck should bandage them anyway. Justice, get one of the sheets.'

'He's going to do this to all of us,' Justice whispered in horror.

'Justice, the sheets,' said Dom firmly.

While he pressed the towel against Con's back, he turned and looked for Sol. He was on the floor, peering around the corner into the bathroom. He chewed his lip as the red and pink rags were exchanged.

'He's got Mercy,' said Wisdom from the other end of the dorm. His breath had steamed up a patch of glass. 'She's next.'

'Maybe the Shucks will get tired,' Merit suggested.

'Maybe we'll all wake up soon,' Concord whispered. The sheets made an awful noise as Dom ripped them into strips.

Another hour passed until they heard the bone-aching roar of the Shucks again. Wisdom returned to the window and cried out:

'Mercy!'

'What?' asked Merit.

'She's back!'

'That's not possible,' he replied. 'It hasn't been long enough. There's no way she could get all the way round in just—'

He paused and listened. Dom knew what was coming: the Doctor's feet on the metal stairs.

The room fell silent as he entered. He looked at Concord, who was on his bed, laying on his stomach, his lips pale and crisp. He looked like Sol after his operation. The Doctor smiled with satisfaction, and then cast an eye over each of them until he found who he was looking for.

'Freedom. The reason we are all here.'

The Doctor gestured to the door. Dom rose to his feet. He saw Sol open his mouth to say something, but he silenced him with a tiny shake of his head. He was determined not to flinch or grimace. He would face it the way Concord had.

Outside a furious wind whistled around every crevice of the house. The Ash House looked like a storm front. The grounds were grey and green beyond the warm glow of the dormitories. Dom strained to hear the Shucks rumbling in their kennels again underneath the Ash House.

He and the Doctor stood by the back door to the house. The cracked concrete of the courtyard was in front of them, with the canteen and classroom off to one side. To the left, a dark path that Dom knew would take him around the grounds he had explored his whole life.

'Concord's time was impressive,' said the Doctor. He was enjoying himself, revelling in the wind and the fear. 'And Mercy surpassed my expectations too, although I don't know how she managed it. Try not to be scared.' He placed a hand on Dom's shoulder. Dom wanted to recoil more than anything, but forced himself to be still and hide his disgust. 'If you hurt yourself, I'll be right here to make you better.'

'Are you going to make Sol race? He's in his chair, he won't be able to.'

'Yes. He will race. This race . . . whatever happens to your friends . . . that is your punishment, Freedom. I made it specially for you.'

The Doctor reached into his pocket, pulled out a crumpled piece of paper and handed it to Dom. He unfolded it and found himself face to face with the picture he'd drawn for the Headmaster years ago. In his panic, he must have left it on the desk, he realized with dismay.

'Next time you go into my study, I'd avoid leaving your artwork where it can be found.'

'It's not your study.' Dom surprised himself with the

anger in his voice.

The Doctor smiled. 'Tell the Shucks.' His timer was a burnished gold pocket watch. He started it with a flick of his finger. 'Away you go. The birds will watch you.'

Dom hesitated. He expected the roar of Shucks to send him on his way. But it was only him, the Doctor and the house. There was nowhere to hide.

The Doctor spoke again, this time so quietly that his voice was swallowed by the gale.

'Go.'

## 24: SOL

The boys abandoned their beds and formed a restless wall at the end of the dormitory, their faces pressed to the vines as they saw Dom on his way. Sol watched them, his head filled with the same thought that had swirled through his mind all afternoon: this was all his fault. Dom could have turned him in, and he hadn't. He'd protected him out of Niceness. But Sol was the one who hadn't listened to Dom's warnings, who'd put his own fear above the rules of the Ash House to try and find the memory box. Perhaps he was the real Nastiness.

He turned away from the boys pressed against the window and wheeled his chair over to Concord's bed. His eyes were closed and his breathing was shallow.

'Um, Con?' Sol whispered.

Concord didn't open his eyes. He simply said: 'Don't call me that.'

'Sorry. It's just . . . are you sure the thing with the

hands won't work?' Sol touched his little fingers together to show what he meant.

A look of intense irritation spread over Concord's face and Sol found himself selfishly glad that Con's injuries meant he was bedbound for the time being.

'Yes. I tried it. It didn't work.'

'I thought the Shucks were here to protect us. How can the Doctor make them attack us?'

Merit appeared behind him and answered the question: 'The Shucks do what the Doctor tells them to. He's in charge.'

'But Libby once told me they belong to the Headmaster. He wouldn't want us to get hurt.'

In a quiet voice, Concord said: 'The Headmaster's not here.' With a low cow-like moan, he turned over and sat up.

'Isn't there a way to stop them?' Sol asked. 'Didn't he give you a way to protect yourselves before he left?'

'Yes. Niceness,' said Concord. 'We remember our Niceness. We live them. They will protect us.'

'Niceness? That's it?'

'Sol—'

'You're not going to try to do something? Not even for Dom?'

'I told you—'

243

'Niceness doesn't do anything! If it did, we wouldn't be in this situation. Look what's happening to Dom right now. He has more Niceness than anyone – you told me that on my very first day,' Sol argued. 'Concord, Freedom, Solitude, Love, Hope, Mercy – these things can't help us! They're just words the Headmaster uses to control you. He controls the Shucks, the ash, all of you, without even being here. You're brainwashed!'

'Shut up, Sol,' spat Merit. 'You don't know the first thing about Niceness.'

'Or the Headmaster,' Concord added.

'I know he can't care about you all that much,' said Sol, made brave by his anger and worry for Dom.

'Take that *back*!' Merit shouted.

'The Headmaster keeps us safe,' Concord growled. 'That's why he trained the Shucks to protect the Ash House in the first place. But they're pack animals. They only listen to one person. When the Headmaster's not here, that's the Doctor. It's not the Headmaster's fault all this has happened.'

'But who protects us from the Doctor?' Sol demanded.

'We protect each other,' said Concord. 'We're pretty good at it. We should have got rid of you when we had the chance, but Dom wanted you to stay because he wanted to teach you about Niceness. We went along with it, but I should have known that you're just like that rabbit Love looks after – a pet Dom wants to keep, which would be better off fed to the Shucks. If tonight proves anything, it's that he was wrong about you. You have no Niceness.'

'This thing with the vault – we know you had something to do with it,' said Merit. 'I don't care what Dom said. I don't care that you're stuck in a chair. Somehow you made him do it.'

Concord and Merit glared at Sol. He turned his chair around and saw that everyone else was looking at him too.

The boys drifted down the room and Sol felt the walls were closing in on him, just as he had on his first day. He tried to wheel himself back to his bed, but Merit was standing in his way, his dark eyes fixed on him.

'I didn't make Dom do anything,' Sol insisted.

Merit stood in front of the chair. 'You're the one who brought the Doctor here. You're the one who needed an operation.'

'And ever since you got here, the Headmaster stopped phoning us,' Justice added.

'That's not my fault,' said Sol. 'None of it is.'

'It doesn't matter,' said Justice. 'Dom might not even

come back from the Shucks. Then who will look after you? Everything we did – taking you to the lake, making you this –' he kicked Sol's chair – 'was because Dom asked us to. But he's not here now.'

The boys closed in around him. Sol felt he couldn't breathe. He wanted to call Dom's name, but Justice was right – he might never see Dom again after this awful night.

He felt the ground lurch beneath him. Justice had grabbed hold of the handles of his chair, reminding Sol that he was powerless, utterly at their mercy. He panicked.

'Fine, yes, I was there too! I went into the Headmaster's study, but only because I had to. And Dom only went because he was trying to stop me!'

Sol couldn't begin to explain all the things that had led them to the study, or that they never meant this Shuck race to happen. But he knew he had to say something. He was agonizingly guilty. He knew that anything the Shucks did to anyone tonight was his fault. If he hadn't gone into the study to find the memory box, none of this would have happened. And he knew Dom had kept the secret about his pain when it mattered, but now he had to break his promise and share Dom's secret.

'Look.' Sol grabbed the wheels of his chair as Justice

started to push it towards the door. 'Dom knows something. He says one of the memory boxes can get the Doctor into trouble. Maybe even get rid of him. Dom didn't want to do it because he didn't want to steal from the Headmaster, but it seemed like my only way to avoid another operation, so I did it anyway. Dom came to stop me, and before we could get out, the Doctor's light came on upstairs and we had to leave, but I swear – I *swear* – we didn't mean all this to happen!'

Justice and Merit seemed less sure of themselves after Sol's garbled explanation. The other boys exchanged confused, fearful glances. They looked at Concord, but he was curled up on his side, ignoring the crisis.

'What's in the memory box?' Justice asked eventually.

'I don't know exactly. But I think the birds saw something the Doctor wants hidden – and Dom knows what it might be. The box is locked in the vault, but he's too scared to steal it himself.'

'Did Dom see this memory?' Merit asked.

'I . . . Well, I'm not sure. He said – and I know how this sounds – he heard about it from someone beyond the fence. A girl.' Sol was desperate for them to believe him. 'But listen, if we can get our hands on the memory box, we might have solid proof the Doctor is doing bad things.' Sol looked from one stunned face to another and for a moment forgot how the Ash House worked and that he was meant to be a part of it, because he said: 'This could be the key to getting out of here!'

Chaos erupted.

Justice lunged for Sol and was pushed at the same time by the other boys, so he tripped and fell. Someone toppled Sol out of his chair and he landed awkwardly – it hurt his left leg, but he couldn't think about what that meant because Merit was on him, pinning him down, while everyone else shouted and shrieked.

'He wants to take us away! He wants to take us away!' Wisdom's voice was high-pitched and hysterical above the noise.

'We – won't – let – him,' Merit insisted through gritted teeth.

Sol tried to cover his face and head as the fists rained down on him. He couldn't crawl away. He certainly couldn't run.

But he didn't need to.

'STOP IT!'

Each of them froze. Concord's voice silenced them.

'Get away from him.'

Feet shuffled away, leaving Sol sprawled on the floor. Merit was the last to let go of Sol's arms and back off.

Concord stood over Sol. A bruise was blooming

across the unscarred side of his face. Someone muttered something about him teaching Sol a lesson.

Then he whispered: 'A girl beyond the fence?'

Concord put his hands under Sol's arms and lifted him back into his chair.

Sol nodded. 'Yes.' He tried to catch his breath. 'That's the thing. Dom . . . well, Dom mentioned Clem.'

## 25: DOM

**D**om decided not to run.

It was not the first time he had been alone in the grounds at twilight with dark shapes slinking at the corner of his eyes. It was also not the first time he had been in the grounds when a Shuck was let loose. He stuck to the rules they always followed when that happened. No sudden movements. Follow the paths. Don't let your imagination run wild.

The dramatic wind covered the noise of his footsteps over the concrete, on to the gravel and then the mud path. The dorm lights disappeared behind him. He headed in the direction of his shed.

He tried to keep his mind clear so that he would know where the shed was that evening, but it was difficult. He knew he shouldn't, but he let the thought enter his head: maybe the Shucks weren't coming. Maybe it was some elaborate test from the Doctor.

The idea unnerved him much more than any snarling, snapping Shuck on his heels.

He took a deep breath and pictured the shed in his mind. It was on long grass, not too far from some trees. It took him a moment to recognize the spot. Then it came to him – it was to the north of the Ash House, a little way from the top of the drive. He doubled his pace and headed straight there.

The shed seemed like the only oasis of safety in the world. Dom knew that from there he could see most areas of the grounds, so he could see the Shucks coming, if they *were* coming, and maybe find out what the Doctor was doing.

He broke into a run when the small, dark shape of the shed appeared in the gloom. The door banged shut behind him as the wind pushed and pulled at it, and the light bulb blinked on. The smell of damp and dust reassured him. He could imagine that it was just another day. He turned the screens on and they hummed as they came to life. The birds' eyes blinked open, beaming black-and-white pictures into the room.

Dom checked the dorms first. The boys were looking out of the window at the far end. Sol was near Concord's bed. The girls were clustered around someone in the middle of their dorm. Dom's stomach squirmed. It had to be Mercy.

He forgot about the outside and became lost in the black-and-white world of the Ash House. He even started to relax. He checked each viewpoint and there was nothing else out of the ordinary. Maybe Justice was right – the Shucks were tired. Maybe the Doctor was testing him in some other way. He could end the madness, go back to the Ash House and explain what happened to the Doctor. He could ask again that only he be punished, not his friends. By not going along with this strange chase, he might persuade the Doctor to change his mind.

He felt so certain about this idea that he turned away from the screens and yanked open the door, letting the screaming wind sweep through the shed. A piercing green light shone through the dark.

Then the wind wasn't the only scream.

No birds watched the shed. It was unnecessary. Only a few people at the Ash House knew how to find it. That was why Dom hadn't seen the Shuck prowl towards him.

The flash of its green eyes was enough to make him shriek with surprise and slam the door shut – the rickety wooden door that couldn't even keep the cold out in winter, let alone a Shuck. Dom pressed his weight against it and looked around for something to block it. The screens were too far away to reach. He only had the chairs, which wouldn't slow the creature down at all.

As if it knew this, it swiped an enormous paw at the door.

Its claws wrenched splinters from the wood and a couple broke right through it. Dom heard its frustrated snarl.

He didn't wait. The next swipe would send a claw into his head. He leapt away from the door towards the screens. The Shuck pushed, and the door crashed open, its flimsy hinges crumpling under the force of the blow.

Dom grabbed one of the screens. His arms could barely fit around it. He pulled with all his strength, feeling every muscle in his back protest, and turned to face the Shuck.

It made the shed look tiny. Its eyes were brighter than the light bulb and left green splotches in Dom's vision. The smell of its fur – damp hair, clay and something metallic that he didn't want to think about – filled the space. Dom's arms shook.

'Why are you doing this?' he shouted, but he sounded more pleading than heroic.

It snarled again, revealing teeth sharpened to delicate points.

As it leapt, so did Dom. He held out the screen – half-shield, half-bludgeon – and shoved it in the Shuck's face. The screen shattered and Dom was thrown backwards. The Shuck was yelping and snarling as the screen, now an empty box, crashed to the floor. Dom had the wind knocked out of him, but he forced himself to stand, clutching his ribs. The Shuck clawed at its own face and he soon saw why. A shard of glass from the broken screen was stuck in its eye.

Dom couldn't explain his overwhelming urge to stay and help the creature. It thrashed and clawed at itself, making it impossible for him to get close. It was also blocking the only doorway.

Dom hid behind the remaining screens as best he could. He worried that its howls would attract the other Shucks. He had been lucky with the screen, but he wouldn't be able to fight off three at once.

The Shuck smashed blindly into the walls, the chairs and some of the lower screens. More glass scattered across the floor. Dust and a few unlucky spiders fell from the ceiling. Glass shards pierced the Shuck's pads, so it smeared blood across the floor with each movement, yelping in pain. Dom couldn't bear the ghastly sound. He was certain he could feel its pain in his own face and palms.

With one great howl, the Shuck swung its head into

the wall. The shed groaned and the whole structure began to lean, crushing Dom into the screens and the desk. He had to get out.

He slid along the wall and tried not to think about how much closer he was getting to the Shuck, which threw its weight against the wall one more time. The wood gave way, the roof rained down around Dom, and the other walls collapsed as if they were made of paper. He threw himself forward.

Dom hit the grass. The cold, damp earth felt miraculous.

He threw his arms over his head as a corner of the roof hurtled towards the ground and caught him on his shoulder blade. He cried out and twisted himself from under it. He felt his shirt and skin rip at the same time.

The smell of the Shuck was nearly overpowering. Clutching his shoulder, Dom got to his feet. The Shuck was furiously rubbing its face into the grass. Its black fur was becoming difficult to see, as the world was beginning to fade into darkness.

Some part of Dom wanted to stay with the Shuck, perhaps out of compassion or guilt or forgiveness. But the green flicker coming from the Ash House was unmistakable. First two, then four foul-coloured irises blinked in his direction.

He ran for the woods.

Branches, leaves and thorns flicked by. Dom felt nothing but the urge to run and run and run. He didn't know where he was going. Towards the fence, it seemed, in a straight line away from the shed and the house. He didn't turn to see if the green glares were gaining on him.

It was only when he slipped and went tumbling into the stream that he was jerked out of his mindless running.

Dom stayed in the shallow water on his hands and knees, panting and feeling the cold, sharp pebbles under his palms. The water was freezing. His shins and shoes were wet, but he didn't care. He slapped some of the icy water on his face. It felt like waking up from a bad dream. He scooped up some more and dribbled it over his throbbing shoulder.

The wind blew in great gusts that died as soon as they started. Dom looked over the bank behind him and could see only a dark tangle of brambles.

'Get up,' he whispered to himself. 'Move.'

But it was as if he had used up every grain of energy. He felt safe in the stream. Leaving it would mean letting the chase go on. He bowed his head, closed his eyes and let the wind ruffle his hair for a moment. He couldn't shake the image of the Shuck with glass impaled in its face. He tried to replace it with other thoughts.

Not so long ago it had been summer. Concord had taught them a new game on the lawn outside the house. The ash on the grass had stained their trousers. They had got sunburnt. They froze milk and ate it with spoons in the canteen. They left the door of the dorm open while they slept and listened to the breeze through the trees.

A sob bubbled from Dom's lungs. And a word: 'Clem.'

He wiped his nose on the back of his hand and choked back another sob. Wistfulness was replaced by anger.

'CLEM!' The name scratched his throat. He looked desperately all around, but there was no sign of her.

Dom felt that ever since the day the Headmaster left, everything he cared about had been decaying. He thought about every bad thing that had happened over those three years – all the hours of watching the drive in the rain, hiding from the Doctor, watching the birds on his own with nobody to talk to – as he scooped up stones from the riverbed and dropped them back into the water. One was long, thin and sharp. He turned it over in his hands. Sniffed up his tears. Then paused.

He squeezed his eyes shut, opened them again, and turned around.

The Shuck was sitting on the riverbank panting. Blood dripped from its eye on to the leaves. Dom could see its teeth, but only because its mouth was hanging open. It had been watching him cry in the stream.

'Why did he leave?' Dom whispered to it. 'Why won't he come back?' A fresh wave of tears choked his throat. 'Why doesn't he want to come back to us?'

He covered his face and let the sobs come. When they settled, he looked back at the Shuck.

'I'm Freedom.' He spoke softly, hoping it would stay relaxed and not realize that it should be chasing him.

He slipped the long, sharp stone into his pocket. The Shuck's good eye hadn't left his face.

'I'm sorry about your eye,' he said to it. 'But I suppose it's what you did to Concord. He has a lot of Niceness. Sometimes. I'm going to stand up now.'

It didn't react as the pebbles crunched under his feet. The cold water dripped down his legs. His shoes were sodden and heavy.

The Shuck's fur was smeared with blood. Its breath rasped painfully and it didn't put any weight on one of its front paws.

'The Headmaster will come back soon,' Dom whispered. 'The Doctor will leave. I know it. And that will be good, won't it? Things won't be so bad then.'

He had an overwhelming need to stroke the Shuck and reassure it. He inched forward, his feet slipping on the wet stones.

'We can call it even, right?' He placed one foot on the bank. 'Tell the Doctor he can shove his Nasty race. Eat some food. Get warm and dry. OK?' He reached out his trembling fingers. They looked bright white against the Shuck's fur. As far as Dom knew, no one had ever stroked a Shuck. The Headmaster maybe, but not one of the children. He'd be the first. He'd go back to the dorm and tell them there was nothing to be afraid of.

'Are you hurt?' His hand shook. The Shuck's fur looked so soft and enticing. 'Whatever you do, don't go to the Doctor,' he joked.

The mention of the Doctor agitated the Shuck. It gave a deep growl, but the rest of its body stayed calm and still. Dom paused, his hand still outstretched. Then he realized that it wasn't the Shuck that had growled.

At least, not this one.

Four stars of bright green appeared in the distance through the undergrowth. A roar swelled around him.

'Got to go,' he hissed, and he ran for his life downstream, deeper into the forest.

## 26: SOL

'He's lying,' Justice spat.

'Clem's gone. Dom knows that,' said Merit. 'You have no right to talk about her. He's just trying to upset us.' He looked around the dorm, waiting for someone to jump in and back him up.

'Obviously it's not Clem. It's nobody else either. There's no one beyond the fence,' said Justice.

'Dom doesn't think so,' Sol replied.

'Did you know about this?' Merit ignored Sol and turned to Concord, who was now sitting on his bed again. His lips were pressed together so hard all the blood had left them. He shook his head.

'We need to talk to the girls,' said Justice.

'No one is going outside while the Shucks are out there,' snapped Concord.

'What if Clem really did tell Dom about this memory box?' asked Wisdom. 'Before, I mean. Could it make the

Doctor go away?'

'Don't be stupid! She didn't tell him anything,' Merit insisted.

'Obviously she didn't. Sol's lying – because Clem's *dead*!' Justice yelled over them.

The word made Sol feel dizzy. He touched his binoculars. They suddenly felt heavy around his neck. No wonder Libby hadn't wanted to give them to him. They were all that was left of Clem.

Everyone began shouting over each other. This time Sol wasn't so sure Concord would step in – he looked ill and tired. The argument swirled ferociously, so the boys didn't hear the footsteps on the stairs outside until they were right by the door. It was like a gong had commanded silence. Then:

'Dom!' Justice cried.

The others groaned with relief, and Merit leapt over Concord's bed to get there first and pull the door open.

Cold evening air swept in. The Doctor came with it. The boys stared with open mouths and sweaty hands as he strode past Merit.

The Doctor looked as polished and poised as ever; only a web of delicate red veins in the whites of his eyes hinted at his stress. He went down the length of the dormitory, looking at the gaps between beds. When he reached the end, he turned and retraced his steps before walking through the bathroom. The others looked at Concord for a reaction or some direction, but he gave no sign. His eyes were glued to the Doctor the whole time, like a cornered animal watching its predator.

When the Doctor finished his tour of the dormitory, he paused and looked at them. Some of them were still breathing heavily from their argument.

'Time for bed, boys,' he said quietly.

It took a moment before anyone moved. One by one they went back to their beds.

Sol didn't touch the wheels of his chair. Concord didn't move either. On his way to the door, the Doctor paused by Concord's bed and looked at the bandages and the bruises on his face. He smiled.

'Such bravery.'

He closed the door behind him and his footsteps became a part of the gale. Concord howled with fury, then he hung his head between his knees as silence settled back over the dorm.

'Are you OK?' Sol asked.

Concord sighed, then nodded.

'What was he doing in here?'

'I think he was looking for Dom,' said Concord. 'Which is the first good news we've had in a while.'

'You think he's lost Dom? Why is that good news?'

It seemed to take Concord a lot of effort to lift his head. 'Because it means he doesn't know where Dom is. He's not in control.'

The waiting made Sol feel like he was going insane. He didn't know how long he could stay in bed, staring at the canopy above him, not knowing where Dom was and if he was safe. He had a million questions for him. Where did he really learn about the memory box from? And was it enough to make the Doctor leave them alone?

When the boys had been quiet for some time, Sol heard a creak from near the door. Concord rose from his bed and walked down the aisle. For a moment Sol thought he had come to speak to him, because he stopped near his bed, but instead Concord crawled on to Dom's mattress and pulled the blankets around him. He was so close that Sol could have reached out and touched his colourless hair.

'I hope he's OK,' Concord whispered. Sol wasn't sure who he was speaking to, but he rested his cheek on his arm and watched him. Tentatively, he asked a question that he'd held on to as his only source of hope.

'Do you . . . Do you think Dom's theory is right? Could there be a memory box that the Doctor is scared people will find?'

'I don't know,' Concord replied. 'I don't know what's been going on in Dom's head since . . . Well, since you got here. And now this thing with Clem. Dom never talks to me about Clem.'

Sol never thought he'd feel sorry for Concord, but seeing him curled up on Dom's bed, questioning his oldest and most important friendship, his face turning different colours from the bruises and cuts, made him want to reach out and pat him and tell him everything would be OK, even though it was becoming clearer by the hour that it wouldn't.

'Concord, is Clem really dead?'

'Yes.'

'So you think Dom's imagining things?'

'He has to be.'

'But Dom always says the Ash House can do impossible, extraordinary things.'

'And what do you think?'

Sol thought back to floating in the lake, the glowing ash and his new friends all around him. The first morning waking up without pain or fear. He'd been in awe of the ash – but nothing could bring back the dead.

'I don't know what to think any more. Maybe . . . Dom wouldn't say this, but maybe it's not the ash.

Maybe *we* could do something extraordinary.'

Concord didn't reply to this. He sighed heavily and turned his head on Dom's pillow. Then he frowned. Sol watched him rummage under the pillow and pull out a folded piece of paper.

'What's that?' Sol asked.

'I don't know.'

Concord unfolded it. He stared at it as if he was trying to memorize the image, then he handed it to Sol.

'Oh!'

'Have you seen this before?' Concord asked.

'Yeah. It's from the Headmaster's study. Dom must have taken it when he came to stop me going into the vault.'

Sol ran his finger down the crease where Dom had folded the photo. It was the one from the Headmaster's desk. There they all were – young, smiling, even though the Doctor stood right there with them.

Concord took the photo from him and cradled it in his palm.

'What was he thinking?' Sol wondered. 'If the Doctor found out . . .'

'Stealing from the Headmaster is a Nastiness,' Concord muttered. 'But look – we're so small. There's Clem, look! Sol, you have to understand how much

Dom loves the Headmaster.'

'What's that got to do with anything?'

'It's been three years. If you had the chance to take something so you could remember someone you love, you would too. If it was that "parent" thing you mentioned?'

'What are you talking about?'

'I get why Dom would want to keep a photo of the Headmaster. The sad thing is, I think any of us would too, if we were given the chance.'

Sol leant forward so he could look at the photo again, its edges held gently by Concord's hands. There were still brown patterns of blood in the cracks of his skin.

Sol felt a blanket of dread drape over him as the answer to his next question dawned on him.

'Um . . . why do you think that's a photo of the Headmaster?'

'I can tell from his expression,' said Concord, touching a fingertip to one of the smiling faces. 'He looks different when he becomes the Doctor.'

## 27: DOM

**D**om was certain he could feel the breath of the Shucks behind him as he ran, but every time he turned around they were still green lights floating in the dark woods. They didn't gain on him, but they were close enough that he could always see them. They weaved and dodged, sometimes further away but always quick to get nearer if he slowed down. As far as Dom could tell, the injured one hadn't followed them. There were the two new ones – one leaner and faster than the first, the other the biggest by far – and they weren't tired or hurt in the slightest.

His feet pounded along the riverbed heading towards the lake as he tried to think through his breathless panic. He knew that the lake was halfway through the forest. He needed to go past it, out of the woods, up towards the driveway and around the front gardens before making his way back to the courtyard. It might as well have been a trip around the moon. He wasn't fit enough to keep up this pace, and his shoulder and ribs were constant reminders of what had happened to the shed.

The stream got wider and its current stronger. The birds hummed overhead, following him. An algae-caked root trapped one of his feet and he had to kick off his shoe. He tore off the other one too. They were heavy and weighing him down. He clambered out of the water so he could run on the mud and avoid cutting his feet on the stones. He glanced back to see a Shuck pounce on one of his shoes and rip it apart as if it was made of gossamer.

Then the Shuck looked up and made eye contact with him. It started moving again. Concord had been right: it was herding him.

He blundered on until the trees parted and revealed the lake. A green glow beamed through the trees and the water caught the light. He decided he didn't have a choice. He waded in.

He was nearly waist deep when the Shucks reached the shore. They emerged from the undergrowth and came into sight, unhurried now they had him in front of them. One let out a shiver-inducing howl, and the other dived straight in, the ash that had settled on the surface of the lake sticking to its black fur. Dom thrashed and splashed as he waded deeper.

The water was up to his chest, but his instinct to get into the water had been a good one. The Shuck was slower in the lake and had to use its enormous paws just to stay afloat. Dom half-swam, half-waded desperately, and although it bought him time, it wasn't enough. He heard the growl behind him, like thunder and earthquakes.

Dom thought of the bloody mess of Concord's back. He turned to face the Shuck.

Its jaws snapped with terrifying speed. Dom yelled and threw his arms over his face, feeling the teeth sink into his forearm. He screamed, but he was so cold that the pain didn't strike straightaway.

He twisted and pulled and writhed, the water flying into his eyes and the air around him. The Shuck growled and held on tighter. With his good hand Dom tried to beat it with his fists. Then he scrabbled in his pocket.

He pulled out the sharp stone. It was slippery and wet. He held it tightly and with all his strength aimed the sharp point at the Shuck's snout. It yelped and let go just long enough for Dom to free his arm and splash away.

The other Shuck was in the water, blocking his way ahead. With one in front and one behind, Dom turned and swam as fast as he could towards the end of the lake near the Lookout. He would climb the steep, wet rocks and go through the rest of the forest on foot, as long as he didn't lose too much blood. His arm was only aching, but he knew it was worse than it felt.

Dom only dared to check on the Shucks when he reached the rocks. The one he'd hit with the stone had climbed out of the water and was shaking itself on the shore. The other was still in the lake and heading towards him like a menacing sea creature – its fur looked like soft, inky seaweed.

There was no strength left in his bitten arm and injured shoulder. He scooped some of the flaky ash from the surface of the lake and rubbed it in, hoping it would heal it. Then Dom gritted his teeth and pulled himself out, just as the Shuck in the water snapped at his feet. He found a foothold and started to climb, using his good arm.

The Shuck howled below him, unable to climb after him. Dom twisted around and couldn't see the other one. Perhaps it had gone into the trees to lick its wound. This thought gave him the strength to haul himself up to the flat rock at the top of the Lookout.

He lay there panting. He was drenched and couldn't tell what was water and what was blood. He wanted to stay there for the rest of his life. The Shuck in the water was still scrabbling at the rocks at the bottom.

Clutching his arm to his chest, Dom got to his feet and started clambering down the far side of the Look-out. Small stones skittered ahead of him. Others wobbled and rolled as soon as he put his weight on them, so he made slow progress. Here and there he saw dark gaps between the larger stones. Water trickled some-where beneath his feet, and the cold made him shiver so hard that the jerky movements hurt his shoulder.

He was nearly at the bottom, still holding the sharp stone he'd used to fight off the Shuck, when he misplaced a foot and sent a rock bigger than his head rumbling towards the earth.

The earth growled in response.

Dom's stomach went cold.

The green appeared – two orbs of it in the darkness, only a few metres from him, waiting, listening, watching him.

'No!' Dom shouted. 'Just leave me alone! Please, please, please, go away and leave me alone!'

The Shuck pounced.

Dom jumped backwards, barely escaping its jaws. Rocks crashed and rolled all around him. The world lurched underneath him. As first he thought he was fainting and would lie there helpless as the Shucks devoured him.

But the feeling continued. He was falling. The large stone he'd been standing on wasn't there any more. The earth swallowed him up. He didn't fall far, but it knocked the wind out of him. He wheezed and coughed and sucked at the air until he finally felt some oxygen had returned to his system.

Something dripped on to his face. He recoiled, and desperately wiped it away, thinking it was saliva from the Shuck's jaws. But when he looked up, he saw that it was just water.

He was lying on bare earth and all above him were dark, wet stones. The sound of running water filled the little cave as it trickled and dripped over the rocks, making its steady way back to the lake.

Dom sat up and cringed at the pain in his arm. A glimmer of green fell on his hand. He looked up. The gap he'd fallen through was blocked up with more rocks. The Shuck was sniffing and scrabbling at it, but the stones did not move.

He was alone, trapped, and perfectly safe. He laid back and his laughter mixed with the tinkling of the water.

## 28: SOL

'COME BACK!' Concord shouted. 'Sol! Solitude! I *forbid* you to go outside.'

'What's going on?' Libby's head appeared from one of the ground floor windows. Sol was shuffling down the stairs, dragging his chair, and was caught between her and Concord yelling from the doorway above him.

'I'm going to find Dom,' he shouted at both of them.

'Sol, what's happened?' Libby asked. 'Whatever Con's said, just ignore him. It's too dangerous to go outside.'

Faces of the other girls appeared in the windows.

'He told me the truth,' Sol replied, bumping on each step as he struggled to drag his chair after him. 'About the Doctor and the Headmaster. They're the same person.'

'They're not the same person,' Libby said in confusion.

'The same body, then!' yelled Sol. 'It doesn't matter

how you say it.'

'We thought you understood,' Concord called down to him. 'Where are you going?'

'I'm going to find Dom and I'm going to take him far, far away from here.'

'Sol, calm down,' Libby pleaded. Sol was nearly at the bottom of the staircase. 'The Doctor will turn back into the Headmaster soon. Some day. Until then, we just have to do as we're told and not make him angry.'

'Three years!' Sol screamed. 'He hasn't been your Headmaster for three years! And there's always the danger he'll change back.'

'What do you expect us to do? If we hurt the Doctor, we hurt the Headmaster. We have to take his Nastiness with his Niceness. Please go back upstairs.'

'I'm closing this door!' shouted Concord. 'Don't even think about coming back, even if you avoid becoming Shuck-meat!'

Sol ignored both of them. As he clambered into his chair, he tried to rethink every conversation, every detail he'd seen since he got to the Ash House. Could he have known? Did anybody tell him?

No matter what Concord said, they knew he hadn't understood. How could he? The Doctor's madness was far deeper and scarier than he'd ever imagined.

His chair was damp with cold. The wind blew tails of smoke off the Ash House. He looked up at it; the lights glowed on the top floor where the Doctor waited for Dom's return. The dormitory door slammed behind him and Sol felt his confidence dip. How could he possibly find Dom and escape when he was stuck in his chair? And even if he did find Dom, the Doctor would stop them and he wouldn't be able to fight him. The others would accuse him of hurting their precious Headmaster and he'd be an outcast. Again. He needed Dom. He needed whatever was in that memory box. Then, if he didn't die trying, he needed to leave the Ash House for good.

Finding Dom out in the grounds in the dark after all this time would be difficult, but Sol knew where he would hide if he was Dom.

He closed his eyes and pictured the shed in his mind, taking in the trees and grass around it, orienting himself in the grounds. Then he set off.

At first Sol thought he hadn't pictured it correctly in his mind. He knew where the shed should have been, but its shape didn't emerge from the gloom. As he wheeled himself closer, he heard a crunching noise and looked down. His chair was rolling over glass. He went faster and then saw that the shed *was* there – what was left of it.

Its walls and roof were crumpled and splintered, like a den that had been torn down by a storm. The screens lay scattered about, some of them webbed with cracks, others smashed in entirely. A few glowed feebly and turned the grass in front of them silver.

'Dom?' Sol called as loudly as he dared. He wheeled closer to the wreckage, dreading seeing an arm or a leg sticking out of it. Huge claw marks streaked the wood with pale gashes. A few boards rocked and groaned in the wind.

'Dom?' he called one last time, but he felt his hopes sink. Dom wasn't going to last long against something that could reduce the shed to splinters.

Sol pressed his knuckles over his closed eyes. He didn't want to look any more. He couldn't go back – he was more terrified of the Doctor than ever, and he couldn't leave Dom wandering out here on his own. He couldn't bear to think what could have happened to him. When he opened his eyes again, pink and purple splotches swam across his vision. His gaze settled on one of the screens that still shone half-heartedly in the dark. It was tipped on its side, showing a wobbly black-and-white image of somewhere in the woods.

Sol tilted his head. He remembered the view, but he

wasn't sure exactly where it was. He thought of Dom taking him to the shed for the first time and them arguing. After Dom had stormed out, he'd seen Libby in that place. She'd appeared as if from thin air. At the time, he hadn't thought much of it, but now Sol couldn't shake the image. He knew he should be worrying about the Shucks and Dom and how the Headmaster was trapped inside the Doctor . . . Finding out about the Doctor's illness felt like piecing together a puzzle that he should have seen all along. He had the same feeling now.

Libby materializing in the woods. Mercy outrunning the Shucks, even though Concord barely could. The day when Libby had taken him to feed the Shucks trapped underneath the Ash House, and the way they could appear from nowhere, as they had the night at the lake.

Sol found himself whispering what Libby had said to him that day: *'There are ways of moving around the Ash House.'*

His palms were blistering by the time he made it back to the dorm. The boys' door stayed shut, but the girls heard him, and their faces appeared at the windows; they looked like they were underwater.

'Libby!' Sol called.

She was there amongst them. There were creases

under her eyes and her hair was clipped untidily on top of her head.

'You came back,' she said, clearly relieved.

'I need to talk to you,' said Sol. 'All of you. Now.'

'OK, but quickly – you should be inside.' Libby disappeared for a moment, and then reappeared, poking her head out of the window a few steps further up. Through the murky glass, Sol could see she was standing on a bedframe.

'What is it?' she asked.

'No,' said Sol firmly. 'Not like this.'

He wheeled himself away from the window and went around to the front of the dorm.

'The Doctor just went out. He could come back any time!' Libby called out.

'Then let me in,' Sol said loudly. It was impossible to see inside – the glass door was entirely knotted over with ivy.

'You know we're not allowed.' Libby's voice came from the other side.

'I don't care. Let me in.'

The door opened a crack – Sol could see only a sliver of Libby's face.

'You can't come in. Now, what is it?'

It stung his hot, blistered hands to grab the wheels

and launch himself at the door, but he managed to throw his arm through the gap. He heard a few girls behind Libby shout with anger.

'Sol, get back! What are you doing?'

'What's going on?' Concord's voice called down from the stairs.

'He's trying to come in!' Libby shouted. She tried to press the door shut on Sol's arm, but he pushed forward stubbornly.

'Concord, get down here!' Sol shouted back.

There was a pause. Sol could imagine Concord hesitating, still in pain, outraged at being told what to do, but also wanting to help Libby against Sol's obnoxious demand. Eventually, they heard his footsteps, as light as he could make them on the metal stairs.

Concord rounded the corner and saw them both wrestling with the door.

'We're not allowed in there! Why is it, every single Nastiness—'

'They can save Dom!' Sol yelled at him.

Concord paused, his hands frozen on the handles of Sol's chair.

'What?'

'You can, can't you?' Sol could still only see a fraction of Libby's face. Her expression was angry, guarded.

'Lib?' Concord asked. 'What's he talking about?'

'The girls can move around the grounds,' said Sol. 'I don't know how, but you can.'

Libby's grey eye flicked from Sol's face to Concord's and back again. Then she sighed and Sol felt the pressure on his arm relax. She opened the door fully. All the girls were standing behind her, ready for a fight.

'If I could help Dom, I would,' she said.

'No, you wouldn't!' Sol insisted. He twisted in his seat to speak to Concord. 'We're all supposed to be fighting together, but they're keeping secrets. Dom was keeping secrets too – important ones. We have to find him *and* we have to get the memory box.'

'Will this memory bring back the Headmaster?' Concord's voice was monotonous from the strain of keeping the hope out of it.

'Um . . .' Sol rocked forward and back in his chair. 'Honestly? No. That's why Dom's so torn about it. It's only worth something if we take it outside. Beyond the fence.'

Libby and Concord exchanged looks and their eyes widened just a fraction. It was the only sign that they were terrified of what this meant.

'Leave the Ash House?' Libby said.

Sol nodded. 'I wanted to. Dom stopped me.'

'You know what happens when someone crosses the fence?' Concord asked seriously.

'I know the stories. It doesn't mean they're true.'

'You're mad,' said Concord.

'I'm right. But I can't do it on my own. Libby, you need to tell us how you move around the Ash House.'

Concord and Sol stared at her intently. Her face was expressionless, unreadable. The girls craned their necks to see what she would do.

'Lib,' Sincerity whispered. 'Don't . . .'

Then Libby stood aside and held the door open.

The girls' dorm was different to the boys'. Upstairs the light felt alive, the sun and the moon always moving and pushing through the foliage. Downstairs, the shadows reigned.

There was no floor, only a soft carpet of moss. The beds were arranged in a circle. Sol could barely make out the bathroom, directly underneath the boys', behind a trailing curtain of ivy and creepers. The room felt warmer, smaller. Near the windows, tiny yellow and blue flowers blossomed on plants that leant towards the windows.

Concord pushed Sol's chair for him. He held his pained hands in his lap and blew on them gently. Libby pointed them to the middle of the room and the girls sat on the ends of their beds. Sol was nearest to Love, who curled her legs under her. The rabbit she looked after was cradled in her arms. Sincerity, Merit's chore partner, who walked down the drive with him every day, was next to her, sharpening a stick that looked too rotten to hurt anybody. Honesty and Happiness sat either side of Mercy, who was pale-faced and shivery with sweat. There was a bowl of water at their feet, along with a pile of bloody rags and a stack of clean ones.

They spoke as if the boys weren't there.

'We're the ones who had to move down here,' Sincerity said. 'Whatever is down here is ours, not theirs.'

'But if we help Mercy and not Dom . . .' Honesty didn't know how to finish her sentence.

'*He's* the one who got sick and made the Doctor come.' Love shifted the rabbit into the other arm so she could jab a finger at Sol. 'All this is his fault. Let him fix it. Don't drag us into it.'

'We're already dragged into it,' said Libby calmly. 'All it would take is one of us getting sick to bring the Doctor here.'

'She's right,' said Mercy. Sol noticed that the fingers of her right hand were strapped together tightly as if they were broken. 'We're all going to have to face the Shucks.

Even if Dom let Clem down, we should help him.'

'What's that supposed to mean?' Sol asked. The girls looked awkwardly at each other. 'What do you mean, Dom let Clem down?'

'It doesn't matter,' said Concord.

'It's between us,' said Libby.

'And now's not the time to—'

Sol interrupted Concord. 'No! No more of this. All these secrets and lies and, "Oh, we thought you knew." If we're going to help Dom together, we need to be honest with each other. And that starts with being honest about the Doctor.' Sol pushed himself forward and turned his chair so he was glaring at Libby and Concord. 'What really happened to Clem?'

Concord took a deep breath. 'OK. I'll tell you.'

'Stop!' Libby exclaimed. The girls were watching her every move. 'I'll tell it.'

Concord held up his hands and took a step back.

'We used to . . . we used to all sleep upstairs. Boys and girls. But when we got a bit older, the Headmaster moved us to the downstairs dorm.' Libby's voice started off quiet but grew in confidence as she spoke. 'He said we were too old to share with the boys, we had to have space. Clem didn't like it. She was loud. Louder than anything. You could always hear her coming.' A smile pulled at Libby's lips as memories came to her. She said to Concord: 'Remember how bad she was at hide and seek? We could hear you shushing her from halfway across the grounds. You were always together.' Concord nodded stiffly and stared at his feet. Libby looked down too, the brightness of the memory fading, replaced by a sadness that almost made Sol regret asking to hear the story. 'She was loud in her sleep too, always muttering and talking nonsense. It got worse after we moved downstairs. She had these night terrors. Screaming, shaking, crying. It was horrible. Then the Doctor arrived, and he heard her at night. He went away again. We were watching for when he'd come back, in case he tried something. We were going to hide her. Dom was supposed to be watching. He wasn't watching the birds when the Doctor arrived, with this new sleeping draught he said would make her better, and . . . and . . .'

'He got to her. She never woke up.' Concord finished for her.

Libby wiped her eyes.

'I'm sorry,' said Sol quietly. 'I really am. But . . . it's not fair to blame Dom for what happened to her.'

'*He's* not being fair, Sol!' Libby insisted. 'Don't you realize that? Dom should have seen the Doctor go to her. We all knew the Doctor didn't know what he was doing.

Look what he did to Con's face! Dom should have tried to stop him. But he didn't. You only just got here, but he was going to do that for you! Clem should be here, not you!'

Tears were falling down her face now, but her voice was clear and dry. Sol was surprised he didn't feel guilty or angry. Instead, he felt he was understanding for the first time.

'It's the Doctor's fault. No one else's. Not yours, not Dom's, not even the Headmaster's. Look, I think Dom had an idea, a plan. But he was too scared to do anything about it. He realized that unless we find the memory box – Clem's *last* memory box – the Doctor will keep doing what he's doing. We need evidence. Proof that we were all here, that the Doctor did what he did, that – that someone died because of him. I'm telling you, no one on the outside will help us without it.'

'What memory box?' Honesty asked.

Sol relayed the whole story as best he could: Dom's promise after his first operation, how he thought some-one lived beyond the fence and spoke to him, how he claimed the idea came from Clem.

'I know it sounds mad,' he concluded. 'But however Dom found out about it, the logic makes sense.'

'He's just imagining her.' Love dismissed the idea,

clutching the rabbit close for comfort.

'Exactly.' Concord spoke up suddenly. He looked intently at Libby. 'He's imagining what she would say if she was here. If Clem was here, what would she tell us to do?'

Libby looked at her feet, and then nodded.

'OK, then,' she said.

'OK, what?' Sol asked.

'I'll show you. I'll help you.'

'Make sure you mean it,' said Concord. 'He's talking about leaving home.'

'This place hasn't been home since the Headmaster left three years ago. It could be again,' she said. 'Now step back.'

Concord shuffled back and pulled Sol's chair with him. Libby stepped into the centre of the circle and bent down. Some of the girls muttered, but none of them tried to stop her.

As she stood up, she lifted a corner of the moss. It came away easily. It lifted higher and higher until she dragged it back.

Then all of them were standing around the entrance of a tunnel that sloped deep underground. It was lined with the blackest ash Sol had ever seen.

## 29: SOL

Concord moved to lift Sol out of his chair. When Sol tried to argue with him, Concord held up his hands and insisted.

'It will slow us down if we need to get out quick. Remember, the Doctor could notice we're missing any minute.'

'If you're waiting for my legs to suddenly work again—'

'Look, we'll just do this.' Concord knelt in front of Sol with his back to him. 'Put your arms around my neck.'

Hesitantly, Sol did as he was told. Concord lifted him easily. Sol shuffled his weight a bit and although his legs dangled awkwardly through the crooks of Concord's arms, the rest of him clung securely to his back.

'Are you ready?' Libby asked. She was standing at the entrance. Amity had supplied her with a torch and some lock picks.

'Let's go,' Sol said.

It was like the Ash House was a creature and it was devouring them whole, alive and moving. The tunnel wasn't deep, but when the girls covered the entrance behind them, it was utterly dark. Only the yellow beam of Libby's torch could guide them. She was relaxed and confident, while Concord was hesitant for once, and didn't point out that Sol's arms around his neck were a little tighter than they needed to be.

'Why did you never tell us this was here?' Concord whispered to Libby.

'We thought about it. At first it was fun to have a secret. We were going to play tricks on you. But then the Doctor came, and Clem . . . after a while we just didn't want to.'

'Where does it go?' Sol asked.

'Everywhere,' Libby replied. 'The house. The lake. Lots of the tunnels have entrances in different parts of the forest.'

'There's more than one?'

'It's a whole system,' she explained. 'It took us months to map them all. There are still some old ones we don't know very well. Some have caved in or flooded or just go in a circle.'

'Does the Doctor use them?'

'We're not sure. The Headmaster made the Ash House, so he must know, but we've never seen him use them. But he doesn't know we've found them, and we want to keep it that way. We try not to use them too much when he's here in case he gets suspicious.'

Sol imagined the tunnels woven like black veins underneath the Ash House. There was a smell of soil, smoke and stale water. He kept his eyes on the yellow glow of the torch, sometimes spotting gaping gaps in the walls where the tunnel twisted or divided. Libby moved quickly, turning this way and that through the maze. Sol was horribly aware of how lost he and Concord would be without her. And without either of them, he'd be stuck almost entirely . . .

Libby suddenly came to a stop.

'What is it?' Concord hissed.

'We're here.' The darkness was uniform and unrelenting. Sol couldn't see any sign of a door.

'Where exactly?' he asked.

'So that's the thing.' Libby turned to face them. The light was thrown carelessly into their blinking eyes. 'Only one tunnel goes into the house itself.'

'Fine,' said Concord.

'It goes into the Shucks' kennels.'

'Oh, no.' Concord staggered back. 'No way. I'm not going in there.'

'But they're hunting for Dom,' said Sol. 'They're not here, are they?'

'Exactly. And it's underground – if we're quiet, the Doctor will have no idea we're there. It's the perfect way in.' Libby turned back and crouched down. She struggled with something for a moment, then stood up and pointed the torch to reveal what looked like a low window in the wall.

'I'll go first. Then you pass Sol to me,' she said to Concord.

'You don't have to talk like I'm not here,' Sol grumbled.

'Lib, I really don't want—'

But Libby didn't pause to listen to either of them. She sat on the floor and went through feet first. They heard her land somewhere beneath them. She reached up and laid the torch on the ground, pointing at them.

Sol found threading himself through the hole awkward and painful, and he was grateful that nobody could see very much. Libby supported his legs, then caught his body and set him carefully on the floor. Then they waited for Concord.

'Con, come on,' Libby called gently. 'It's fine.'

'No. I can't. I'm not going back in there...'

In the faint glow of torchlight, Sol looked around and tried to imagine how terrifying it must have been for Concord when the Shuck dragged him inside. The Shuck kennel was vast and ice cold. A grating at the very top – the one Libby had pointed out to him – showed that it was dark outside. The air was filled with thin smoke and clouds of their breath. Sol saw enormous chains slung across the far wall.

'You can.'

'Just wait.'

'Is he crying?' Sol asked Libby.

'Don't you dare make fun of him,' she snapped.

'I wasn't!'

'Con, you can do it. I'm here. Do it for Dom.'

They could hear Concord breathing through the gap in the wall. Finally, his trembling hands appeared and he climbed through and joined them.

'Let's get out of here,' he said.

Concord picked Sol up again. Sol could feel him shaking. Libby didn't stop to look round; she marched them fearlessly towards the chains and the thick metal door that hung open next to them.

'This way.'

They went down a narrow, dark hallway. The torch

showed Shuck prints in the ash that coated the floor. A tight spiral staircase led them up and up, until they were standing in the main hallway.

All of them breathed out with relief.

'Now where?' Concord whispered.

'It's Sol's lead from here,' said Libby.

'Take the stairs.'

Concord moved towards the stairs that led down to the assembly room.

'No, no. Upstairs,' said Sol. 'To the first landing. We have to be extra quiet.'

Sol felt Con exhale, but he didn't complain. They climbed up and Concord placed Sol on the top step.

'Have you been up here before?' Sol asked.

'Once with the Headmaster,' said Libby.

'Me too,' said Concord. 'I was very little.'

'In there –' Sol pointed – 'is the study with the vault. Up there is the Doctor's office and some other rooms. I don't know what else is up here. The Headmaster's apartment, possibly.'

They took it all in silently.

'Let's try the vault first,' said Sol. 'The Doctor might have changed the code. We'll need time to work it out.'

Concord scooped Sol up and Libby led the way into the Headmaster's study.

'Careful not to knock anything,' Sol whispered as they entered the room. The sight of it stopped Concord and Libby in their tracks.

'Woah.'

'What the—?'

They froze under the gaze of the birds, the eyes all shining shades of gold, tawny and black.

'What is it?' Sol asked.

'I've never been in here,' Libby whispered. 'Only Dom was allowed.'

'What are these things?' Concord asked.

'Birds,' Sol said.

'These aren't birds,' Libby objected. 'Con, don't they look just like—'

'Like Dom's badge,' Concord said with amazement.

'They're birds in the world outside. Now don't touch anything,' Sol said again. 'Go this way.'

He tried to direct Concord, who kept pausing so he and Libby could look at the birds. Libby reached up to gently touch the tip of a wing, and Sol slapped her hand away. He pointed towards the door of the vault at the end of the room.

'Look!' Libby whispered excitedly when she saw the workbench. 'That's where he makes our badges.'

'All these names . . .' Concord said in wonder, as he

sized up the door. 'Who are they?'

'The new people, maybe,' said Libby. 'The Head-master used to talk about them, but they never came. Until you,' she said to Sol.

'The names are the code,' Sol explained. 'Libby, bring me that chair.'

Libby pulled the Headmaster's desk chair over and Sol found himself once again in front of the impervious metal door. He reached out and clicked the notch next to his name. Nothing moved.

'I was right. The Doctor's changed it.'

'To what?' Concord asked.

'I don't know,' he growled. 'It's a vault.'

'And all the memory boxes are in there?' Libby asked.

'Yes. This is where Dom puts them.'

'We need to hurry,' she reminded them. 'The Doctor mustn't catch us in here.'

Sol tried more combinations, but none of them worked. The time crawled by and Sol's fingers were becoming slippery with nerves as they pressed the notches. Libby crouched next to him and watched every move with interest, while Concord paced behind them.

'You must know something,' Sol insisted eventually. 'You've grown up with him! How would he think?'

'Remember, the Headmaster didn't set this,' said

Concord. 'It was the Doctor.'

'They're the same!'

'They're *not*. I explained—'

'Boys!' Libby snapped. 'Concentrate. Sol, didn't you say the Doctor's office was upstairs?'

'Yeah, so?'

'*So*, maybe there's a clue in there.' She turned around to look at Concord, who groaned into his hands.

'All right,' he said. 'I'll look there. You two stay here. And Sol, you're clearly useless at that – let Libby try.'

They listened to him stomp away.

When he was out of earshot, Libby said: 'Not to be Nasty, Sol, but he might be right.' She moved him gently, took his place in front of the door and started pressing the endless combinations.

It was a relief to sit back and watch her for a while. Sol was so tired he could feel his eyelids dip. The clicking sound was almost soothing. Then something made him sit bolt upright: the sound of a door downstairs opening and closing.

'What was that?' he whispered to Libby.

'What was what?' She was too focused on the maze of Nicenesses in front of her.

'I thought I heard . . .'

Sol pushed himself off the chair and crawled behind a

cabinet filled with delicate wrens. He was suddenly very aware of how easily they would be cornered. He hoped there was another door he'd never noticed, or perhaps a cupboard to hide in. He looked around. Nothing. There was an old blocked-up fireplace opposite him, with a set of fire irons next to it. He took a poker without quite knowing why. It felt good to have something he could defend himself with.

Then he heard the mechanical whirring and clunking of the vault door.

'I did it!' he heard Libby whisper.

'What was the code?'

'Everybody at the Ash House except for Dom, Concord and Mercy. Everyone who hasn't raced yet. He must have only just changed it.'

Sol felt the hairs on his arms and the back of his neck prickle.

'Sol, we're in.'

There was a creak out on the landing. Unmistakeable this time. Someone was there.

'Libby,' Sol breathed. 'Find the memory box.'

He turned and crawled back to the vault, still clutching the poker. Libby was standing in front of the open door. In the gloom, Sol could see endless racks of dull metal hard drives going on and on into the depths of the house. Libby stepped nervously across the threshold.

'Is that Concord?'

'I don't know. Just find it. Quickly.'

Footsteps came into the Headmaster's study, walking purposefully in their direction. Before Libby could protest, Sol grabbed the door, and, using all his strength, swung it closed, shutting Libby inside.

He was just in time.

'Solitude.'

He turned. The Doctor stood before him.

'I hope you're not trying to steal my memories.'

His smile was strained. His eyes looked crazed and sleep-deprived. His hair and shirt – usually so neat – were rumpled and spattered with raindrops.

'He's been out for hours. Too long,' said the Doctor, as if finding Sol next to the vault in the Headmaster's study was the most natural thing in the world. 'I've been out in the grounds looking for him. The Shucks haven't come back either.'

'Maybe they ran away together.'

'How did you get in here?'

'I walked.'

The Doctor stared at him. Sol expected to feel flooded with terror, but something stronger was rising up within him: loathing.

'Are there others in here?'

'No. Just me.'

'Is Freedom here with you?'

'What? No, I just said—'

The Doctor didn't wait to hear him out. An enormous crash split the air as he threw the cabinet of wrens to the floor. The glass smashed, and the heavy wood crushed the tiny bodies of the birds.

The Doctor's frenzy was only beginning. He flew around the room, overturning furniture, until the air was thick with feathers and down.

With each act of destruction, he shouted: 'Where is he? Where *is* he?'

Sol cowered and realized two things. First, he had to distract the Doctor so that he didn't try the vault and find Libby inside. And second, if he didn't move right then, he was likely to get crushed to death by an ugly piece of furniture.

Sol started to crawl through the room, the poker tucked under one arm. He hoped Libby stayed safely shut in the vault and that Concord had heard the commotion and had the sense to stay away.

Halfway to the door, he was hit on the back, on the exact spot of his surgery wound. He screamed.

The Doctor was pressing his knee between his shoulder blades.

'Tell me where he is! Bring him back here.'

'I can't . . . I don't know . . .' Sol choked. His face was pressed against the dusty carpet.

'You didn't get in here alone. I know he helped you.'

'Get off – please, get off, please . . .'

The Doctor stood up and Sol breathed again.

'If this goes wrong, it's because of you,' the Doctor told him.

'It's because of you!' Sol yelled. He twisted around to see his face. 'I know the truth about you.'

The Doctor's lips twitched.

'I really can heal you, you know.'

'I know all about what you've been doing here,' said Sol.

'The hiccup with your legs is unfortunate . . .'

'And you can't do it for ever. I'll find a way out. I'll tell people.'

'But with a few more weeks, I really think I can correct it. You said yourself that your back doesn't hurt any more.'

'I'll get proof. Then everybody will know what you did to Clem!'

'What was that?'

The Doctor's face froze. Sol had said too much. He used his elbows to inch towards the door.

'Nothing.'

'Clemency . . .'

'I – I don't—'

'Who told you about Clemency? Who has been telling you Nasty, *Nasty* stories about Clemency?'

'No one,' Sol tried desperately to placate him. 'I just heard you tried to heal her too . . .'

The Doctor's eyes were wide and bloodshot as he whispered, partly to Sol, partly to himself: 'It wasn't meant to happen. I just wanted to heal her. I only wanted her to get better. But then I hurt her – I didn't mean to, but I hurt her – and they hate me, and all I do is love them. I'll make them love me again. I'll heal all of you, you'll see. That's what the Ash House is here for. I made it for them. A paradise. Here they'll always be safe, and I'll help them be smarter, braver . . .' The Doctor looked down at Sol with something like affection in his eyes. '*Nicer*. Then they will go out and heal the rest of the world. A world filled with Niceness.'

The hope and kindness in his eyes gave Sol an idea.

'I need to speak to the Headmaster.'

'He's not here right now.'

'I know you're in there. This other person you

become is hurting the people you love, not healing them. They miss you – they *need* you.'

'I said, the Headmaster is not here right now.'

'They want you to come back. Leave the Doctor! Come back!' Sol screamed as though his voice could penetrate the skin, the membrane, the thoughts of the Doctor and reach the Niceness of the Headmaster that he hoped was stored somewhere deep within him.

'COME BACK!'

Something seemed to snap inside the Doctor. More furniture rained down.

'Freedom will be lost in the woods, that's all,' the Doctor muttered. 'I can't find him through the birds. They've lost sight of him. The Shucks are there by the lake. But he's not there. Where *is* he? He knows nothing about Clemency. The birds would never show him. The memories are *mine*!'

The Doctor's mind was running away. Sol tried to calm him, trying to imagine the handsome face softened with fondness for the children.

'Maybe we can find Dom together?' Sol said. 'You could call off the Shucks. Let's just get Dom back and he'll tell you himself: no one knows anything about Clemency.' The Doctor's foot was so close he could hear it lift and press on the carpet. 'Then we can get back to lessons,' said Sol. 'And Niceness. You can finish whatever it is you've started. We'll do whatever you say.'

The Doctor stopped walking. The frenetic energy seemed to leave him, and Sol realized that Concord was right: his face did look different when he became the Headmaster.

He looked dazed, like someone stepping into sunlight after a long time in darkness. His eyelids looked heavier – the wide, staring gaze was gone. His breathing deepened, his back straightened.

He looked around the room. He swiped a shining shoe through the dust on the carpet, a curious expression on his face. Then he noticed Sol at his feet.

The Headmaster's hand fluttered to his collar and he took a small step back, seeming suddenly unsure, afraid – shy even.

Sol had the distinct feeling of looking not at the Doctor, but at a perfect stranger.

'Here,' Sol said. 'Let's tidy things up in here. We'll find Dom.'

'Dom?' the Headmaster whispered.

'Yes. He's been looking for you.' Sol's hand trembled. He kept his voice low. 'We should go and find him.'

'Perhaps . . . perhaps that would be for the best . . . Perhaps . . . yes. Thank you.'

Sol pointed to himself. 'Solitude.'

'Solitude.'

The Headmaster beamed at the sound of his name. He held out his hand. Then his head jerked forward, his eyes rolled back, his knees buckled, and his full weight collapsed on to Sol.

Concord was standing behind the Headmaster holding a heavy picture frame with a painting of a falcon inside it.

The Headmaster groaned. Sol struggled to free himself, but the man was heavy and woozy, holding his head in his hands.

'What the hell!' Sol yelled at Concord, who was staring in disbelief. 'He'd changed back! He was about to call off the Shucks!'

'How do you know?'

'He was going to let us help him find Dom,' Sol cried with dismay.

'And when we find him? He'll be as good as dead anyway. Where's Libby?'

'She's in the vault. I locked her in, we have to let her out.'

The Headmaster groaned again and pushed himself on to all fours, breathing heavily. He looked up, and Sol saw that the kind, shy man was gone again.

The Doctor's wide-eyed, blood-shot gaze cast around the room. Concord rushed forward to lift Sol, but as he bent over, the Doctor's hand shot out and grabbed him by the throat.

Concord's yell was squeezed into silence. He grabbed uselessly at the Doctor's hand and made an awful dry gurgling sound.

The Doctor climbed to his feet, tightening his grip around Concord's neck. Sol could see a dark patch at the back of the man's head and blood seeped from his hair on to the white of his shirt collar.

Sol watched helplessly from the floor as Concord's face turned red, purple and white. His eyes were wide and watering. He was staring at Sol's hand.

Sol grabbed at the Doctor's legs, but he might as well have been a fly. With one shake, the Doctor threw him off.

Concord choked desperately, trying to say something.

'You will regret doing that,' said the Doctor. His spit landed on Concord's face. 'But only after you tell me what Nasty stories you've been telling about Clemency.'

He slackened his grip to let Concord speak.

His voice sounded like glass scraping against metal: 'S-S-Sluh . . .'

304

The Doctor shook him manically. 'Tell me!' he insisted. 'Tell me right now!'

Sol tried to dig his nails into the Doctor's legs, but it was pointless.

'S-So...'

Sol realized that Concord was trying to say his name. Concord's eyes were still fixed on his hand.

Or what was near his hand, on the floor.

Sol picked up the poker. He hesitated – he couldn't help it – but only for a moment. He lifted it up in both fists and stabbed the Doctor's foot as hard as he could. The Doctor grunted, but the poker hadn't pierced his shiny leather shoe.

Sol did it again, and this time the Doctor screamed. He staggered back, trying to find something to hold on to, before his knees buckled. He fainted.

Concord fell motionless on the floor. His face was clammy with sweat and his lips were still purple. Ugly marks were forming on his neck, blending with his bruises. Sol shook him.

'Con, we need to get Libby!'

Concord groaned, then nodded. Slowly, he staggered to his feet and headed to the vault.

'All of us except you, Dom and Mercy,' Sol called out to him. 'That's the code.'

The door whirred and then it was open. Libby's palm slapped Concord across the face, adding fresh sting to his injuries.

'OW!'

'You shut me in!'

'That was Sol!'

Libby sprang out of the vault and hugged Concord tightly.

'Are you both OK? I heard the Doctor.' She took in the devastation of the study. 'What happened?'

'Did you get it?' Concord croaked.

She held out a hard drive. 'I think this is it. They're organized by our badges. This was the last one in Clem's. Sol!' She ran over to Sol, her voice filled with concern.

Libby stopped in her tracks when she saw the Doctor curled on the floor. He let out a low groan as he started to come around. 'What – what did you do?'

Concord went back to the fireplace. He picked up another poker.

'This. This was a good idea,' he said. He handed it to Libby, then bent down to pick up Sol.

The Doctor opened his eyes. The three of them were nearly at the doorway when he spoke. The poker stuck out of his foot.

'Concord. Liberty. I wouldn't have expected this

from you,' he gasped. 'Where are . . . you going?'

Concord tensed. Neither of them replied.

Then the Doctor laughed. It was a pained, stuttering sound that made Sol nervous. He wished he could back away, but he was trapped in Concord's grip.

'It doesn't matter!' the Doctor croaked. 'This is our home. There's nowhere you can go that I can't get to. We will find Freedom together.'

He started to push himself up.

'Run,' Libby whispered. 'Just run.'

## 30: DOM

It was peaceful under the rocks. The Shucks grew tired of clawing at the stones and sticking their snouts into the hole. The water sang all around, finding its way back to the lake. Dom pressed his arm against one of the wet rocks and sighed as the cold water washed away some of the brown blood.

The cave's floor was sand, mud and long-dead grass, and was as deep and wide as Dom was tall. He sat with his back against a solid rock wall. Facing him was another wall made up of a pile of smaller rocks. Some were covered in black ash. He tried to see through the gaps between them but couldn't decipher the darkness beyond. It was like there was a tunnel disappearing towards the fence, but Dom had never heard of such a thing.

He didn't know how many hours he sat there. The only thing that kept him from sleep was the bitter cold.

His clothes and hair didn't dry, and his body complained with random, violent convulsions. Through the hole above him he could see a corner of sky turn from black to blue.

Dom wondered if the races had continued after he didn't return. He hadn't heard any more noise from the Shucks or in the woods around him, so he hoped that meant everyone was still safe inside. Maybe the Doctor had called it off. Maybe they would come looking for him.

He examined all corners of the cave, wobbling and moving rocks to see if it was possible for a Shuck to bash its way in, or for him to bash his way out, if it came to that. It was secure. A worry nudged at the edge of his mind – what if they never found him? He pushed it away. Better to see the cave as a sanctuary, not a prison.

He couldn't stop Clem's last night playing through his mind. He'd offered to stay late and watch the birds – she was exhausted from the night terrors and wanted to go to bed early, alone in the dorm. The Doctor had been visiting more and more, so Dom should have been on the lookout for him, but that night it was a full moon and he wanted to see the ash glow. He was standing outside in the frost, the golden fragments of ash glittering all around him, so he didn't see the black car arrive.

He didn't see the Doctor go to the dorm and speak to Clem, who had no warning, no place to hide. He didn't see her take the sleeping draught he'd made her, in his madness, his desperation to help her. He didn't see her fall asleep for the last time.

He skimmed the surface of sleep, but woke up often, imagining he heard Shucks in the cave or his friends' voices far away, calling for him. At one point it sounded as though Clem was right in his ear, whispering: 'Did you find it?'

Dom woke up shivering from the dream and the cold. He stood up and waved his arms and jumped as much as he could without banging his head. His feet tingled as the blood started to move again. The corner of sky he could see was now definitely lighter.

'I can't stay here for ever, Clem,' he said. 'I can't change what happened.'

Clambering to the top of the cave wasn't difficult. The rocks were well placed and offered good grip, despite their damp surface.

When he reached the top, he couldn't ignore his predicament any longer. The gap was big enough to fit his arm, but not big enough to climb out of. He'd have to push his way out from below without causing the whole cave to fall in and crush him.

He raised a hand through the hole. Nothing happened. He shifted himself higher and threaded his good arm further through the gap and started feeling around for rocks to move. He needed to shift the ones on top so that he could make the gap bigger and pull himself through.

After some blind scrabbling, he felt one of the larger rocks move. It was hard to get enough force behind it – he was holding the wall with his bitten arm and couldn't grip as well as he'd like. He shuffled his weight to improve the angle.

But before he could give one more push, a piercing howl echoed through the cave. A paw was on his arm and a slick of drool was swiping his skin. Dom screamed and snatched his arm back, let go of the wall, and fell to the ground. His breath was thumped out of him.

A black snout snuffled through the gap and strings of drool swung above his head.

Now he really was stuck.

He wished the cave was big enough to pace in. Instead he tossed a pebble from one hand to the other and thought. He could wait and hope. But what if it got dark again? He'd survived one night in the cold and wet, but he didn't have high hopes for a second one.

He sat back down and tried to keep the tears at bay.

He stared at the dark gaps in the rock pile in front of him until they blurred and his eyes grew heavy.

He couldn't allow himself to fall asleep. He had to try again. He picked up a stone and tossed it through the gap above him. He heard the Shuck growl and snap at it.

Finally, one of the stones Dom threw made the Shuck scrabble over the entrance of the cave, dislodging one of the larger rocks. It felt like being inside an earthquake. The rocks scraped against each other as they reorganized themselves. The gap half opened and half caved in, allowing Dom to wriggle free before he was crushed and his hiding place was sealed up for ever.

His eyes watered in the light. He swayed in the fresh air. When was the last time he ate or slept? It felt like weeks. It was impossible to believe that his bed was only behind the trees.

The Shuck spotted Dom and growled. Dom stumbled and slipped down the rest of the Lookout, heading towards a tangle of brambles, wishing to be nowhere near the lake. But it was as if his feet weren't listening to the instructions from his brain, because he soon tripped and fell, ripping open his trousers at the knees and grazing his palms. He came to a stop, splayed on his front. He put his arms over his head and curled his knees into his chest. He couldn't run. Couldn't fight. Couldn't shout. He just wanted to sleep and sleep in the weak sunshine.

The Shuck howled in victory, sprang down the scree and launched itself at him. Dom could smell its earthy scent. He could feel its breath.

Then its howl turned into a high-pitched, animal scream. A girl screamed back.

Hot saliva dripped over Dom's shoulder, neck and cheek.

But the Shuck didn't bite him. He wondered if the cold had made him so numb that he couldn't feel pain.

'Dom!'

A hand was clapped on his back. He recoiled, assuming it was the Doctor. He rolled over and saw the silhouette of a wild-haired girl bending over him.

'Clem,' he murmured.

'Dom!' The girl shook his shoulder. She moved so she wasn't blocking the sun any more. It was Libby, red-faced and breathing heavily, with Concord as pale as snow behind her.

'Libby? Con?'

'We've been looking for you all night! Were you hiding in the tunnel?' she asked.

Dom uncurled and sat up.

313

'Tunnel? No, I . . . Where are the other Shucks?'

'We saw them heading back towards the kennel,' said Libby.

'How did you find me?'

'We saw the Shucks packing here,' said Concord. 'It's been quite a night.'

Concord pointed to where Sol was waiting in his chair at the edge of the lake. Something had changed about him. He looked calm, determined. He started to wheel towards them.

The day was cold and clear. The ground beneath Dom was rock hard and the trees and plants all around him glittered. The lake was smooth as glass. Smoke hung in the air, carrying flakes of ash. Winter had arrived.

Dom saw that it wasn't saliva that had dripped on him. Jewels of Shuck blood shone on his skin. The Shuck itself was within arm's reach. It was dead. Some sort of blade was sticking out of its neck. Dom crawled closer, half expecting the Shuck to burst back into life. Its fur looked wonderfully soft and warm. Then Dom saw that it wasn't a blade at all. It was a poker.

He reached out and finally got the chance to bury his hand in a Shuck's fur. He watched his skin disappear into its darkness.

'I'm sorry,' he whispered to it.

'Hey!' Sol cried out as he got near. 'Look at the house!'

Dom looked up. The Ash House was just visible over the trees. As the wind blew, a plume of flame flickered into the sky. The house was becoming darker, more solid – as if something was burning beneath the ash.

'The Shuck – it's doing something to the ash,' said Libby, failing to keep the fear from her voice. 'The house is catching fire.'

'Fire . . .' Sol's voice trembled. 'It can't be – not again . . .'

'Because you killed it!' said Dom. 'You did a Nastiness and it's destroying the house!'

'I didn't mean—'

'You remember your Niceness, Dom!' said Concord. 'She saved your life!'

'We don't have time for this,' said Sol. 'The Doctor's hurt and slow, but he's still coming after us.' He held up the dull metal box that lay in his lap.

'You let him take it?' Dom turned to Libby and Concord.

'It was the only option we had,' said Concord defensively.

Dom looked at the poker sunk deep into the Shuck. He gulped. He was trembling all over when he stood up.

Concord held out his arms, ready to catch him if his legs wouldn't take his weight.

'Will the Doctor say I'm done?' Dom asked, dizzy at the idea of it. 'Is it someone else's turn?'

'No,' said Sol. He tucked the memory box under his arm and put his hands on his wheels. He looked determined, but his eyes were shining with sadness as he spoke. 'No more Shucks. No more operations. We're getting out of here.'

Dom felt sick. He wanted to go back to the dorm and sleep until summer came around again. He didn't want to argue with Sol about this.

'We can't do that,' he tried to explain. 'The other Shucks could be here any minute. When the Headmaster comes back—'

'When the Headmaster comes back,' said Sol, '*if* he comes back, we'll still be trapped here, knowing he could turn back into the Doctor at any moment.'

'The Headmaster might stay,' Dom mumbled.

'He's not able to,' Sol was speaking like Concord, as if what he said was right and true.

'He's right, Dom,' said Concord. 'I think . . .' He took a deep breath. 'I think even if the Headmaster does come back, we can't stay here with him.'

'Shut up. You don't mean that.'

'It's been years. He's left us. Whether it was his choice or not—'

'Listen to yourself!' shouted Dom. 'He'd never leave us. He's coming back, any day now, he'll come back.'

'Even if he does, he isn't safe!' Concord shouted back. 'We know it's not safe here. We don't know about the outside . . .'

'The unknown has to be better than this,' Sol insisted. 'Look at us.'

Dom looked from Sol in his chair, so much thinner than when he'd first arrived, to Concord, in his bloodstained clothes with a dark, furious network of bruises choking his neck. There was Libby, standing over the Shuck she had just killed. Then he looked down at himself. Drenched, exhausted, his arm almost useless.

'Sol said that sometimes you go to the fence and speak to Clem,' Libby said quietly. 'Is that true?'

'Yes,' Dom said weakly.

'But Clem died.'

'No. I stopped it. She's just beyond the fence.'

'But I remember,' she claimed calmly.

'I remember. I stopped it.' Dom pleaded with her to agree with this memory: 'I saw the Doctor through the birds, I warned her, I got her to the fence so he couldn't reach her . . .'

'You didn't. You couldn't. And – and that's OK,' Libby said awkwardly. 'It wasn't your fault.'

'It was all my fault,' Dom said with despair.

'Wherever Clem is – beyond the fence, in your memory – she's telling you how to stop all this. And you've told us.'

'We can't cross the fence,' Dom whispered. 'We just can't.'

'We don't have much choice,' said Sol.

'We don't have much time either,' said Concord. 'Look.'

Framed against the morning light, a monster was staggering towards them, shadowed by a Shuck. It limped over the grass, leaning heavily on a stick, from the direction of the Ash House.

'Dom, you take Sol,' said Concord. He pulled Dom behind the chair, ready to push. Libby started preparing for another fight. She picked up the poker and started gathering any sharp rocks she could see.

'What are you doing?'

'Libby and I will slow them down. You have to save Sol from the Doctor. He'll never stop trying to heal him. Take the memory box through the fence. Get help.'

Sol gripped Concord's arm. 'We will.'

'You can't,' said Dom, flooded with panic. 'We can't, you can't.'

'You must. Courage is the only Niceness that matters now.'

## 31: SOL

**D**om half-heartedly pushed the chair, while Sol pulled with frustration at its wheels with his raw palms.

'We have to go faster,' he insisted, but Dom was too scared, his eyes flicking between where they were going and what was behind them.

Libby and Concord stood defiantly on the rocks between them and the Doctor and the Shuck. Libby had handed Concord the poker, and he made a menacing silhouette as he faced his greatest fear – all hint of boyhood had left him. Libby stood tall, a jagged rock in each hand.

The Doctor came to a standstill. The outline of the house billowed and pulsed behind him. The flames were clearer now and gaining height. The Shuck lengthened its stride and went on without him.

'They can't fight a Shuck,' said Dom.

'They don't have to. They just have to slow it down.' Sol wished he could drag Dom, but he needed both hands to move his chair. Dom dragged his heels, his eyes on the scene behind them, then stopped.

'I'm going to help. I'm sorry, Sol—'

'No!' Sol grabbed Dom's wrist. 'Concord told us to get help.'

'I can't leave them—'

'They can take care of—'

'They're going to hurt him!'

'Hurt who? The Doctor, or the Headmaster? Wake up, Dom – he's not your Headmaster!'

'CON!'

They saw the Shuck leap for Concord at the same time as Libby ran past it and dived for the Doctor. She looked tiny compared to him, but she knocked his stick aside and threw him off balance. He staggered back on to his injured foot, the rock she held connected with the side of his head and he fell to the ground unconscious.

Meanwhile, the Shuck skidded, flinging frozen grass and pebbles into the air, turned on its back legs and snapped at Concord again. He swiped the poker in front of its dripping jaws and backed away. The Doctor lay still on the ground. Libby was kneeling beside him, tears carving bright tracks through the smudges of ash and blood on her cheeks. She was holding his hand.

Sol tugged at the wheel of his chair with one hand – Dom's wrist was still in his other.

'Please, *please* move, Dom,' he begged.

The poker caught the Shuck in the face. It yelped horribly and for a moment Sol felt sorry for the creature. Dom's eyes were shining as he watched. Concord swiped again, but this time the Shuck knew better. When his arm was outstretched, it pounced and knocked him flat.

Sol had to restrain Dom with all his might. There was shouting and yelping from both Concord and the Shuck. When the animal stood back, Concord jumped back on to his feet, but his face was a mask of red. His eyes found Dom and Sol.

'I told you to run!' he roared.

This seemed to break the spell that held Dom in place. He grabbed the handles of Sol's chair and soon they were hurtling deeper into the woods.

Through the saplings and trees, the fence came into view.

Dom brought them to a halt a few metres from the wire.

'She's not here,' he said. 'She should be here.'

Sol tried to surge forward but found he was stuck.

Dom was glued to the spot, the chair's handles still in his grip.

'Dom, what are you looking at? We have to go!'

'No one's ever crossed the boundary.'

'Then we'll be pioneers.'

There was a yell behind them. Then the familiar green points of light. The Shuck burst through the thicket, but Concord was right behind it. He threw himself on to its back and wrapped his arms around its neck. Sol could feel the Shuck's growl in his bones.

'I can't hold it!' Concord yelled. 'Go, go!'

Sol thought of the day when Libby took him to see the Shucks caged underneath the house.

'You can hold it,' he insisted. 'Convince it you're in charge.'

'What!'

'Sol's right,' Dom exclaimed. 'The Doctor won't be in charge any more. You will!'

'You can do it. You have more Niceness than anyone,' Sol insisted.

A hundred emotions crossed Concord's face: fear, sadness, overwhelming gratitude. He buried his bloody face in the Shuck's fur. Its growl started to soften.

Dom turned back to the fence and shouted into the void: 'Help! Now! Help us!'

'Who are you talking to?' Sol demanded.

Then the Shuck gave a howl – the most guttural, mournful noise Sol had ever heard – and sank to the ground. Concord was still on its back. He was whispering to it. Its lips folded down over its teeth. Its panting grew heavy and tired. It didn't want to attack them.

'Come on,' said Sol.

'I can't go any closer,' Dom replied.

'Just to below the wire.' Sol pulled at his wheels. 'We can do it.'

Dom started to inch forward.

The memory box shone on Sol's lap. Dom pushed him and leaves crunched under the chair's wheels. Then he heard something behind him.

Something yanked Dom off his feet just as Sol pushed himself forward. The wheel of his chair bounced against a root and he felt it disappear from under him. He was thrown forward into nettles. The memory box flew out of his hands. The fence was only a metre away.

'Sol!' Dom called out.

He twisted and saw that the Doctor had grabbed Dom by the collar and thrown him to the ground. The chair was toppled over on its side, its wheel bent at an awkward angle, hanging off the frame. Sol found that the sight of it hurt his heart. Concord was still restraining the Shuck, unable to let go and help them.

'No!' Libby's shriek cut through the woods. She came running. There was an ugly red mark on the side of her face and her lip was split and scarlet.

'Libby, help!' Dom called out.

Concord and the Shuck stood between her and the Doctor. She hesitated.

'Don't hurt him,' she begged, but Sol wasn't certain who she meant.

'Wait!' he said. 'I'm coming.' Sol started to crawl towards Dom.

'You will spend the rest of your days with the Shucks!' the Doctor spat at Dom. 'You will never see the birds again! You won't touch another memory box!'

Sol was covered in mud. Every root, bramble and creeper seemed determined to slow him down. He spotted a round, heavy stone and picked it up. He knew the Doctor's weak spot.

The Doctor didn't notice Sol crawling through the dirt until he smashed the stone into same foot he'd stabbed with the poker. The Doctor made a noise like a Shuck and fell to the floor, clutching his foot.

Dom took the chance to stand up again.

'How did you—'

Concord called to them: 'Make sure you get over

the boundary.'

'Help me carry Sol,' Dom said to Libby.

'No,' said Libby. She was next to Concord, helping him restrain the Shuck. 'We're not coming.'

'What!' Dom and Sol shouted at the same time.

'The others – in the dorms,' Concord panted. 'They need us. We can't leave them.'

'You're the one who said we have to cross!' Dom yelled, suddenly furious.

'You two have to,' Libby said. 'Sol will need you.'

Sol closed his eyes. He thought of the boys clustered together by the dorm window, staring at the courtyard. He thought of the girls leaning over the tunnel entrance, listening for all they were worth. His heart lurched. They were the friends who had shown him the way out of his pain, and suddenly he was scared he'd never see them again. But Concord was right. He and Libby belonged with them.

'Con, listen,' he said. 'We'll come back. I swear. As soon as we can get help, we'll come back.'

Concord's mouth became curved like his scar.

'No need,' he said quietly. 'The Ash House is ours now. For good. You did that. It's time for you to go. Sol, I'm sorry. The pig and everything, I—'

'That's OK,' Sol said, too quickly.

'We're not leaving you. Not with the Doctor,' Dom said. At the mention of his name, the Doctor began to uncurl himself and let go of his foot. 'Libby, tell him! We have to stay together.'

Libby slowly let go of the Shuck, the inky fur slipping through her fingers, and shook her head. 'Sorry, Dom, but he's right.' Then she said to Concord: 'It's now or never. Let it go.'

Concord nodded and whispered something to the Shuck. It bristled and growled. Its lips curled and its jaws snapped, its eyes brighter than ever. Blood was still pulsing from the Shuck bite on Concord's face.

'One...'

'Con, you can't!' Dom said. 'We do everything together. Please. *Please!*'

'Two...'

'Dom, I'm sorry—' said Sol.

'Just run! PIG!'

He released the Shuck and pointed. It hurtled towards them with astonishing power, like a pent-up tornado of fur, muscle and teeth. But it wasn't interested in them. It had eyes only for the Doctor, who had just staggered on to his bleeding, broken foot.

Concord looked at Sol. 'Remember your Niceness.'

Then Libby took his hand and they were gone,

sprinting back through the trees towards the Ash House.

The Doctor started screaming.

Dom picked up the memory box and placed it in Sol's hands. With a huge effort, he crouched down, picked Sol up, and staggered to his feet.

'Dom, you don't have to . . .'

'I do. For Clem.'

Above the trees, flames erupted into the sky. They could feel the heat blowing through the leaves. Black smoke billowed into the air.

The Ash House burnt.

## 32: DOM

Buried alive, burnt alive, evaporated.

Dom thought of the stories they'd told for their whole lives. There was a story from the early days, when one of the girls strayed too far during a game and decided to cheat by hiding beyond the boundary. She was never seen again. In another, a boy with no name forgot his Niceness, and the Headmaster banished him to walk outside of the boundary for ever and ever.

They were myths, not memories, but Dom knows what he believes. That if he crosses the boundary, he'll evaporate. Every moment he spent at the Ash House, every friendship, every night watching the creepers above him, every day staring at the screens that let him watch over them all – it will all stop existing.

No one knew the name of the girl in the story. Perhaps when you cross, the memory of you gets evaporated too, he thought. It would be like a spell lifting. The others would all look up at each other and wonder what they were waiting for. Concord and Libby would hold hands all the way back to the dorm, then let go, not knowing why they'd held on so tightly or where the blood had come from. They'd be confused, in pain, but not missing him one bit. Their lives would go on.

Dom looked at the wire. He couldn't explain any of this to Sol. He simply said: 'Once we cross, we can't come back.'

'I know.' Sol was looking at the wire too. 'But that doesn't mean we shouldn't cross.'

With Sol in his arms, Dom couldn't wipe his face. His voice was high-pitched and pleading. 'I don't want to leave.'

'I know,' Sol whispered. 'Me neither, really.'

Then she was there. Dom was so relieved that he couldn't even be angry with her for keeping them waiting. A miasma of smoke was reaching out to him. Her eyes glowed. The smoke and ash that surrounded her was darker than ever. It wavered in the air, tremoring with a strange energy.

'I could stay,' Dom whispered. 'You go.'

'No. I can't do it without you.'

Dom peered over Sol to look at the leaves on the other side of the boundary, his face crumpling.

'I'm sorry I didn't save you.'

'You did,' said Sol with surprise. 'Look where we are.'

Dom couldn't explain that he wasn't talking to Sol. Clem's eyes flared red from within their soot-stained sockets.

'I need help,' he said.

'I'm here,' Sol told him. 'You're not alone.'

Buried alive, burnt alive, evaporated.

Evaporated.

But he couldn't evaporate. He had Sol. Even if the rest of it disappeared, they wouldn't disappear from each other. Dom felt certain of that.

Clem reached out and took hold of his wrist. Her fingers scorched his skin. She pulled him forward and Dom carried Sol under the wire. Dom felt the soft heat radiating from Clem.

'Hey, it's warmer here,' Sol murmured, closing his eyes for a moment.

The smoke was lightening from charcoal to dove-grey. It was spreading everywhere, through the trees, the leaves, their hair. The fire turned the sky pink and orange. There was the sound of cracking and roaring flames.

Clem walked right past them, then paused under the wire. Dom spun around to watch her. He held Sol tightly.

Before he could ask where she was going, she slipped under the wire. Her wild hair and fiery eyes softened, and blurred, and then she was made of ash: grey and fine and beautiful. The shape of her dissolved in the air, just as the wind picked up and carried her back towards the house and the flames.

## 33: EVALUATION SESSION #1.016

The list of names sits on the table between them. His new doctor leans forward and nudges it closer to him. She says that one of the names is his real one from before.

'Do you know which one? Can you point to it?'

Letters wriggle on the paper like spiders burrowing through sugar.

'No,' he says.

'Look carefully. Take your time.'

He reads them one by one, trying each one on in his mind, but it's like putting a plaster on wet skin. They slip away as soon as he applies them.

He looks up and shakes his head. She smiles sympathetically.

'Would you like me to tell you?'

'No,' he says again.

The room is designed to be cosy, but he finds it too small, he has to sit closer to her than he'd like. A gas fire burns on fake coals in a blocked-up fireplace, and over-stuffed bookshelves stretch from floor to ceiling behind her. A plant – he can't see whether it's real or fake – sits on the shelves too, its pale leaves spilling from its pot. Certificates on the wall say that she's qualified to psycho-analyse children and adolescents.

He can't tell if he's in a hospital, like before. 'Before' is still an untrustworthy place that never comes fully into focus for him. The police picked them up from the phone box on the main road and brought them straight here. She's the only doctor he's spoken to.

He's exhausted. He has spent the last few nights sleep-ing in a room on his own. There's no greenery in it. He eyes her plant enviously.

'Let's carry on,' she says. She shuffles and taps the papers in her hands, then pulls out a thick notebook and a pen. 'I want to go over what you remember one more time. It's important you say exactly what happened.'

'I did.'

'I know, but just one more time.'

'That's what happened,' he insists.

She taps the first page. He can't read the writing from where he's sitting. 'You haven't left anything out?' she asks. 'You're not keeping any secrets?'

'No.'

She writes something down in the notebook. She puts the loose pages of his statement and the names back into a thick file with a green cover.

'What's in there?' he asks.

'This is you,' she places a hand on it. 'Ever since the fire, when you went into the system. Everything we could dig up while you were missing.'

'Who knew I was missing?'

She blinks, surprised. 'Staff at the hospital. They checked on you in the morning and you were gone. Everybody has been very concerned.' She lets these facts hang in the air, waiting for him to elaborate. When he doesn't, she says:

'I can't help but wonder whether what happened to your parents in the fire has anything to do with all this.'

'All what?'

'What you've told me about where you were. I understand that some things are easier to say with –' she waves her hand – 'stories.'

'It's not a story,' he says defensively.

'I'm sure it's not,' she says. 'I just have to be thorough.'

She asks questions about numbers. How many children were there? How many days did he think he was there?

How many names were on the wall in the classroom?

He struggles to concentrate. She is gentle and smiling, waiting patiently for his answers and not minding when he is snappy or rude, but she is still a doctor and he cannot forget it. He fiddles with his badge, which is pinned to the new jumper they gave him, running his thumb over and over the wolf's familiar face.

'No one will tell me if Dom is OK.'

'He's perfectly safe,' she assures him. 'We're trying to keep him calm and to understand what happened, just like you and I are doing.'

'Can I see him today?' he presses.

'When we're done with this. We need to get both your accounts independently.'

'OK. It's just – I've been on the outside before and he hasn't. He might be scared.'

She pauses after he has finished speaking and then notes something down.

'You know, if you let me look at that hard drive, it might help with some of my questions.'

He can feel the weight of the metal box in his pocket. He hasn't let go of it once. He sleeps with his hands wrapped around it.

'I told you, you can have it when the others get here. When you rescue them too.'

'I don't see why—'

'Because it's ours to hand over together,' he snaps. 'You said you'd find them. Where are they?'

'We've sent people, and . . . Well, this is one of the things we need to speak about today.' Her voice softens and he begins to feel apprehensive.

'What?'

'We've retraced your steps and followed your directions, but . . . We can't find the Ash House.'

'I'll tell you again.'

'No, dear, you don't understand.' She leans across the table and slides a hand towards him, but he doesn't take it. 'It's not there.'

The room lurches horribly for a moment.

'Because it burnt down?' he whispers.

'Because there's nothing there at all.'

He remembers the rushing heat of the flames. Even with the fire, there was no way it could vanish. Perhaps it was like the shed, popping up in a different place overnight, but always there, always the same.

'But the others . . .'

'It's been wonderful to hear this fantastical story of yours. I can't help but—'

'Fantastical? You think I'm making it up?'

'No, not at all,' she says quickly.

'You do!'

'Perhaps it means something else.' She runs her hand over the notes. 'Perhaps you're adding these wonderful details, these wonderful children and this terrible doctor to explain a different set of circumstances.'

'I'm not.'

'Think carefully,' she tells him.

'I don't have anything to—'

'The mind can do extraordinary things. Imagine things. See things.'

He scowls. 'That's what the Doctor told me.'

'I'm not like him.'

'No,' he agrees. 'You're not. Because he believed me. He may have been . . . I know he was . . . but at least he believed me.'

'That sounds important to you.'

'He was important.'

'From what you've told me, he was evil.'

'What he made there was important. And he wasn't evil, not through and through. His Niceness just got . . . trapped.'

He imagines the others silhouetted against the flames, tearful and soot-stained, holding hands around a new grave next to the pig's, the photo Dom stole placed lovingly on top of the mound. Stories about happier times. A golden badge with a rising phoenix etched on it, shining under an orange sky.

'Your leg is itching again.'

He hadn't noticed himself rubbing his knee. 'It's nothing,' he says. The room feels far, far too hot. 'Can we open the window?'

She continues speaking as she pushes the window opens and fastens the latch.

'You know, our doctors here want to help you. If you'd just let somebody look at your back and examine you properly—'

'NO!' His shout explodes unexpectedly out of him.

'We just want to help.'

'I don't want it!' he snarls. The tingling feeling in his leg is unbearable, like an itch he can't reach. 'I'm not going to be prodded and tested and judged—'

'But you want to be believed,' she reminds him. 'To be believed we have to be honest. We can't use riddles or fairy tales.'

'What do you want me to say?' His anger boils over, it spits from his lips at her calm face, her unblinking gaze. He feels crushed under the heaviness of everything that has happened.

'Something believable, then? Do you want me to say that the Shucks are dogs?' he demands. 'Fine, tell people they're dogs. Tell them the shed didn't move – there are just lots of different ones and cameras that never stopped. Tell them the fence is two-metres high and topped with razor wire. Tell them the pig was a human intruder. Tell them I still dream about the smell of clay and a dead body.'

He breathes heavily. The only sound that follows his outburst is the gentle whooshing of the gas fire.

'And the Ash House?' she asks quietly. 'What was the ash, really?'

He relaxes his shoulders, only now realizing that they have been hunched around his neck.

'The ash is . . . how it felt to be together. To play in the woods every summer, to be loved by the Headmaster, but controlled by him too, to wake up next to your best friends every single day and know that all you need is there.' He nods. 'The ash is how it feels to be home.'

They sit in silence for a moment. She doesn't add to her notes.

'But you left.'

'Yes. I left. I want to see Dom now.'

She looks at the clock.

'Now,' he insists.

'OK. I think we've done enough.'

She starts to tidy away her notes.

'Is he OK?' he asks.

'He's been stitched up and rehydrated. Mostly he's being treated for shock. I haven't spoken to him, but I gather he's not doing as well as you, so you should be ready for that.'

He looks at his fingers. They're so pink and clean he still has trouble recognizing them as his own.

'I'll help him,' he says.

'I'll be just a moment.' She stands up and scoops up the green file. Then she pauses and takes out the sheet of paper with the names on it. She circles something on it and places it on the table.

'It's the one I've marked,' she says. 'If you're interested.'

She leaves, the door clicking shut behind her. He stares at the electric glow of the fire until his eyes ache. Then he uses the new chair they've given him to inch forward and slap his hand on the piece of paper. He picks it up. Scrunches it. Throws it at the fire. It skitters over the floor, unburnt.

He meant what he said. He doesn't want it back.

His name is Solitude.

While she's out, he wheels towards the bookcase and picks up the plant. Its rubbery leaves reflect the light. Up close he can see that it's real after all. He puts it on his lap and goes back to the table.

When the door opens again, she ushers Dom in. They have only been apart for a few days, but he looks older than Sol remembered, his face less round.

'You're here,' Dom says.

'I'm here.'

'I'll give you two a minute,' says the new doctor. 'I'm just down the corridor if you need me.'

'Thank you very much,' says Dom.

Her eyes linger on the crumpled-up piece of paper on the floor. When she looks at Sol, he shrugs. She closes the door behind her.

Dom crosses the room and hugs Sol tightly with the arm that isn't strapped in a sling. His hair presses into Sol's ear, and his chin clamps over his shoulder.

'You smell of smoke,' Sol whispers.

'What?' says Dom as he pulls away.

'I said, are you OK?'

'Not really.'

He sits in her seat, opposite Sol. It clearly feels too far away, too formal, because he then drags it around the table to be nearer to him.

'I've been talking to this man. Question after question after question,' Dom tells him. Then he bends his head towards Sol and whispers: 'They think the Ash House doesn't exist.'

'I was speaking to that woman,' Sol replies. 'She thinks the same thing.'

'The man said it's likely the Shucks were "a projection of my innermost terrors and conflicted feelings about my role in running away".'

Sol can't help but smile. 'Yeah?'

'I don't think I could make up Shucks.'

'No. I don't think I could either.'

'I kept a secret from them,' Dom says suddenly.

'What secret?'

Dom reaches into his pocket and unfolds a piece of paper.

'They gave me pens to draw things for them,' he explains. 'But they didn't see me do this one.'

Sol recognizes the Ash House grounds in one corner. The phone box is clearly marked. Squiggly felt-tip lines and arrows lead to a box with a bedroom inside it.

'Is this a map?' Sol asks.

'In case we can't find our way back.' Dom nods. 'I tried to memorize all the turnings when we were in the car with the lights on it.'

'The police car.'

'I didn't show the man who was asking the questions.'

'The psychiatrist.'

'Sol, this isn't what I thought the outside would be like.'

'I know.'

'But that's OK. It's not your fault. We'll just go back, won't we? The others won't mind we left; they'll understand. And Libby and Con will be in charge now. It will be strange without the Headmaster, but remember when I told you in the library that if we learn enough Nicenesses, we could run our own Ash Houses one day? Well, I think that's finally happened, because—'

'Dom.' He places a hand on his friend's shoulder. 'We're not going back.'

Dom's grey eyes widen.

'What?'

'They won't let us.'

'Then we'll escape!'

'We can't. It's a good map, but we'd never find our way, and even if we did, they'd come after us and bring us back.'

'B-but . . .' Dom's voice cracks. 'We have to. I have this feeling.' He presses the heel of his hand to his chest. 'Every day it gets worse.'

'It's called homesickness,' Sol explains. 'But don't worry. It's nothing a doctor will try to cure.'

'But what about the others?'

'We'll find them.'

'Promise?'

Sol hesitates, then shakes his head slightly. 'No. I just

hope, that's all.'

Dom covers his face with his hands.

'Here, I got you a present.' Sol seizes the chance to cheer him up and picks up the plant from his lap.

Dom sniffs and looks. He smiles with delight.

'Oh! It's *such* a Niceness.' He takes it and runs his fingers fondly over its leaves.

'It'll keep you company when we're not together.'

'I don't have anything for you.'

'I don't need anything.'

'You can keep the map. You'll know the way better than me anyway.'

'OK. Thanks.'

They sit in silence while Dom places his plant on the windowsill, tilting it back and forth, trying to find the perfect spot for it.

'I keep hearing that noise,' Dom says. 'What is it?'

'What noise?'

'That noise. The nice one.'

They stop speaking for a moment.

'That's, um . . .' Sol hears it. He blinks hard, startled by the question and the tight feeling it creates around his heart. 'Dom, that's birdsong.'

Dom leans against the window, trying to see where it's coming from. 'The birds here sing?'

'Yes.'

'Maybe it's not so bad here, then. Just different.'

'Maybe.'

'I let them think I made it all up,' Dom blurts out, turning away from the window to look at him again. 'They kept nodding and talking about stress. And eventually it was easier to agree. But we didn't make it up, did we?'

'No.'

'It was real.'

'It was real.'

'She didn't make you doubt that, did she?'

'For a second, maybe,' Sol says.

'Me too. Sort of. For a second.'

Dom closes his eyes and silver tracks of tears roll down his face. It's more than Sol can bear.

'I wish Concord and Libby were here,' Sol says. 'They'd know what to do. I wish . . .' He was looking at the plant, but he notices something behind it on the windowsill. It gives him an idea – one so fragile he's scared to mention it to Dom in case it's impossible.

'I wish we could phone them,' he says. 'Dom, the phone!'

'What?'

'That thing! Pass it here!'

It's newer than the one at the Ash House, and Dom looks at it with fascination as he takes it from the windowsill and moves his chair next to Sol's.

'Another phone . . .'

'You never rang anyone on the phone, did you?'

Dom shakes his head.

'Well, it's easy. All we need is the phone number. It'll have eleven digits. Did the Headmaster ever mention it to you? How he called you?'

Dom chews his lip and thinks.

'He never told me a number.'

Sol feels his thin hopes drain away.

'But – there was . . .'

'What?'

'I can't remember if it was eleven—'

'Dom, what?'

'Don't shout at me! The sticker.'

'What sticker?'

'The one on the side of the phone at the Ash House. It had numbers written on it . . .'

'Can you remember them?'

'Of course.'

'Come here.' Sol holds the receiver between their ears. 'Now, tell me.'

As Dom says each number Sol presses it on the

keypad. There are eleven digits.

They wait.

They hear a ringtone.

They lean in closer, their heads touching. Sol breathes in the lingering scent of smoke that's somehow coming from Dom.

At the end of the line the phone rings and rings.

He imagines the others reaching out for the phone, for them, the flames dying down, knowing it's him and Dom – because who else would it be?

It rings on. Sol is certain it's been too long. Nobody is answering.

The tone goes quiet.

Then Dom's damp cheeks pop with a smile as wide as the sun.

A girl's voice crackles through the receiver: 'Hello?'

## THE END

**Angharad Walker** grew up on military bases in the UK, Germany and Cyprus. She studied English Literature and Creative Writing at the University of Warwick and the University of California Irvine. She now lives in London, and works in charity communications.

# ACKNOWLEDGEMENTS

I'd like to thank my brilliant agent, Rachel Mann, the first person to say 'yes' to *The Ash House* and bring Dom and Sol's story into the world. You saw what this book could be even in the moments when I couldn't see it myself. Thank you also to Jo, Donna and Milly at JULA, for all your kindness and support.

It is a joy to watch *The Ash House* arrive in the world as a Chicken House book. So, to my astonishingly talented and thoughtful editor Rachel Leyshon, thank you. It's been a privilege to wander the Ash House with you. Barry Cunningham, your encouragement and kind words about this story will always stay with me. My heartfelt thanks go to the rest of the coop: Rachel H., Elinor, Esther, Laura, Kesia, Jazz and Sarah. I'd also like to thank my eagle-eyed copy editor Daphne and the team across the pond at Scholastic. A special thank you to Olia Muza for such darkly beautiful illustrations.

Over the years there have been too many wonderful teachers to name individually, but I'd like to mention my teachers and fellow students from the Warwick Writing Programme at the University of Warwick and the Creative Writing team at the University of California Irvine.

To my CBC group in cyberspace, your emails and support are the sort of fuel a writer can never have too much of.

Nikoline Nordfred Eriksen, my dear friend and very first champion, this book would quite simply not exist without you. Sophie Shorland and Alice Porter, how lucky I am to have friends who are such generous and intelligent readers. Thank you.

To my wonderful parents, the list of things I should thank you for could fill an entire book, so I thought I'd dedicate this first one to you.

And finally, a thank you to the greatest example of Niceness I've found in this world, Callum. Our story will always be my favourite.

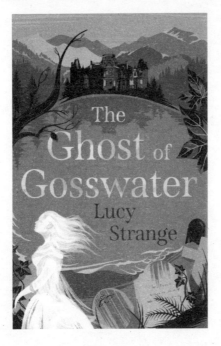

## THE GHOST OF GOSSWATER by LUCY STRANGE

### THE LAKE DISTRICT, 1899

The earl is dead and cruel Cousin Clarence has inherited everything. Twelve-year-old Lady Agatha Asquith is cast out of Gosswater Hall to live in a tiny, tumbledown cottage with a stranger who claims to be her father. Aggie is determined to discover her real identity, but she is not alone on her quest for the truth. On the last day of the year, when the clock strikes midnight, a mysterious girl of light creeps through the crack in time; she will not rest until the dark, terrible secrets of the past have been revealed . . .

Paperback, ISBN 978-1-911077-84-8, £6.99 • ebook, ISBN 978-1-913322-61-8, £6.99

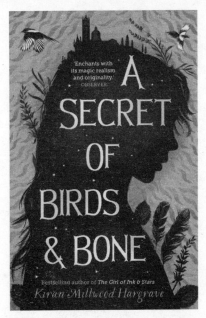

## A SECRET OF BIRDS & BONE by
## KIRAN MILLWOOD HARGRAVE

Sofia lives outside the city of Siena with her mamma, little brother Ermin, and their pet crow Corvith. Her mother is a bone-binder, famous for her keepsakes and charms.

But ever since an unexpected visit from a silver-veiled stranger, Mamma has not been herself. She no longer takes pleasure in her work, nor will she let Sofia help her.

When Mamma is arrested on Sofia's birthday, the children are taken to the city orphanage. It's there that Sofia decides she is no longer a helpless child. Clutching her mamma's gift, an intricate bone locket, she sets out to unravel the secrets that bind her family to Siena itself: its catacombs and towers, its birds and rivers. Its rulers and people. A journey to darkness, danger, destiny – and hope.

*'A dark and mesmerising historical adventure . . .'*
THE BOOKSELLER

Paperback, ISBN 978-1-913322-96-0, £7.99 • ebook, ISBN 978-1-913322-63-2, £7.99

## THE PURE HEART by TRUDI TWEEDIE

### *The purest heart is easy prey . . .*

Summoned by a wealthy merchant to be his daughter's companion, Iseabail is taken from her island home – and the boy that she loves – to an isolated grand mansion in the Scottish borderlands.

Unnerved by her gifted young charge and the house's strange secrets, Iseabail soon wonders why she's really been brought here – and whether she will ever make it back home . . .

'[A] wonderful, twisted gothic novel . . . [an] evocation of a weird and wonderful world with compulsive characters and a cracking mystery at its core.'
THE TIMES

'. . . a deliciously chilling Elizabethan tale with an injection of horror.'
THE OBSERVER

Paperback, ISBN 978-1-912626-00-7, £7.99 • ebook, ISBN 978-1-912626-73-1, £7.99

# PILLGWENLLY